this last
kiss

Madeleine Reiss was born in Athens. She worked for some years in an agency for street performers and comedians and then as a journalist and publicist. She has two sons and lives in Cambridge with her husband and her younger son. *This Last Kiss* is her second novel.

Also by Madeleine Reiss

Someone to Watch Over Me

this last
kiss

madeleine
reiss

ZAFFRE

First published in 2016 by

Zaffre Publishing
80–81 Wimpole St, London W1G 9RE
www.zaffrebooks.co.uk

A CIP catalogue record for this book is available from the British Library.

ISBN: 978-1-7857-6154-6

also available as an ebook

1 3 5 7 9 10 8 6 4 2

Printed and bound by Clays Ltd, St Ives Plc

Zaffre Publishing is an imprint of Bonnier Zaffre,
a Bonnier Publishing company
www.bonnierzaffre.co.uk
www.bonnierpublishing.com

For my dear mother Valerie Unsworth,
with love and kisses.

'The promise of such kisses . . . where would it carry us?
No one could tell what lay beyond the closed
chapter of every kiss.'

Lawrence Durrell

PROLOGUE

December 2012

She knew he was waiting for her back at the house and so she packed quickly, dismantling her old life – or what was left of it, after strangers had lived there and put their own mark on the place. There were only a few more boxes left to fill and then it would be done. She would take a deep breath, step out of the door for the last time and leave the key under the mat for the removal men.

She looked around at the empty room in which she had lived a half-life for so many years and she felt the pull of him still. She thought that maybe she always would. There were days when the sadness of the past took hold of her; when she thought of all the ways that she might have made things better, but she was beginning to understand that sorrow and regret for things left undone and unsaid were part of the deal. All she could do was hold love as close as possible, so that in the end it was worth the pain of its loss.

She took the last book down, the one right at the back of the shelf. She had time before she left for a quick look, just as a way of marking this ending and this beginning. The brown leather cover was worn, the gilt-edged pages a little swollen from a careless placing near a wet window, or maybe she and her grandmother had taken it to the beach. She couldn't remember now. *The Book of Kisses* – some of the tooled gold letters were rubbed, but inside the images were as vivid as ever. As she carefully lifted the fragile tissue paper covering each of the captioned pictures, they glowed out at her as if they had been waiting for the light.

On page ten, Guinevere, her hair threaded with flowers, leaned down from her horse to kiss a glossy, armoured Lancelot.

'*Sir Lancelot stole a forbidden kiss from his Queen.*'

In another picture, Snow White's stepmother, her eyes dark and mad, stood with her plum-coloured lips fastened to the mirror.

'*She knew she was the most beautiful woman that had ever been born.*'

A buxom Maid Marion, her skirt tucked into the tops of her stockings, presumably for greater ease when climbing trees, swooned on a spring-green bank under Robin Hood's ardour.

'*The lovers embraced and a bird sang deep in the wood.*'

As a child, Rora had imagined her own life illustrated and captioned in this way, with her key moments taking place in forests and in rose-filled gardens, moments that were important enough to be rendered in deep red and teal and gold and covered in tissue paper.

The book also contained famous works of art . . . Rodin's lustrous marble lovers with their lips not quite touching; the clutching, ugly embrace of Judas in Caravaggio's frozen moment of treachery, *The Taking of Christ*; the fused faces of Mary Cassatt's *Mother and Child*; Brancusi's cubed essence of a kiss, his homely stone lovers cemented together for eternity. What captured Rora's imagination was that the kisses, in all their variety – maternal, illicit, erotic, sorrowful and duplicitous – were not an end in themselves, but rather a moment in a story that told of what had been and what was yet to come.

'I knew as soon as I kissed him.'

Rora could hear her grandmother Isobel's voice as clearly as if she was in the room.

'I couldn't tell where my body ended and his began.'

It was always this book that Isobel used to reach for when she was thinking about her late husband, and although the two of them were supposed to be doing Rora's homework, Rora probably learned more than if they had stuck to cracking long division. Looking at the book always felt like a ceremony. The volume was opened with reverence so that its smooth pages were not marked, and then the green silk ribbon that served as a bookmark was delicately retrieved and laid across her grandmother's lap. Isobel would flick through the pages in exactly the same fashion each time, until the book fell open as if by magic at the very place she claimed she was looking for. Rora learned to recite great chunks of poetry, and she became familiar with all of Shakespeare's most famous love scenes.

Sometimes, inspired by the film quotations in the book, the two of them would make a note of the afternoon films in the *Radio Times*, making sure not to miss such breathless moments as the interrupted but extended kiss in Hitchcock's *Notorious,* which Isobel timed as two-and-a-half minutes on the face of the Cupid clock in her living room, or Burt Lancaster and Deborah Kerr's passionate surf-lapped clinch in *From Here to Eternity.* It was from the book and from her grandmother that Rora acquired the notion that love and romance, done properly, was central to everything. It made flowers twist in extravagant abundance. It made the sea foam. It turned marble into flesh.

'How many kisses will you remember when you're old like me?' Isobel had once asked her granddaughter, smoothing Rora's unruly hair off her forehead and holding her chin up towards the light, as if she was reading something in the girl's face.

'You may not believe it now, but you are looking at a woman with more than a few significant kisses to her name,' she'd continued, with an arch glance.

'Some of the kisses I remember with happiness, others not so much, but they are all part of my story, threaded together over the years like beads on a necklace.'

Even though Rora wanted to get back to him, longed for the feel of his arms around her, she was unable to stop the past from intruding and it held her there in the room. She sat on the dusty, wooden floor, marked all around by the ghosts of missing furniture, and memories filled her like a sky suddenly thick with swifts or the wriggling push of sheep bursting into a field. It was her version of *The Book of Kisses* that she remembered – the story of how she had arrived at this day, in this room, replete with the prospect of home and him, and a Christmas tree to decorate. The pictures she conjured up told their own story of loss and joy and had their own gleaming splendour.

PART ONE

Kiss 1

'She had woken to find his lips on her mouth.'

15 May 1996

The first time she kissed him was when she had just turned fourteen. Rora had barely talked to him before then. She had seen him once on Hastings pier with a group of other boys. He was showing off – bumping into his companions, balancing along the tops of benches, playing the fool. Something about his swagger and the way his dark hair fell over one eye had caught her attention, and she found herself staring after him. He didn't notice her looking, but one of his friends did and gave his companion a shove in her direction and made some jeering comment that made Rora blush and turn away. She heard one of them say his name . . . Carl. It suited him, she thought. It sounded compact and tough, as if everything would slide off him and leave him untouched.

He had joined her school in September, but although she watched him a lot, she never spoke to him. It seemed to her that he was always right in the centre of things, and she preferred the quiet edges where she could sit unseen. In the second term, they went on a school trip to Fairlight, a wooded area on the cliff to the east of the town. Their challenge was to identify four different types of fern and four wild flowers and press

5

them between blotting paper and cardboard under a flat stone. In a little clearing by a stream, they had learned how to put up tents and build a fire to cook foil-wrapped baked potatoes. She recalled the smell of damp, and rubber ground sheets, and the dry, sweet perfume of the ferns and the sensation of running fast, the earth soft under her feet. Above all, she remembered holding within herself an overwhelming anticipation of life and joy to come.

With the exception of Rora's best friend, Hannah, who eschewed boys in favour of a rather tired-looking pony called Rust, the rest of the girls in Rora's class were fixated on the quest to secure a boyfriend. Being away from the confines of the classroom had only served to intensify this obsession and the camp was rife with intrigue. Rora had caught Carl looking at her more than once and was both dazzled and terrified by his attention. The thought that he might at any moment come over and talk to her and that she then would have to find the right words made her feel queasy. She was torn by her desire to be near him and her desire to keep him away.

When the opportunity arose she slipped away. She went deeper into the woods, straight through the undergrowth, leaping over the low shrubbery, ignoring the nettles that stung her ankles and the stray branches that swung back and hit her face. A long swathe of bramble had caught the underside of her arm and fastened itself cruelly into the soft skin, drawing bright red pinpricks and livid scratches on the white. She sucked the blood from the wound, tasting the metal tang on her tongue. Although the beech and oak canopy blocked out much of the sun, she had stopped just at a point where the trees thinned out slightly and she felt the last of the day's heat on her upturned face. This was the place where the bluebells were at their thickest, the mass of them seeming to hang in a purple mist above the ground.

She remembered being overcome with a feeling of heaviness as she rested against a tree trunk, as if the crashing run through the wood had used up the last of her energy. Her breathing was still quick after her exertions, and she could hear the low hum of life around her – the small stirrings in the leaves and twigs on the ground, the sound of water running thinly over rocks and a bird somewhere making a strange, trembling noise, as if unsure of its own song. She smelled the musk of earth trapped under its layer of vegetation and the mushroom scent of crumbling wood, and sensed the movements of wood lice, tiny legs exploring the crevices, wriggling through the bright moss.

It was as if everything she felt and saw that day was more pronounced, more vivid than usual – the sting of the scratches on her arm, the burning sensation of nettle rash spreading on her exposed calves, the blood beating in her neck, the way her new bra with its synthetic lace, bought optimistically a size too big, rubbed against her nipples, making them feel hot and sore. Her hair had fallen down while she was running and was warm against the back of her neck. She felt a tightening, a kind of clenching in her stomach when she thought about Carl, the way he swept his hair out of his eyes with the side of his hand and the set of his shoulders, straight and ready, as if he was always expecting a fight.

After a while she slid down the length of the trunk and rested her head against its sun-warmed expanse, and then when that didn't provide rest enough, she lay flat on the ground, her head cushioned by ferns. The leaves above her had a quick, lime brightness to them, as if their sticky new-ness had caught the sun on their shining edges. She didn't know what to do with the feeling she had about Carl. She couldn't even pin it down. It moved in her – a kind of excitement, a kind of fear – even, though she couldn't quite explain it to herself, a kind of shame. Although Isobel and she had made romance their specialist subject, she hadn't been able to equate the glossy illustrations they looked at so often with the ragged, wounded way she felt. Young as she was, she had at least known why she had run from him. Running helped to keep the shivering longing away.

She wouldn't have imagined that she could fall asleep in such a place, but it was as if she had been drugged. She didn't hear his stealthy approach through the woods, nor did she see him standing looking at her as if what he saw made him fearful. She woke to find his lips on her mouth. Her first impulse was to push him away, but she saw his brown eyes, shining and intent above her, and felt his fingers in her hair, holding her head gently, and she closed her eyes again. And it was exactly as Isobel had said it would be. She felt the same melting softness her grandmother had described. She no longer knew where their bodies ended and the earth began.

May 2010

It wasn't like May weather at all. The taxi was unbearably hot. The vanilla-scented cardboard tree hanging from the mirror did little to disguise the smell of sweat and a hastily eaten lunch. The driver had thick black hair, which glistened where it lay against the back of his neck.

'Here on holiday?' he asked in a vague attempt at politeness, although he could probably see from Rora's face that she wasn't the type to encourage conversation.

'We are visiting my grandfather,' said Ursula. 'I've never met him before.'

Ursula was nine years old and sometimes a little too fond of imparting information that Rora would prefer to keep to herself.

'He's very ill,' Ursula continued, tucking her hair behind her ears in that endearingly prim way she had, as if she felt let down by her head of wayward dark curls. By rights Ursula should have been born with a neat, sleek bob.

'We are on an errand of mercy,' she said.

'Is that so?' asked the taxi driver, looking at her in the mirror and smiling.

'Yes. We have to give him medicine and drinks and check that his pillows are plumped up,' Ursula said, and turned her attention once more to the contents of her purple, furry handbag.

Rora had lost count of the number of times her daughter had done this meticulous inventory during their journey from London: laying out the small pink hairbrush, the packet of unopened sweets, her best doll, a colouring book, a lucky stone, a feather, a box of plasters and – particularly important – the packet of wet wipes that she was forever pulling out with a triumphant air to mop up even the most minor of spillages and smears. Rora was concerned about her daughter's constant need to check and recheck her possessions. She thought with a pang that perhaps this was part of what they had done to Ursula at school – made her feel as if her things might be taken away from her at any moment. She felt a familiar spurt of helplessness and anger. She should have protected her better.

Rora opened the window of the taxi and leaned out, breathing in the sharp tang of the sea rising clear above the smell of stalled traffic and the medicinal scent of the marigolds in the municipal beds. She felt the old dread. It lined the streets, it hung in the curtains of the passing windows, it lay like a mist over the golden, sandstone cliffs. She carried it with her always but, driving along these streets that she remembered so well, it was as if the story she had been trying to forget had come back into terrifying focus. When she was away from the place it had been possible to smudge the past and render it less vivid, but here there was no escaping it. She felt a rising panic, an irrational, almost chemical reaction, since surely now there would be nobody left to remember what had happened. It was a long time ago, she said silently in her most sensible, soothing voice, but she didn't feel reassured. Looking out of the window the fear of it was as vivid as if it had happened yesterday.

When Hannah had rung to tell her the news about her father, her immediate instinct had been to stop listening, to stick her fingers in her ears and make a chanting noise as she used to do as a child.

'He's very ill, Rora. I don't think he has long,' Hannah had said tentatively on the phone a month before, knowing that she was stepping on dangerous ground. 'He has leukaemia. I spoke to one of the nurses as she was coming out of the house.'

'And I'm supposed to care, why exactly?' said Rora, holding her phone away from her ear. Hannah had an unnecessarily loud telephone voice.

'I know you don't owe him anything at all. Nothing. It's just that you'll not get this chance again,' she said.

'What if I don't want the chance?' said Rora, knowing that she was sounding childish, but unable to hide her resentment.

'I'm thinking as much about you as about him,' said Hannah, persisting even though she could hear the ice in Rora's voice.

'I've barely spoken to him for years. Why do you imagine I would want to see him now?' she asked. 'The man's a cold bastard, and I don't much care that he's on his last legs.'

'Rora!' said Hannah, shocked at her harsh words. 'You don't really mean that.'

'I do, you know,' said Rora, smiling slightly at the outraged tone in Hannah's voice.

'Well, just think about it. If it's too much to actually stay there, you're always welcome here.'

'I know I am,' said Rora, her voice softening as she thought of Hannah's warm, noisy house. She could picture her friend standing in her bright yellow hallway, scuffmarks all along the walls from muddy boots and bicycle handles. She would no doubt be wearing one of the appliquéd sweatshirts she was so fond of.

'He's the only father you've got. Anyway, I've got to go. The cat's just crapped on the carpet,' Hannah said, and rang off.

Hannah was surprised when Rora called a day later to say that she was coming back after all.

'I'm so glad you decided to do the right thing,' she said approvingly.

Rora wasn't at all sure that she *was* doing the right thing. It had been an impulsive decision. One born not out of feelings of duty towards her father – she felt no such bond – but provoked simply by her desire to take Ursula to a place that was free of unhappy associations for her. Sea air, a new school, time spent together, just the two of them – these things might be enough to restore her daughter's happiness. She didn't stop to think about the damage that coming back might do to herself.

Once she had made the decision, Rora did everything as quickly as possible so that she wouldn't have a chance to change her mind. The ease with which she made the arrangements to leave London revealed to her exactly how little there was attaching her to the life she had created for herself and Ursula there. She had done her research carefully before they left – ringing all the possible schools in Hastings and having lengthy conversations with a series of head teachers. The junior school she most liked the sound of, and which Hannah's daughter currently attended, was in the catchment area of Rora's father's house, and she had used the address and the fact of his illness to plead Ursula's case. At first she was told there were no places available and that it was too near the end of the year to be a practical option. But another phone call in which Rora mentioned that she wrote historical books for children and would be happy to come give to the school and do a talk, and even run a small workshop – plus the employment of a strategic wobble in her voice when talking about her ailing father – did the trick. The head teacher finally capitulated.

Rora let out her flat in Lewisham on a six-month contract and put a few personal possessions and the contents of Ursula's bedroom into storage. She was leaving behind no relationships that mattered – it required too much effort to create the necessary intimacy. She had finished her latest project the month before – a children's book written from the point of view of a girl of eight who was employed at Henry VIII's court as an acrobat – and she was able to take a break for a while until she thought about what she wanted to write next. There would be a bit of a tour around schools and a few readings, but she could do that from anywhere. It wouldn't be long before Rora thought of her next idea – her head teemed with stories and she knew she was good at creating characters and situations children could identify with – but her priority now was to get Ursula away from her old life.

She could have gone anywhere, and yet she had come back to Hastings. Sitting in the taxi, letting herself be taken where she had vowed never to return suddenly seemed like madness. Perhaps she should tell the driver to turn around and take them back to the station. He would grumble and she would feel foolish, but she could still save herself. Her life had been easy to set aside and therefore just as easy to restore. She could find another school for Ursula in London, even if it meant selling the flat and moving somewhere else. She almost spoke her thoughts out loud, but just then Ursula turned to her with the wide, hopeful smile that her mother hadn't seen for a long time.

'It's going to be brilliant, isn't it, Mum?' she said. 'An adventure.'

And so Rora sat back and let the taxi drive on.

They turned off the seafront and started the ascent through the streets of the Old Town, passing a mixture of medieval timbered buildings and Georgian houses. It seemed that this part of town had no bearing on the rest of Hastings with its wind and sea-spoiled houses. It was as if the real living happened elsewhere, and these streets and their haphazard history no longer represented the true character of the place, but simply remained for show – the last vestiges of a grandeur that belonged to another time. She didn't allow herself to think about what it would be like to see her father again, but she had a sudden image of the house, shuttered and dark, waiting for them. She thought of the attic set into the eaves, its tiny window high up in the wall. The room that none of them had gone into afterwards. The shock had never left her and she could feel it now, fizzing through her arms, making her throat tight.

When she was a young child she had loved the house's creaking floors and sloping ceilings and the fact there were so many places to hide. Coming home after being away, it had always seemed to embrace her because everything about it was known and loved – the warm patch on her bedroom floor above the boiler, the silky smoothness of the kitchen table against her arms, the gulping sound the water made as it came through the taps at bath time. A school friend had once stayed the night and had woken in terror, seeing shapes in the crumbling plasterwork on Rora's bedroom wall.

'Those are not monsters,' Rora had said of the imagined creatures, picked out of the cracks and dents. 'They're my friends.'

But everything had changed at the turn of a door handle. What she had witnessed that afternoon had taken away the safety and comfort she had always felt there. Overnight, the house had become strange and heavy with half-understood secrets – his secret and hers, and all the others that followed. The taxi stopped suddenly, causing both mother and daughter to lurch forward, but Rora was so deeply submerged in the past that she barely noticed. She was still a child in a house that no longer felt like home.

'Are we nearly there?' asked Ursula, who had put her possessions back into her bag and was now sitting with her face pressed up against the window.

'Yes, almost,' said Rora.

'Bloody kids,' the taxi driver said irritably, as a couple of skateboarders crossed the road, rubbing the back of his fat neck as if he had been stung by a wasp.

'Bloody is actually a swear word,' said Ursula reprovingly.

Rora smiled and squeezed her daughter's hand. Was it this habit she had of saying exactly what she felt that had caused her to be picked on by other children? What was it about Ursula that provoked such venom? Then Rora chastised herself for the way her thoughts were going. None of it was Ursula's fault.

They inched along the High Street, stopping and starting in the snarled-up traffic. The metered minutes seemed to turn over more quickly when they were not moving at all. Saturday shoppers searching for old chemist's bottles and felt cushions walked slowly, imagining their houses transformed. A man threading his way along the congested pavements caught Rora's eye. It was his walk that she recognised first – a slightly rolling gait, wide-stepping and fast. She froze. It couldn't possibly be him. Dwelling on the past had made her pluck phantoms from the air. He was surely just a trick of the light. He stopped to make way for a couple coming in the other direction and he turned his head briefly. She saw the side of his cheek, the dark hair across his forehead. It *was* Carl. She had not thought for one moment that he would be back in the town. She almost said his name aloud, but bit it back. It was strange after all this time that her instinct had been to call out to him. Her heart turned in her chest. He looked harder and older, but still had the same intent purposefulness about him. She hunkered down in her seat, her heart hammering, her face flushed. She hoped he would not turn again and see her there, staring out of the window at him. If the feelings of dread had been acute before, now they threatened to engulf her. Why hadn't she followed her instinct and stayed away? When she looked again he had moved past them, and the taxi found a stretch of clear road and accelerated.

Kiss 2

'The world cracked open under her feet and she was lost.'

9 July 1996

After their kiss in the wood, it seemed to be taken for granted by them and by their classmates that Rora and Carl were a couple. They spent every lunch hour together, Rora often sharing the doorstopper sandwiches that were Isobel's specialty, since Carl never seemed to have any food of his own. People got used to the sight of them walking close together, heads down, talking. Hannah, who now had to share the friend she had been able to monopolise before, was predictably dismissive of Carl.

'Can't see his allure,' she said loftily as she and Rora walked home one day. She was very fond of the word allure and used it in all sorts of contexts, particularly when describing her lust for Mr Brampton, their science teacher, who arrived at school in the morning on a motorbike, clad in faintly ridiculous leather. He only lived ten minutes away and Rora thought he didn't really need to dress as if he was taking part in the Grand Prix.

'He understands me,' Rora said, and then seeing Hannah's face fall she added 'You understand me too, but you have a million people in your family and Carl's a bit lonely, like me.'

'He's fearfully immature,' said Hannah turning into her street with a toss of her head. 'And a little grubby,' she added meanly as she walked away.

'What do you two find to talk about?' asked the English teacher, exasperated that Carl and Rora were whispering to each other in class again rather than paying attention to Malvolio's cross-gartering.

'Nothing,' said Rora, who until her alliance with Carl had been reliably studious and attentive but who was now regularly reprimanded for chatting and inattention.

'I started it,' said Carl, sliding down inside the grey collar of his school shirt; already singled out as a troublemaker, he had nothing to lose and was glad to take the heat off Rora.

On Saturdays, the day it was possible to slip out of the house without attracting too much attention, she would meet Carl and they would walk up the steep steps to the café on the West Hill and make a Coke last two hours. From this vantage point, with its view over the town and the sea, they felt as if they owned the world. Sometimes they followed the paths of the Country Park above the town and on down to the beach along a sloping, perilous track they had discovered, taking care when they arrived to avoid the naturists in strange-shaped hats and terrible sandals. On other days they would set up camp in the deserted cabin on the edge of the cliff, an old lookout post now left to lovers and rabbits and the wind that blew off the sea through its open window.

When the weather was very bad they would take shelter on the pier. Damaged by a severe storm the year before and teetering on the verge of bankruptcy, the patched-up walkway and its view of Pelham Crescent and the castle above it had always featured in Rora's childhood as a place of glamour and excitement. It had become increasingly shabby over the years and was now mostly frequented by anglers, bingo players and elderly dancers in their best shoes, who moved with stiff grace across the ballroom floor on Friday afternoons. But there were still the arcades, which were warm and fusty on rainy days, and the delicious smell of frying onions, and a fortune-teller who had a curtained outlet next to the sweet shop on the apron of the pier. Her name was Sophie and she was an acquaintance of Isobel's. She wore her hair in an elaborate topknot. Sometimes Rora and Carl peeped in through the purple velvet drape, stifling their giggles as she bent her head, odd hairdo bobbing, over the hands of her visitors, all with the same sunburned shoulders and hopeful questions. Carl used to mock the absurd theatricality of it, but Rora, always less cynical, was impressed by the secret solemnity. She was moved by the way people allowed themselves to believe that their future was visible in the cloudy glass ball and in the markings on their palms. She understood how eager they were to hear their stories. Once Carl almost gave them away by sneezing so loudly both occupants of the room looked up sharply and the fortune-teller came to the entrance and saw them running away.

'You're always sneezing,' Rora said accusingly, after they had run far enough away and she had caught her breath. 'You'd be useless as a spy. You'd give the game away every time.'

'I can't help it,' he said. 'I sneeze when my eyes go from darkness into the light. I read about it. It's called photic sneezing and twenty per cent of the population has it. It's genetic. I'm a sun worshipper and a sun sneezer.'

Once they had a go on the 'Love Detective', a machine in the arcade that tested couple compatibility. They had to give their star signs and provide other information, such as their favourite colour and which animal they most resembled. Rora and

Carl had scored a ninety-eight per cent match, which made her wonder what the two per cent was that prevented them from being a perfectly one hundred per cent pair. Sometimes when she lay in bed at night thinking about him, she worried that the missing percentage would turn out to be the thing that broke them up. It rankled that this potential flaw in their relationship was something she couldn't identify and therefore couldn't put right.

Carl may have been unconcerned with percentages, dismissing her worries as being based on unscientific data, but he had his own way of testing whether or not Rora was a keeper. Hardly a week went past when he didn't present her with a new and frightful task. Although he never admitted it, even to himself, he used Rora's willingness to do the outlandish things he suggested as proof that she wanted to be with him.

When he initially suggested the cliff challenge, Rora refused even to contemplate it. She had already, among other things, played shoplifting bingo (five pilfered red items in under an hour), climbed to the top of the statue of Queen Victoria in Warrior Square and garlanded the sovereign's head with a length of tinsel, shaved off an eyebrow, rearranged the items on the altar in the local church, and pretended to faint in assembly. After all the effort she had put in, she felt she had earned her stripes.

Rora's parents, who had a dim grasp of her activities for much of the time, had insisted that Carl should come round for tea so that they could meet the person who was leading their daughter astray. Rora had been worried that they would think him a wild, unsuitable friend, but she was amazed at Carl's previously hidden social skills. He had eaten three helpings of Sandi's vegetable curry, told Isobel that he wished he had a grandmother, and talked to Frank about the history of Hastings Castle. When he left Sandi said he had eyes like river water and the fingers of an artist.

'You'll be perfectly safe,' Carl said, tickling the inside of her ear with a length of grass as they sat on a bench on the West Hill.

'Safe, how?' she said. 'You want me to walk, blindfolded, along the edge of the cliff above Rock-a-Nore? The bit with the steepest drop?'

'I'll be guiding you all the time,' said Carl. 'I'll tell you exactly where to put your feet.'

'Why do you want me to do it?' she asked.

'It's the ultimate test. After this, I'll know that you would put your life in my hands. How about I do it first? That way we'll be equals.'

'I don't want you to do it and I don't want to do it,' said Rora. 'I'm going home.'

Such were Carl's powers of persuasion that a week later Rora was standing on the edge of the cliff wearing the sleep mask he had stolen from Boots expressly for the purpose. She was very nervous; she had never been comfortable with heights, but she knew that Carl's challenge was nothing to do with testing her courage, and everything to do with testing her devotion. The sensible part of her resisted the idea of subjecting herself in this way, but the other part found it difficult to turn him down. Besides, she wasn't without pride and had a wilful determination not to lose face.

Although she couldn't see, she could feel the empty space to her right and the breeze that stirred the grass at her feet. She was aware of the crumbling rock at the edge of the cliff, pockmarked with caves and cormorants' nests. Over the melancholy sound of the ice cream van and the blithe hum of the summer town, she could hear the beating of her heart. Carl took hold of her hands and spun her round three or four times so that she was completely disorientated.

'Now take one small step forward,' instructed Carl, 'and another.'

She shuffled her feet, feeling the slide of the grass under her flip-flops.

'Now, just turn slightly to the left,' he said, 'not too much, just a fraction.'

'How far am I from the edge now?' asked Rora.

Last summer a dog had dragged a woman off the cliff at this very spot. Behind her mask, Rora could see the thrown stick, the leaping dog, the owner tied to the lead by devotion and habit. Rora put her arms out as if she feared she might be approaching a wall.

'There's nothing in front of you,' said Carl, 'just keep on going exactly the same way. Don't deviate.'

'How much longer?' asked Rora.

'Twenty steps,' he said. 'Twenty small steps.'

'Left a little. Right a little,' said Carl, no longer able to keep the laughter out of his voice. She shouted out when she felt the rush of him knocking her over onto the grass.

'Carl! What are you doing?' She lay breathing heavily, her heart in her mouth. He pulled the mask off and his grinning face was above her, so close she could see the downy hairs above his curved top lip and feel his breath on her face. She was lying a safe ten feet away from the edge of the cliff in the opposite direction from where she thought she had been going.

'Did you really think I would've risked you falling?' he asked her.

'Let me get up. I'm lying on something sharp,' she said at last, when the way he was looking at her had begun to make her feel even more breathless. He pulled her to her feet.

'I wouldn't have let you fall,' said Carl again earnestly, and he touched her disordered hair gently, moving it off her face and tucking it behind her ear.

'I know you wouldn't,' Rora said, and kissed him. His lips were dry and he tasted sweet and sour. She could feel the shape of his bony shoulders under her hands and the way his body leaped at her touch as if he had been burned. The world cracked open under her feet and she was lost. It was as if she had fallen off the cliff after all. Their kiss might have lasted a minute or an hour, the dizzying swoop of it made it hard to tell, but when she stepped away from him he smiled.

'I could do that all day,' he said.

'You'd get nothing done,' she said, since being brisk helped to bring the world back into focus and stilled her hammering heart.

'Who cares?' he said, and swung himself onto his hands and she stood and watched as he did one perfect, straight-legged cartwheel after another, all the way down the hill.

May 2010

The taxi came to a halt at the bottom of Pilgrim Street, a walkway lined on one side with narrow Regency terraces in various states of repair, and on the other, a strip of a park with a bench and a patch of green. Some of the houses had clear signs of gentrification: glossy black iron railings, front doors painted the requisite olive green and vaulted glass roofs filling up side returns. Others had remained largely untouched, with weeds pushing through the cracks in the pathways and window frames blistered by the sun.

'This is the nearest I can get you to the house,' said the taxi driver and reluctantly unfolded himself, releasing a fug of yeasty, unwashed flesh, to make heavy work of taking their suitcases out of the boot.

'I'd help you with your luggage,' he said, 'but I have a bit of a back.'

Rora tipped him too much regardless, and felt a familiar disgust with her own cravenness and eagerness to please. She still felt shaky, almost tearful after the shock of seeing Carl, and her weakness made her feel even less prepared to confront her father.

'I can't stop you,' is what he had said to her on the phone when she rang to tell him that she and Ursula were planning on coming. During their brief conversation, she hadn't mentioned that she had shut up her life behind her, preferring to make the visit seem like a casual, spur-of-the-moment thing, something that she could cut short at any time. She pulled her suitcase up the street, its wheels catching on the uneven paving. Ursula, with her handbag now strapped efficiently across her chest, followed behind with her own luggage, a small case fashioned to look like a ladybird, another receptacle in which she took an inordinate amount of pride.

Rora stopped at the bottom of the steps that led to the front door of 14 Pilgrim Street and gazed up at the house. It looked exactly as it had when she had last seen it; the cream stucco was marked with traces of damp, the sixth step broken right across, as it had always been, the roof tiles green and patchy. The front garden and what she could see of the back were overgrown with nettles and convolvulus and rampant ivy that twisted its tendrils up from the bottom of the wall. It was as if the outside was encroaching on the fabric of the building, softening the edges, making it indistinct. Despite the obvious neglect and its shuttered, watchful air, the house had elegance; the windows were placed a pleasing distance apart, one next to the front door and then two by two on the remaining floors. The windows at the top of the house were headed with two curling scrolls, like eyebrows. The second floor had an ironwork balcony, onto which both rooms opened, which was so delicate it looked like filigree. Rora thought it was a wonder it hadn't rusted away.

'Stay with the suitcases just a moment,' she said and climbed the steps to the arched front door of her father's house, which was glazed with a pattern of coiled ferns and framed by peeling Doric columns. She pressed on the bell but didn't hear it ring. There was no doorknocker, so she rattled the handle on the letterbox. After a few seconds a middle-aged woman in a pale green uniform opened the door. She had heavily pencilled eyebrows and a severe fringe, which made her look as if the top half of her face didn't belong to the rest.

'Can I help you?' she said. She spoke quietly and with a slight local accent, the edges of her words blurred.

'I've come to see my father,' said Rora. The woman gave her a sharp, assessing glance.

'He never mentioned that he was expecting visitors,' she said. 'I suppose you'd better come in.'

She stepped aside, leaving Rora and Ursula to drag their suitcases up the steps and through the front door.

'He's in the living room,' she said once they were inside the hallway. 'I'll leave you to get on with it.'

The door to the living room was shut, and Rora found that she was holding her breath. If Ursula hadn't been there, she might well have turned round and left the house without seeing him, but her daughter was looking expectantly at her and she had to muster at least the semblance of grown-up behaviour, even if being there made her feel like a child again.

The house caught her up in its grand, forlorn air, as if it had been waiting to show itself to her and had felt neglected by her absence. The weight of the place bore down on her, the rooms heavy above, the tangled greenness of the garden pushing against the walls as if conspiring to seal the place up. There was a fetid, trapped quality to the air, and yet the nurses who looked after him must have opened windows and aired the bedding. It was what nurses did. Her hand hesitated on the doorknob. After the years of silence that had lain between them like a dark river it seemed suddenly impossible that she would enter the room and make small talk. Maybe he would think she had forgiven him, although he ought to know that she never would. What he had done had been the start of all the fear and sadness she now associated with this house, this town. She swallowed hard and pushed open the door.

Her father was sitting in an armchair by the empty fireplace as if he was waiting for another season, when it might be cold enough to warrant the blaze of logs and the pine cones her mother used to burn because of their sweet resin smell. Rora was surprised to see how small he looked. It was as if someone or something had pressed down on his head and shoulders as he sat there in the chair.

Until his retirement, Frank had been a part-time history lecturer at the University of Sussex, but for much of Rora's early childhood the real focus of his efforts had been on writing a book about Hastings, a lengthy work that seemed always to be just a chapter away from completion. He had been absent-minded to the point of absurdity, regularly mislaying keys, hats, cars, pets and on one occasion young Rora herself, whom he left on a bus in her Moses basket. He spent his time immersed in details: researching the way fishing nets used to be made in early Victorian times or mapping out the narrow passageways, better known as 'twittens', which laced the Old Town. He had been a benign presence around the house, forgetting to eat or button up his clothes or change out of his slippers when walking into town. When he emerged from the past long enough to allow conscious thought about his circumstances, he felt himself to be a lucky man, with a wife he adored and a daughter who was the apple of his frequently befuddled eye.

That man no longer existed. His diminished stature was emphasised by the high ceilings and elaborate cornicing of the room. She could see, even in the dim light, that the illness had claimed him. His skin had a yellowish tinge and his eyes had been stretched wider by his weight loss, giving his face a strange new openness. Despite the way she had armoured herself, the sight of him made her falter. He seemed vulnerable in a way that she had never allowed herself to imagine.

'You've come, then,' he said, and his voice was expressionless, without expectation.

'Yes,' she said. 'Hello, Dad.' The word felt unfamiliar on her tongue.

'This must be Ursula,' he said, looking beyond Rora to her daughter, who was hovering behind her.

'Ursula, meet your grandfather Frank.'

Not for the first time, Rora was grateful for Ursula's matter-of-fact manner and lack of apparent shyness.

'It's very nice to meet you,' she said, and came and stood in front of him, readying herself for inspection. Frank looked at her gravely for a moment.

'You look just like your mother,' he said. His voice had gained some warmth. 'Why don't you go into the kitchen, along the hall and down the stairs on your right, and ask Pauline – she's my nurse, you know – if she has a glass of juice? You must be hot after your journey,' Frank said, and Ursula obediently complied.

'If you've come because you heard I'm ill,' he said as soon as the door closed behind Ursula, 'you don't need to feel obliged.'

'I don't feel obliged,' she said. 'I thought you might need some help.'

Any softening she had felt when she first arrived hardened again and she reverted to seeing him as he had been before death had begun to drag him away and prompted her fleeting pity. She was consoled by her anger because it made her stronger, more able to deal with him.

'I've got all the help I need,' said Frank.

As if on cue, the nurse came into the room and hovered protectively by his chair, then began fussing with the blanket he had over his knees. Ursula followed her in, drinking from a glass.

'Your father shouldn't be disturbed,' Pauline said. 'He's not used to visitors.'

'Don't worry, we won't stay here,' said Rora. 'We'll go to Hannah's for the night.'

'Aw, Mum!' said Ursula, her face falling. 'I don't want to go anywhere else. I haven't had a chance to meet Grandad properly yet.'

'We can come and visit tomorrow,' said Rora as calmly as she could. The tick she got whenever she was particularly tired or stressed started to flutter over her left eye.

'Please let's stay here,' said Ursula in her most irritatingly wheedling voice.

Rora looked at her father and noticed his tight, triumphant smile, even though he bent his head to disguise it. He was enjoying her discomfort.

'OK,' she said at last. She had no choice really. It would look odd to go so soon after they had arrived and Ursula seemed set on staying. 'Just for a couple of days.'

After making Ursula a meal of pasta and tuna from the rather sparse contents of the kitchen cupboard, Rora unpacked the ladybird suitcase and settled her daughter into what had been her grandmother's room. Tired from her journey and the excitement of being somewhere new, one story was enough to set Ursula's eyelids flickering.

'There's an awful lot of stuff in this room,' said Ursula, gazing around at the paintings that covered almost every inch of the walls.

'Your great-grandmother was a bit of a collector,' Rora said, feeling suddenly bereft. She remembered the way Isobel used to tell tall tales of her amazing exploits. Part seductress, part spy, her grandmother had turned down the marriage proposals of fifteen panting young men, smuggled important documents in the lining of her bra, fought tigers bare-handed and trained herself to hold her breath underwater for fifteen minutes. Rora wished Isobel was there now and could tell them one of her stories or perhaps get down *The Book of Kisses* and banish everything else for an hour or so.

'It's a funny house,' said Ursula, pushing off the quilt that covered her. Although it was seven o'clock in the evening the heat had not diminished, and Rora pulled open the sash window to let in what little breeze there was.

'What do you mean?' she asked.

'It smells strange,' said Ursula. 'A bit like Burney Bear did when we left him out in the rain and didn't dry him properly. There are rooms with all the furniture covered up. It gives me a weird feeling.'

'Well, your grandfather has been living here by himself for quite a long time and he doesn't use most of the rooms anymore,' said Rora.

She stayed until Ursula fell asleep, and then went to her old bedroom and lay down on the small bed, immediately recognising its loose headboard and lumpy quilt. Rora had been christened Aurora by parents who had given little thought to how an unconventional name might be received in the playground. She was named in honour of the Northern Lights, the Roman Goddess of the Dawn and Disney's Sleeping Beauty. The young Rora had been unable to pronounce her own name, her mouth struggling with the awkward sound, and she had shortened it to Rora, a nickname that had stuck over the years, despite her parents' best efforts to call her by her given name. In fact, its short, slightly prickly sound was much more suited to Rora's personality. She had a mass of blonde curly hair and wide, green eyes, but her whimsical appearance belied her serious soul. From a very young age, it was all too apparent to Rora Raine that if any sort of order was to be maintained she would have to be the sensible one in her family of dreamers and storytellers.

The ceiling still bore the traces of where she had stuck the fluorescent stars that had glowed all the way through her nights until she had left home. The dressing table with its oval mirror was still in the corner where the ghost of a teenage Rora sat applying eye shadow and religiously turning the gold studs in her newly pierced ears. A seagull started up its insistent cry, and the sound was so loud it was as if the bird was in the room with her. She got up and went over to the window and pulled aside the curtain. It was sitting on her windowsill. It turned an unperturbed eye towards her. She banged on the glass and after a last insolent stare, the creature flew off to splatter roofs and rummage through bins for chips and steal the warm pasties from children's fists.

At some point Rora must have fallen asleep, because she woke to the sound of her father and Pauline climbing the stairs. She could hear him breathing heavily and the nurse making encouraging noises as she helped him up. He stopped to gather himself on the landing outside her bedroom, and she remembered the many nights she had lain on this bed in this room wanting someone, somehow, to put right all the things that had gone wrong. He had never come into her room, even though she sometimes heard him make this exact same pause outside her door, as if he was thinking about it. It had been an unhappy house in those years after her mother had gone, and the fabric of the place had seemed to reflect the sadness: the walls, left too long unattended, flaked plaster onto the floors, and the condensation trickled down the windows like tears.

*

It seemed that Frank was making some kind of protest about her arrival at the house, because the next day he didn't come downstairs.

'He's very tired,' Pauline said as she washed up his breakfast dishes, and Rora could hear the barely veiled censure in her voice.

'I've hardly seen him. You can't blame me if he's taken it into his head to stay in bed,' Rora said.

'You've been away a long time,' said Pauline. 'Your arrival has been unsettling for him.'

She leaned her not inconsiderable bulk against the kitchen sink and dried her reddened hands on the tea towel. She gave Rora one of her assessing stares, as if she was contemplating a purchase and was finding the object wanting.

Rora noticed again the strange dislocation between the two halves of Pauline's face. She looked as if someone had glued her together.

'Well, we wouldn't want Frank upset, now, would we?' Rora said bitterly.

'He's very ill,' said Pauline. 'It's my job to make his last days as comfortable as possible.'

'How long do you think he's got?' asked Rora, and then wished she hadn't been quite so blunt.

Pauline seemed unperturbed by the question. She was obviously used to the vagaries of relatives, even one like Rora, who had shown up at the last minute and who clearly didn't have any of the attributes associated with a loving daughter. Rora wondered if the woman's hostility was due to her suspecting Rora had only turned up to cash in on the spoils of death.

'It's very difficult to put a time limit on it,' she said. 'It could be a few days, but it could be as long as a few weeks. It depends on the course of the illness and on what the patient hangs on for.'

'What do you mean – hangs on for?' asked Rora.

'Well, some folks just give up, and others cling to the prospect of a certain day, like the birth of a grandchild, or sometimes they wait until someone close to them can be with them before they go.'

She looked meaningfully at Rora.

'Oh, he's not been hanging on for me,' said Rora. 'He doesn't even want me here.'

'You'd know better than me,' she said shortly, and with a last energetic swipe at the kitchen surfaces she went out of the room.

Pauline's departure for the day left Rora at a loss. Hannah had come round earlier with her two daughters to take Ursula out for a few hours, and Rora was unwilling to go and see her father until he asked for her. It seemed nothing had changed between them; they still butted up against each other's stubbornness the way they always had.

She wondered again at her decision to come home. She knew that being here was only going to open her up to fresh hurt. She could already feel the beginnings of the ache, as if a long-frozen limb was becoming warm again, bringing with it the dull throb of life. She thought about the fact that Carl was back and what, if anything, she should do about it. He hadn't tried to find her, so she assumed he didn't want to. What if she bumped into him? What would she say? When she thought about meeting him again, all the old feelings of guilt rose up in her, as strong and as desperate as ever. Over the years Rora had become an expert on feeling only as much as she allowed herself to. Her work frequently absorbed her, requiring as it did total immersion in whatever subject she was researching, but that was as close as she ever came to losing herself. In all other areas of her life she held back, only doing the bare minimum needed to make herself appear like a regular person with ordinary preoccupations. She had never lost her reluctance to stand out. She attended certain tried and tested social gatherings with people she knew and who asked little of her. As soon as a crisis hit and someone required more than an evening drinking wine and talking thinly about work and yoga and whatever book or film was doing the rounds, she would hastily retreat. She avoided emotion in others as assiduously as she avoided it in herself.

As she moved around the house she had the sensation, despite the familiarity of her surroundings, that she was an interloper. She found that she was consciously softening the sound of her feet on the floor and was opening and closing doors tentatively, as if she knew she shouldn't really be there and was nervous of being discovered. In the front reception room the light came through the slats in the shutters like knife blades. She opened them and secured them against the wall and the room seemed to come suddenly alive. She tried to unfasten the window but the thing was stuck fast. It was still breathlessly hot. She knew she should be glad for such weather by the sea, but this heat was oppressive, choking.

The sofa and chairs were shrouded in sheets and she tugged one of them off, releasing a cloud of dust. The chandelier, obscured with dirt, was laced between its branches by swathes of cobwebs. The mirror over the fireplace was mottled around the edges. She caught sight of her face in its reflection and thought she looked pale, as if the house had leached the colour from her skin and hair. This room would have to wait, she told herself.

She needed to attend to Ursula's room first and make it clean. She felt better now that she could see a purpose for herself. She paused for a moment in the hallway and let the colours from the glass in the door play over her hands and her arms. These same yellows and greens had passed over her when she was a child, and they moved on her now in the same way they always had, oblivious to the changes in her.

She took a basin of hot water up to Isobel's old bedroom, where Ursula had laid out her possessions neatly on the bed. The objects in plastic pinks and purples looked out of place amid the faded glories of Isobel's clutter. She cleaned the tops of the paintings, each wipe transferring a thick skin of dirt onto the cloth. She dusted the golden curves of the Cupids on the clock whose dimpled crevices were lined with grey, and wiped the glass case containing the taxidermy owl, so that its eyes glinted at her as they had done when she was a child. She sponged the furred insides of the lampshades and rubbed the brass finials at the ends of the bed. She went downstairs again and found some crusty lavender polish in the kitchen cupboard and restored the chest of drawers and the wardrobe to their old sheen. She took up the silk rug and carried it into the garden and shook it out, wondering if the particles she released still contained vestiges of her grandmother.

Satisfied that the room was now clean enough, she began to explore the rest of the house. The two further bedrooms on the first floor were shrouded as downstairs had been. On the second floor, she took care not to step on the creaking board outside the room that her parents had shared and in which Frank now lay in defiant silence. The room next door to his was full of boxes of books and papers and abandoned bits of furniture propped up against the wall. She looked at the flight of steps that led up to the attic bedroom. She knew then that this was where she had been heading all along.

She felt the same trembling of her limbs and constriction in her throat that she had experienced in the taxi. It seemed that the passage of the years had done nothing to lessen her feelings of fear and helplessness. She hesitated, then forced herself to walk up the narrow steps – the treads curved and slippery where feet had worn them smooth. She was too old to be spooked by ghosts, and if she didn't go there now, the room would wait for her, like a job unfinished, a letter unopened. She spoke aloud to herself.

'It's just a room, Rora. Just an empty room.'

She tried the handle of the door, but it was locked. She felt along the top of the doorframe for the key she knew was always kept there, but it was missing. She turned away with a kind of relief. It seemed she wasn't going to have to go back after all. The past was going to stay where it was, sealed up like a corked bottle or a bunch of old lavender stitched into linen.

Although she was tired and would have been glad to rest until Ursula came home, she couldn't settle and so she resumed her cleaning frenzy in the kitchen. As she slopped water and wiped surfaces she knew that this desire for order was a reaction to coming home. Each twist of the mop head as she squeezed it against the bucket seemed to bring her greater ease. She got down on her knees and scraped at the cracks between the wood of the parquet floor until she was sore and stiff with the effort. She plunged her hands into bleach and hot water so that they became rough and red. It felt like a kind of purging and a kind of penitence.

The pantry was full of canned and dried goods that were past their sell-by date. She pulled the bin across the kitchen floor and started throwing away rusting tins of chickpeas and bags of flour that were older than Ursula. She dragged the whole lot round to the wheelie bin in the passageway. In the dining room she rubbed polish into the battered oak table and then began sorting out the drawers in the Welsh dresser, which were full of random debris. Stuck in the crack down the side of one of the drawers, she found a single earring. She prised it out and held it flat in the palm of her hand. The raindrop-shaped garnet set on a small silver hoop was instantly familiar to her. Her mother had worn these earrings almost every day of her life, even leaving them on overnight, so that in the morning she sometimes had the shape of a teardrop embedded in her neck. Closing her eyes, Rora could still see her mother's ears, pale and flat against her dark head, the crimson droplets looking almost black. She checked in all the drawers to see if she could find the other one, but it wasn't there.

Standing in front of the mirror in the hall, Rora took out the silver stud she was wearing and replaced it with her mother's earring. She wondered what her mother would think if she could see her now. Would she forgive her for what happened then and afterwards and for all the ways she hadn't properly lived, vivid and wholehearted, as she should have? It seemed as if her life had been made up of more holes than solid ground, and now it felt like it might give way at any moment. She thought again of her glimpse of Carl through the window of the taxi and how just the sight of him had sent her reeling helplessly back. He had known her in the years before all the promise had been rubbed out.

Kiss 3

*'It was the jasmine she smelled now as her lips touched her
mother's smooth cheek.'*

10 September 1996

Rora didn't know that today would be the last time she would
kiss her mother. If she had known, she would have made the
kiss better. She would have pushed her face closer and harder.
She would have told her how much she loved her – and she did,
more than she could describe – even though her love for her had
always been complicated by anxiety.

Rora's mother, Sandi, carved tiny boats and birds from sal-
vaged beach wood in the days when there were very few of the
galleries and gift shops that were now common in the town and
which sold such things in bulk. Consequently, her mother's
earnings were erratic, many of her creations remaining unsold
and taking up space on the windowsills and mantelpieces in the
house. When Rora thought of her mother, she saw her as a kind
of blur. Seldom still, she was propelled by a nervous energy that
made her quicker and larger and noisier than anybody else's
mother. She often initiated spontaneous excursions to places
via what she called 'the holiday route', which involved sending
Rora's father on the most scenic but convoluted way to their
destination. They extended this haphazard approach to money.
Frequently unsure of how they were going to survive until the
end of the month, they used to shrug their shoulders and say,
'Something will turn up,' just as if they had thrown away the

map and were happy to arrive at whichever destination presented itself.

As she grew older, the obvious affection her parents had for each other became a source of embarrassment to Rora. They would hold hands when walking down the street, sometimes even swinging their arms as if they were about to start skipping, and she developed the habit of walking a little way behind them and looking the other way.

'Your mother is wonderful,' Frank would say to Rora, regardless of who might be listening. 'She lights up my life.' And he would pinch her mother's bottom, or spin her around the kitchen floor in a ridiculous waltz when certain dreamy songs came on the radio. Sandi would pretend to hate the attention, slapping away his straying hand or frowning at him when he became excessively amorous, but her face would crack with the effort of staying stern and the love she felt for him would blaze from her. Cautious, watchful Rora would worry at the intensity, the sheer transparency of her mother's feelings, and wish that she felt and showed less.

On the good days, Rora and her mother would walk on the beach and bring back pieces of oily wood in the shape of dragons and mermaids and sea-smoothed glass and fragments of china. Sandi would paint the walls of the house in bright colours and hang mobiles and sun catchers and strings of beads from the ceilings and above the windows. Best of all, as far as Rora was concerned, was when her mother told stories, the words tumbling out of her as glittering as the beads and the mobiles. Stories of battles and impossible challenges and castles on the sides of dark, pine-covered mountains, monsters under the sea and in lakes and rivers, black-hearted villains, and long-haired maidens with delicate bone structures but wills of iron. Rora loved the stories but knew deep down that they were shields to keep the darkness at bay, and that they only worked for as long as it took to tell them.

These periods of colourful exuberance were often followed by days and weeks when her mother stayed silently in bed, beset by a crippling inertia that left her barely able to lift her head. Sandi thought that her daughter was unaware of these periods, but Rora always knew by a quick check of the still-warm sheets that her mother had only dragged herself up and out of bed just in time for her return from school, and that despite her attempts to help, despite the good marks and the jobs quietly done, her mother had somehow fallen away from her again. Each time this happened, she felt as if she had let her tender, noisy, lovely mother down.

She sometimes escaped to her grandmother's shaded, patchouli-scented living room on the first floor of the house. She lay on the balding chaise longue in the mass of dusty velvet cushions and listened to the tick of the clock with its golden cherubs. When she was in her grandmother's room, she didn't need to worry about how she could make her mother feel better or whether her father had remembered to pay the electricity bill. She could even forget about the worrying crack that now ran the entire length of the kitchen ceiling, about which both her parents seemed completely unconcerned. Being with Isobel allowed her to relinquish responsibility for a while. Their post-school sessions were lit by lampshades draped with silk scarves and, when her grandmother was feeling particularly flamboyant, candles in a dripping candelabra. These lighting arrangements, though atmospheric, were a source of anxiety to Rora, who would creep around after Isobel had gone to bed, licking her thumb and index finger, anxiously pinching each wick and taking scarves off hot bulbs.

Isobel owned a bright yellow beach hut, which bore the name Kiss Me Quick above its door, and sometimes the two of them would go there with a picnic packed up carefully in a wicker hamper. The moment Rora liked the best was when the door to the hut was unlocked and she got her first smell of warm wood and mildewed canvas – odours she associated with happiness all her life. They would put the folding chairs on the porch and spread the picnic out at their feet and eat and talk and watch the changing colours of the sea. Rora was entrusted with the task of coaxing the reluctant stove to produce enough heat to boil water for tea. It was often when they were at the beach hut that Rora talked about her mother. It seemed safer to share her feelings when there was no possibility of being overheard. Despite her volubility, Isobel was a very good listener because she seldom rushed to give advice. She held her granddaughter's words carefully, turning them over to see what was on the other side, in the same way that Rora checked the shells she found on the beach, for flaws or for any creatures that might still be wriggling inside.

'What makes Mum so sad?' Rora asked one day. 'Is it me?'

'It's never, ever you,' said Isobel. 'Something very sad happened to her several years ago. She's tried lots of things to make herself better, but nothing quite works.'

'What was the sad thing?' asked Rora.

Isobel hesitated and then spoke.

'Five years before you were born your mother had a baby. The doctors said that the baby was sick and that Sandi shouldn't have her, but she decided to go ahead anyway, and very sadly the baby died a week after she was born.'

Rora was astonished. Another baby! Why had her mother never told her? She wondered for a moment if this was just one of her grandmother's stories, but Isobel seemed very serious when she was talking about it so Rora thought it must be true.

'She pretends it never happened, and I think, that's why the sadness of it has got deep inside her,' said Isobel.

'Didn't having me make her feel happy?' asked Rora, aware of feeling different now. She wasn't the only one after all. Before her there had been another child that her parents had wanted and loved.

'There are some things that are very hard to recover from, even if you have someone as gorgeous as you turn up,' said Isobel. 'Sometimes it's just the way you are made. I had a cat once called Bonnie,' she said, leaning her elbow on the arm of her deck chair and tucking her little finger against the corner of her mouth, the way she always did when she was beginning to tell a story. 'A tortoiseshell, which everyone knows is the trickiest of cats – so moody and unpredictable. Bonnie loved being stroked. She would lie in my lap and purr and purr and rub her face into my skirt in a kind of rapture, but every now and again, even though I touched her in exactly the same way each time, she would bite my hand. Dig her teeth in really hard so that she left marks in my skin. It was as if the sensation of being touched had suddenly overwhelmed her. The joy of it had somehow become unbearable and she would jump off my lap and go and find a quiet corner to lie in. And she would stay there until she was hungry or a fat bird caught her eye or she could see a warmer patch of sun in another place in the room. Your mother is a little like Bonnie. She can only take so much rapture and then the darkness comes down on her and she has to find somewhere to hide.'

It seemed to Rora that over the past couple of months the periods of time her mother spent in bed were getting longer, and she knew that even her father, who hardly seemed to notice anything at all, was worried. He had always been laughingly indulgent about what he termed Sandi's 'periods of recuperation' and treated his wife's absences as just one of her many eccentricities.

'She's just plotting her next move,' he would say, when Rora mentioned her concerns. 'She'll be back to her usual mischief before too long.'

But Rora could tell that something had changed. She thought it might have been something to do with what she had seen when she had walked into her parents' bedroom a couple of weeks before. The image of her father's face with its strange, stunned look, as if he had been hit, was still clear in her mind. She caught her father looking at her mother in a new, cautious way. There were raised voices during the night, and the sound was so unfamiliar to Rora that she would lie awake worrying long after her parents had gone to bed. There were lots of empty wine bottles in the bin, and bunches of flowers that made her mother cry, and then a sudden, uncharacteristic decision to take a trip away in the middle of the school term.

They stayed in Alnmouth in Northumberland in a house with a bay window looking out onto the estuary. It was atmospheric but chilly, and Sandi spent most of the time sitting wrapped in a blanket. One afternoon Rora had been out alone, walking on the beach, and when she returned, something about the low, secretive tone of her parents' voices made her stand outside the door of the living room and listen to what they were saying. When they had been happy, she had never felt as if they left her out – she had always been part of the celebration, but now that they didn't seem to be getting along, she had an only child's sense of feeling excluded.

'You don't love me anymore,' she heard her mother say in a despairing voice.

'Don't start this again. Please don't start this again,' Frank said. He sounded tired. Not the sort of tired that he seemed when he had been up all night poring over maps and yellowing scraps of paper, but the sort of tired someone gets when they have run out of things to do. When they have walked round and round the wall looking for cracks wide enough to get through and not found any.

'We shouldn't have had her,' he said.

'Don't say that. How can you say that?' Sandi said.

'It took too much of a toll on you.'

Rora felt a queasy twist in her stomach. She was a toll – something heavy and hard to bear. Something you had to pay for when you didn't want to. Her father thought she was the reason why her mother was so unhappy. Having Rora had tired Sandi out and made her sadness worse. Rora felt like crying but packed her tears hard inside. This hiding of emotion was something she had learned to do only recently.

'Hello, darling, been to the beach?' Frank asked when she came into the room. He had the too loud, friendly voice he used when he was pretending.

'Yes,' she said, and gave her mother the handful of fragments of blue and white china she had picked up on the beach. They gathered in the fold of her mother's skirt, pulling it down.

On their last night in Alnmouth they made a barbeque on the beach and cooked burgers. Rora stood in the sea with her mother while they ate the smoky, savoury meat. The sky and sea were suffused with hot pink and threads of dark purple, and as they stood in the shallows the colour licked up almost to the tops of their wellington boots so that they too were part of the otherworldly shimmer. Her mother's sadness seemed to have disappeared.

'Hang onto this moment,' Sandi said, turning to Rora, her beautiful navy eyes wide with delight. 'If you fix it in your mind now, it will stay with you forever.'

And Rora fixed it as she had been told to do – the taste of the salty, charred meat, the sensation of cold through her boots, the extraordinary colours of the sky, the way her mother stood with her hands held out as if she had at last discovered what it was she wanted.

Now it was a rainy Monday morning and Rora was furious that Sandi had not bought the black T-shirt and leggings she needed for her dance class that day. She considered that being fourteen with braces and no curves to speak of was bad enough without having to present herself in the school hall in her hockey skirt and PE top, which meant the boys would be able to see her knickers if they stood at the edge of the stage while she danced. Isobel, who often helped out with this sort of thing, was away on one of her coach trips to see churches or stately homes. She would come back from these holidays full of hair-raising stories of near disasters and intrigues. Rora had trouble believing that a group of men with clicking dentures and hair growing out of their noses and women in lumpy cardigans would be capable of such behaviour, but her grandmother said, 'Passion lies in the most unlikeliest of breasts,' which made Rora feel a bit funny when she thought about the cardiganed breasts of Isobel's companions.

Not having the right kit would only give the two girls she hated the most in the world more ammunition. Katie Simmons with her neat nose and perky bottom would no doubt arch her over-plucked eyebrows at her and smile in a superior fashion. Katie wore an immaculate black leotard and sugar-pink legwarmers and was given to unnecessary displays of the splits and much leaning against the wall while flexing her feet. You could tell she thought she was a proper dancer, instead of just a kid in a school hall. She had serious delusions of grandeur. Her sidekick, Moira Templeton, was an own-brand version of Katie; she was slightly less groomed, slightly less clever. Her role was to giggle in appreciation and, from time to time, hand her mentor the lip balm from her pencil case. The girls put their identical sleek, blonde ponytails side by side and cupped their hands and looked at Rora while they whispered, and although she despised them with every fibre of her being, she wanted very much to know what they were saying. She also wanted a sleek, blonde ponytail.

'Be a leader. Don't run with the herd,' was her mother's advice when she had tried to tell her about Katie and Moira, which was terrible advice when Rora considered that her chances of being a leader were slim to nothing. She was lucky if she could just get by without drawing too much attention to herself. She despaired of her uncontrollable hair, her inability to bite her tongue when she thought someone had made a mistake, her round face and wide green eyes, which made her look as if she was much younger than she was.

'You promised you would buy them for me,' said Rora as she stood at the door of her parents' bedroom. She was already late for school, and if there was one thing Rora hated more than factual inaccuracies, it was lack of punctuality. Their feeble grasp of the time was one of the many things about her parents that drove her mad. 'I reminded you about fifteen times.'

'I'm sorry, darling, I forgot,' said Sandi, her head still under the duvet. Her voice had that muffled, dead quality that usually acted on Rora as a warning to walk quietly and not make any demands, but this time the sound of it enraged her.

'You always forget everything,' said Rora, and when her mother didn't answer, she went into the room and snatched the duvet off the bed. At the sight of her mother's body, her legs long and thin, and her nightdress rucked up to the top of her thighs, she felt instantly remorseful, but it was too late, the damage was done. It was always like this, lately. She would find herself going further than she ever intended, and once she had started there seemed no way back. It was as if someone else was in control of her.

'You're a useless mother. I may as well not have a mother at all,' she said, her voice low and hateful. Sandi didn't respond, she just curled her body up tightly as if against an incoming blow. Rora could smell the jasmine perfume that Sandi wore behind her ears on the good days, but the odour was overlaid now with something sour, like the smell you get on your hands from touching the top of the milk bottle. It was her mother's vulnerability, lying like this without any care for how she looked, with her tangled hair and her mouth ridged with some sort of white crust, that made Rora cruel.

'Why don't you just get up?' she said. 'Why don't you *do* something?'

Rora stood for a moment more and then turned and left the room.

She had got almost all the way to school before she allowed herself to think about what had just happened. Until then she had been propelled by fury at her own powerlessness. She thought about her mother lying in the still room, her white limbs cooling, Rora's words burning her, and she turned back even though she knew it would mean she would get another late note on her report. Sandi was lying exactly as she had left her, and Rora had the feeling that she could lie like this forever, until she crumbled like bones in a desert whitened by the sun and then cracked by the cold, on and on until there was nothing left but sand. Rora covered her up and tucked the duvet tightly around her mother's neck.

'I'm sorry,' she said, 'I didn't mean any of it.'

She bent over and kissed her mother gently, the lightest and most penitent of kisses. It was the jasmine she smelled now as her lips touched her mother's smooth cheek.

When she got back from school, Rora thought her mother was hiding from her. Sandi often emerged from behind curtains and out of cupboards, shaking with glee and triumph, refusing to believe that Rora had heard her shifting around behind the door or seen her feet sticking out from the bottom of the curtain. Unlike Rora, Sandi found being still a difficult thing to manage.

'Mum, where are you?' Rora shouted when she had looked in the living room and kitchen. She had brought a peace offering – a big bar of Sandi's favourite Turkish Delight chocolate. Her mother always did a kind of comic belly dance when presented with the confection, and her foolish gyrations never failed to make Rora laugh. She thought with a sinking heart that her mother had perhaps not managed to get out of bed yet. It usually meant it was a really bad day if she wasn't up in time for Rora's return, but when she poked her head around the bedroom door the duvet was smooth and the cushions had been placed in an orderly line against the headboard.

She wasn't in the bathroom either, and Rora had just decided that perhaps her mother had gone out to the shops forgetting that Isobel was not at home, when she saw that the door to the attic stairs was slightly ajar. Although there was a bed in there somewhere, it had been years since anyone had actually slept in the room. Now it was simply a repository for everything that was waiting to be fixed or which no longer had a place downstairs.

When Rora first saw her mother's feet, she thought she was playing one of her games. Did she really imagine that Rora couldn't see her? She climbed up the first few steps and then stopped. Her mother was not standing at the top as she had first thought; she was hanging from the bannister. Rora dropped the bar of chocolate. If she hadn't recognised her feet, the toes painted with sparkly nail varnish, Rora would never have known this was her mother. Her face was swollen, as if mosquitoes had been feasting on her, and her eyes were dark and wide. Panic took hold of Rora in its terrible electric grip, so that at first she didn't know what to do. It took some time for her to realise that the strange wailing noise she could hear was coming from her own mouth. She climbed further up the stairs and put her mother's arms with their clenched fists around her shoulders and tried to hold her up around the waist, but the silky material of her dressing gown was too slippery and she couldn't get enough purchase. There was something wet on her mother's chin. Rora lifted the edge of her sweatshirt and wiped it off. She tried to let go of her mother's body gently so that it didn't bang against the wall. She didn't want her to be hurt any more. Although she ran to the telephone and remembered to talk clearly and calmly, stating all the necessary facts, she knew it was too late. Her mother had decided the rapture was not worth the pain.

Rora remembered the days after her mother's death as a series of frozen moments. The urgent, almost instinctive way she had set off running to the school to meet Carl to tell him what had happened. The way he had held her against his chest as if she had a new shape. Her father coming back from the hospital with a blank face, as if his features had been pixelated. Her mother lying in the chapel of rest with her hair parted on the wrong side. Isobel sitting in her chair, her narrow shoulders shaking as if she was trying not to laugh, but then her mouth stretching open like she was about to swallow something whole. People gathering around her, then dispersing.

Rora knew what had happened was her fault, but she couldn't talk to her father because she thought that perhaps her mother's death was his fault too, and she felt filled with a kind of embarrassed fear at the prospect of hearing him try and make it right. She didn't want to see him looking ashamed while he struggled to find words that she would understand, when she knew already he wasn't the person she had thought he was. Isobel looked too fragile, suddenly too old to burden further. She wasn't sure in any case that she could actually admit to anyone what she had done. She remembered her words to Sandi with terrible shame. 'I may as well not have a mother,' she had said, and she had made it happen.

A few weeks after Sandi's death, Frank went away to Yorkshire and took the urn that had been Rora's mother with him. He told her he wanted her to stay behind and look after the house and her grand-mother. Rora thought that he would return after a few days, but the days turned into weeks, then months. Although she wasn't even sure she wanted him to come back, the house felt too big with only her and Isobel. It felt like she no longer had a proper family.

'Why is he staying away for so long?' she asked her grand-mother after yet another phone conversation with her father, during which he had been vague about when he was coming back. Isobel did her best to make sense of it to her.

'He loved your mother so much,' she said, stroking Rora's always tangled hair, 'that he can't bear to come back to the house without her in it just yet.'

'But I'm in it,' said Rora, 'and you are.'

'I know, darling,' said Isobel, 'but your dad thinks that having him around being unhappy will only make you unhappy too.'

'I'm unhappy already,' said Rora, taking herself away to her room and closing the door firmly against Isobel's offers of cheese on toast or a hot water bottle. When he hadn't phoned for a fortnight, she took matters into her own hands and rang him up. When he answered, he sounded as if he had been asleep, although it was the middle of the afternoon.

'When are you coming back?' she asked him.

'Pretty soon,' he said.

'Where are you?' she asked, imagining him in a draughty house like Wuthering Heights, or in a black and white landscape similar to the one on the front cover of her copy of *A Kestrel for a Knave*. She had never been to Yorkshire.

'I'm staying in a B&B,' he said. 'I'm trying very hard to get myself better, Rora.'

*

When he eventually returned, he had changed almost beyond all recognition. It wasn't only that he looked thinner and older and moved as if his body hurt, it was as if he had gone away and sent back a rough approximation of himself, someone who sounded like him but behaved quite differently. He had always been vague and studious, but now he shut himself in his study for most of the day and barely spoke to either Rora or Isobel. All his sweetness seemed to have gone. Once or twice she tried, in a scared, tentative way, to talk about what had happened. She thought if he spoke to her about what he had done then she would be able to share her own guilt with him, but he shut such conversations down before they had even begun and the silence grew between them, wider and broader every day so that there was no way back. She remembered that he had called her a toll, and she supposed she was even more of one now that her mother wasn't there to intercede for her.

'Where did you put Mum's ashes, Dad?' she asked him once, since he had never mentioned it.

'Under a tree,' he said, looking down at his hands placed on either side of his plate on the kitchen table.

'Was it a special tree?' she tried.

'It was all a long time ago,' was all he would say on the matter, and they carried on with their meal in silence, the clock ticking loudly on the wall, the evening light from the window turning grey then blue and holding them there until the food was finished and she was able to escape.

After a while Rora gave up trying to talk to him about Sandi or expecting him to show any curiosity about her own life and what she was doing. She gave up expecting any comfort from him at all, and she knew she couldn't comfort him. The old way they used to talk together, easy and teasing, was like another language and she had lost her grasp of the vocabulary. Isobel always showed up for the school plays and prize-giving ceremonies, dressed in silk frocks and pastel-coloured cashmere cardigans, and did her valiant best to fill the gaping holes left by Rora's parents, even though they both knew that was impossible. They kept up their sessions in Isobel's living room, even sometimes reading *The Book of Kisses*, which was still a comforting ritual, though Rora felt increasingly that it mattered more to her grandmother than it did to her. The kisses and swooning moments in the book had changed since her father had acquired his new, ashamed face and her mother had died. They were nothing like what actually happened in real life.

May 2010

It had been a long time since Rora had seen Ursula so calm and contented. It seemed that all the unhappiness of the last few months had disappeared. Her daughter took the little jobs she was given by Pauline with great seriousness, carrying cups of tea and jugs of water up the stairs to her grandfather with an air of self-importance, and although he didn't talk to her much, she seemed to enjoy sitting on the end of his bed, chattering away to him. Rora kept thinking that she would rent somewhere in town for the summer, just as a temporary measure until she could decide what they were going to do next, but Ursula was insistent that they stay.

'I like it here,' she said with a purse of her lips that signified she had made up her mind.

'What do you like so much?' asked Rora.

'It feels safe,' said Ursula, as if the matter was settled, and Rora was so glad to see her daughter's face flushed from a day at the beach, her hair in a salty mess around her head, that she put aside her misgivings. It was difficult to be back, but if it made Ursula happy to be here then they would stay. Ursula hadn't mentioned her own father for weeks, which Rora took as a sign that she had really started to move on. Over the years Ursula had always initiated conversations about her absent parent when she was feeling particularly low, as if she blamed this gap in her life for everything that ailed her. When Ursula had grown old enough to notice the absence Rora told her that he had gone away – that he and Rora had broken up before he knew she was going to have a baby.

'Why don't you ring him up and tell him about me?' Ursula asked once, her little face puzzled. 'I'm sure he would come if he knew I was here,' she said.

'I don't know where he is,' Rora said, thinking the answer was inadequate, but not knowing how else to explain it. A few days later she heard her daughter telling a friend that her daddy was lost and they couldn't find him. She made it sound as if they had left him at a station by accident or he had wandered off one night and forgotten his way back. Ursula never abandoned the idea of him and of the family she imagined they would have been, and when she was cross with her mother she sometimes used her longing as a source of blame.

Ursula deliberated for a long time about what she should wear for her first day at her new school, even though she only had to choose something plain to go with her uniform, which was a navy sweatshirt embroidered with a little red tree.

'You only have to choose between the grey skirt, the black trousers or the navy shorts,' said Rora, glancing at the clock. They had half an hour left and she wondered if she was going to be able to get Ursula there on time.

'It's important to get it right,' Ursula said and started to worry away at the patch of raw skin that had developed on the corner of her mouth. Rora stilled her daughter's hand.

'Don't pick, Ursula. You'll make it sore. You're going to be fine. They are going to love you even if you turn up in a plastic bag with a tea cosy on your head.'

Ursula gave a wan smile and shook her head doubtfully.

'Listen to me, my darling girl . . . there are more good people than bad people in the world, but you just happened to stumble upon a bunch of nasty ones at your old school. It wasn't anything to do with what you were wearing or what you said. You are perfect.'

Rora took her daughter in her arms and held her close. She could feel the beat of her heart as fast and near the surface as that of a bird's. It was Ursula who finally pulled away.

'I'll wear the grey skirt,' she said decisively, 'and you'd better go and get your shoes on. We don't want to be late.'

'I'll be fine, Mum,' she said as they walked up to the entrance of the low building with daffodil yellow walls and trees in pots placed around the playground.

'If you don't like it you don't have to come back,' said Rora.

'Don't worry about me,' said Ursula. Although her voice was determinedly cheerful her face was set and pale.

'I'm going to stay at the back of the classroom for a while,' said Rora.

'You don't need to. Nobody else's mum will be there. They'll think I'm a baby,' said Ursula.

Ursula's teacher, Miss Prentice, was a thin woman with a slightly dishevelled air – her slip was hanging down at the back of her skirt and she had what looked like porridge on her cheek, but she welcomed Ursula warmly and introduced her to the rest of the class.

Rora sat on a small chair at the side of the classroom and was reassured by the friendly touches she could see all around her: the teetering models of castles with egg box drawbridges, the pegs along the walls adorned with the photographs of each of the children, the nature table with its motley collection of stones and bits of vegetation. It seemed the most benevolent of places, but then she had thought that about Ursula's last school and its effect on her daughter had been devastating. Two girls with the faces of angels and the hearts of witches had tormented Ursula for months – jeering at her in the playground, throwing her lunch down the toilet, whispering to the others about things she hadn't done. The terrible thing was that Rora hadn't realised it had been going on until they had made Ursula ill with their malevolent attentions. What sort of a mother was she to have been so without proper instinct? Mothers were supposed to know as if by osmosis what was going on with their children. The news that Ursula had been so systematically bullied and for so long came as a complete surprise. Her daughter had always seemed so self-sufficient, rather like she had been as a child. It should have been a warning, not a reason for complacency, given Rora's own experiences.

'Why didn't you tell me?' she had asked a feverish Ursula, from whom the sorry tale had finally poured out one night. It had started with the sound of heartbreaking wailing coming from her daughter's room, as if Ursula had reached some sort of saturation point and been unable to keep the pain inside any longer.

'I could have stopped it,' Rora said, lying stricken next to her sobbing daughter.

'No one can stop it, Mum,' Ursula said with pitiful earnestness. 'They say that I am a person to hate. But I don't even know what I did to start them hating me. That's what I don't understand. I asked them, but they wouldn't tell me.'

After Rora had been in the classroom for about ten minutes Ursula made a kind of jerking motion with her head to indicate that her mother should go, and so Rora mouthed that she would see her at going home time and left quietly. She felt tempted to go straight back to the house. Some memories travelled alongside you – they were caught up in your days, in the lines of your face, in the things you no longer allowed yourself to do. Although she was used to what she had to carry with her, walking around these streets would be like rolling up a blind and looking more closely than she thought she could bear at the scared, shamed child she had been. And what if she saw Carl again? It was unlikely, but not impossible. Despite herself she felt an echo of the old shivering longing. Instinctively, her hand went to the charm she wore around her neck, the little key that Carl had given her. It was the only thing she had allowed herself to keep. She wore it as part talisman and part warning, even though there was no danger she would ever forget what they had done. She decided to walk on despite her fears. There was nothing to do in the house and her father was still keeping up his obdurate silence.

Her decision to come to Hastings had been made so abruptly that she hadn't really thought enough about what she would need and had only packed a few jumpers and a couple of pairs of jeans. Rora felt hot in the knitted top and narrow trousers she was wearing. She took the jumper off and tied it around her waist, aware that the T-shirt underneath was past its best, its pale green now a much-washed grey. She ought to buy some lighter summer things, but the thought of going into a shop and choosing items and then standing in front of a mirror to try them on wasn't appealing. She couldn't remember when she had last taken anything but the barest glance at herself. She only gave herself enough time to scrape back her hair, still as blonde and curly as it had been when she was younger, pass some cream across her face and quickly poke at her eyelashes with a drying mascara brush.

She thought with longing of the sensation of cool water on her feet and decided to walk through the town to the sea. She passed some buildings that she didn't recognise, but in between these new additions were the old, familiar places. She saw herself at different ages – in a new checked dress, waiting for Carl on the corner of the street by the Flower Makers' Museum, where they still stamped out silk petals and leaves for wreaths and corsages; or, when she was much younger, her hair restrained into a plait, walking to the public library with her father, a Saturday treat made even better by the ice cream they always had afterwards in a green-tiled café by the pier, where the waitresses wore little black aprons and kept their pens tucked behind their ears. She passed the garden created to commemorate the bombing of the Swan Inn in 1943. She had sat there on a bench just after her mother had died, feeling bewildered and guilty, waiting for someone to make things right again. Rora had always found it a strange place, as sites that mark an absence often are. The sign at the entrance to the garden stated that the destruction of the pub had happened at midday on Sunday; the information immediately and unhappily conjuring up hard-won leisure and the hot, companionable haze of the bar and the sound of glasses being put down on tables. She remembered now that a little girl had died there too – the landlord's five-year-old daughter, who had been washing up glasses behind the bar when the bomb hit. They were all here at once – those men with their glasses raised to their mouths, the girl standing on a stool over a sink full of soapy water, and Rora too, as she was now and as she had been.

Five minutes walk saw her on the Stade, the stretch of seafront and shingle beach that ran from the Old Town as far as the car park on Rock-a-Nore Road. It was from here that the town's fishing fleet launched their boats, working in the same way they had for centuries, pulling the vessels from their hardwood blocks across the stones and into the churning shallows, although now rusting tractors were used to shift the bigger boats rather than horses.

She walked a little way beyond the boats and sat down on the pebbles and took her sneakers and socks off and rolled up her trousers. At first it was painful to walk – the stones hurt her feet and the water was breathtakingly cold despite the heat of the sun, but then the pebbles gave way to a more sandy patch and Rora was able to walk along the beach comfortably, the water lapping at her ankles. The soft drag of the shingle as each wave receded was a soothing sound and the sea shone in great sheets of beaten silver. Despite growing up on the edge of this sea and watching its changes every day, she had never learned to swim. One of her many childhood preoccupations had been the potential danger of tides and currents. She had once heard tell of someone who had been caught by an incoming tide and had described the water as moving faster than a racing horse, and the image of that desperate run to safety, the steaming flanks and wild eyes of the horse as it ran just behind, had stayed in her mind, even though the tides were gentle here. When she had Ursula she thought about finally getting swimming lessons so that she would be in a position to save her daughter if she ever got into trouble in the sea, but the old aversion was too entrenched, and now Ursula could swim like a fish and she was still marooned on dry land.

She was so deep in thought and so lulled by the water and the sun that she didn't see him until he was almost upon her.

'Beautiful day!' he said. 'Perfect for paddling.'

With her eyes cast down, looking at where she was putting her feet, she had almost bumped into him coming the other way. He looked incongruous, dressed in a suit, with the trousers rolled up to his knees. He stopped in front of her, forcing her to stop too.

'Yes,' said Rora, wondering why it was that she so often found herself falling into conversation with strangers. She thought it must be the cat effect – the more you didn't want them jumping up into your lap, the more eager they were to do so.

'No time to swim today, so I thought I would just have a leg dip,' he said.

He had a slight accent, Eastern European she thought. She shaded her face with her hand and looked at him. He had an open, suntanned face and closely cut hair that was just turning grey.

'You'll get your suit wet,' she said, and he smiled widely, apparently delighted at her response. Maybe most people simply ignored him when he accosted them in the sea.

'I have an appointment this afternoon. Have to be booted and suited,' he said. 'People believe you more when you wear a suit,' and he smiled again revealing white, even teeth and a dimple in his cheek. Rora couldn't resist pricking his bubble. He was far too happy for her liking.

'I don't think a suit is necessarily a sign of trustworthiness,' she said. 'Lucky Luciano was a snappy dresser.'

For a moment the man looked a little crestfallen, but quickly rallied.

'I concede the point,' he said with quaint formality. 'I've always thought there was something dodgy about Colonel Sanders. So secretive about the recipes and always the white suit, even though we all know that frying chicken is a messy business.'

She laughed despite herself.

'I've got to go,' she said, turning towards the beach.

'Me too. I must dry my feet ready for the bank manager,' he said and then extended his hand. 'My name's Krystof,' he said. 'I hope we meet again.'

Rora shook his hand, but resolved to keep her paddling to the other end of the beach in future. She wasn't in Hastings to make new friends and he was clearly more than a little eccentric. What sort of a person shook hands in the sea? As she put her shoes back on and watched him splash away into the distance she wondered what he needed money for – gambling debts perhaps, or a demanding ex-wife, or maybe some pie-in-the-sky project that would never come to anything. She found herself hoping that the bank manager would look favourably on his request, but she rather doubted it. His suit had been most dreadfully creased.

When Rora got back to the house Pauline was in the hall.

'Oh hello, I was just leaving,' she said, unrolling the sleeves of her uniform. 'I've made him comfortable, given him a wash.'

Her tone was a little perfunctory and her face was set in an expression that Rora thought of as professional compassion.

'How's he doing?' she asked.

'Well . . . not too bad, considering,' Pauline answered, again that exactly pitched voice somewhere between practical and personal.

'Don't let it get on top of you,' she said, putting on a cardigan and looking, as if for the first time, into Rora's face.

'We don't get on well,' said Rora, 'we never have. We fell out over something that happened a long time ago.' As she said the words she felt the anger simmering in her.

'I don't even know if I should stay. If I can bear to.'

'You're here because you need to be,' said Pauline.

'But I don't need it,' said Rora, resenting the presumption the nurse was making. 'I wouldn't even have come if it hadn't been for my daughter.'

She wondered as she spoke if she was being completely truthful. She had certainly needed to take Ursula somewhere new, but no one had made her come back to Hastings. Hannah herself had spoken as if she thought that it was unlikely, so why had she decided to return? Some instinct that she denied almost at the same time as she sensed it had brought her home.

'It's difficult saying what you feel,' said Pauline, and she must have seen something in Rora's face because she put out a hand and touched her lightly on the shoulder. At the almost caress Rora felt her eyes filling with tears. As she closed the door behind the nurse she wondered what it must be like to go from house to house, easing people towards death, adapting to cope with all the different ways that grief was expressed.

As she went up the stairs Rora heard the thud of something hitting the floor in her father's bedroom and rushed up the last few steps. Frank was lying on his side by the bed and he was so still that for a moment she thought he was dead. She bent over him. His eyes were closed and his lips were working, as if he was trying to dislodge food from between his teeth. At first convinced he was having some sort of stroke, she saw that the movements of his mouth and face were caused by the fact he was trying not to cry. All of his diminishing strength had been put into preventing himself from doing so. It was as if he was lying there fighting with himself. The sight of his imminent tears alarmed her more than anything else. She had never seen her father cry before. Any crying he may or may not have done following Sandi's death and in the years after had taken place behind closed doors.

'What happened?' she asked. 'Did you reach out to get something?'

He didn't reply, just turned his head away from her.

She saw that he had wet himself and she felt a sudden and unexpected surge of pity for him.

'Let's get you straight,' she said and put her hand on his shoulder. Frank shrugged her off.

'Go away,' he said. 'Just fucking go away.'

'I can't leave you on the floor,' she said.

She hated him; the way he lay there so helpless with his thin, white ankles sticking out of the ends of his pyjamas. The resident seagull had followed her upstairs and was now mewling at the window like a cat wanting to be let in. There seemed suddenly nowhere for her to go and no peace to be found. She got down and lay silently on the floor beside her father. After a while he moved his head towards her until they were lying face to face. The blue of his eyes had faded to an indeterminate grey and his nose and ears were more prominent. Her mother wouldn't recognise him if she saw him now. She would be in her long skirt and scarf, making one of her goofy expressions. He was only a ghostly version of the man her mother had known.

'Why are you here?' asked Frank.

'I don't bloody well know,' she said wearily.

'If it's my money you're after you are going to be sorely disappointed. Most of it's going on the wretched nurses.'

'I don't want your fucking money,' said Rora furiously, sitting up.

'What do you want then?' he asked.

She didn't know the answer to his question. It suddenly seemed absurd that she should be here in this room, at this time, with a man she barely knew. What she wanted was intangible. From deep inside her she felt a childish wail, long suppressed and yet hard to deny.

'I want to get you up off this floor,' she said with a firmness she didn't feel, and got up and bent to help him back to his bed. He resisted her at first. She could feel his thin shoulders and arms become rigid. She was reminded of the way Ursula used to lock her body in an arc when she didn't want to be put in the pushchair. Then he suddenly capitulated as if he was too tired to fight and she manoeuvred him so that he was lying down.

'You'd better phone Hattie Jacques and tell her to come back,' he said. Smiling slightly at his description of Pauline, Rora left the room. He needed the attentions of someone who loved him or someone who had been paid for the task, and she didn't qualify on either count.

Kiss 4

'Carl took her hand and traced the lines on her palm with his finger.'

12 February 1997

Carl was the only person other than her grandmother who allowed her to talk about her mother's death. When she had returned to school two weeks after it happened she became briefly popular. Groups of girls who had ignored her up to that point gathered round her at break time, talking softly, touching her arm, drawn to the aura of tragedy that hung over her. Even Katie Simmons had approached her with a pious look and put her arms around her as if she was trying sympathy out for size. But after a while the glamour of it wore off, and everyone reverted to being exactly as they had been before. Even Hannah started to get impatient when Rora went over what had happened for the fiftieth time, trying to make sense of it.

'It's the most awful thing and you will always miss her, but you have to try and move on a little,' Hannah said. She had asked her mother, who was a counsellor, how she should deal with Rora's grief and had been furnished with the necessary phrases.

'You have to somehow make it part of your life without it taking you over,' she said, wishing Rora would change back into the friend she could talk to about normal stuff, rather than this new, splintery person she always had to be careful with in case she broke apart.

Carl, on the other hand, seemed to have an endless capacity to listen. He placed his chalky hand on hers – he had spent the last few months doing pavement drawings, huge copies of old masters that he had cut out of magazines and that took him hours to reproduce; his way of earning some cash from the 'stoopids', as he called the tourists – and let her talk.

'We had an argument,' she told him, her voice so quiet he had to strain to hear her.

'It wasn't even about anything important. Mum had been low for weeks and I was bored of it. Bored of worrying about her. Bored of never going anywhere anymore, just the two of us. I was mean to her. I can't even tell you the things I said.'

Rora trailed off, her eyes filling with tears, and Carl produced a dodgy looking tissue that had been balled up in the pocket of his jeans.

'Can't have been that bad,' he said.

'It was. It really was,' she whispered. 'It was like once I'd started I couldn't stop. I didn't even mean the things I was saying.'

'That's what girls do,' said Carl calmly. 'To each other, I mean. They get rid of it. Boys keep it mostly inside.'

Rora wasn't so distracted by what she was telling him that she couldn't object to his sweeping generalisation.

'Actually, Carl,' she said repressively, 'I know plenty of boys that can't stop jabbering.' Then she carried on talking until a sudden realisation made her pause. 'I was the last straw,' she said in a small voice.

Carl stroked her hand. His eyes were sad and he suddenly looked much older than his years. 'I would lay money,' he said, 'that the row you had and her killing herself are two completely unrelated facts.'

Rora took comfort from his straightforward approach.

'Adults do the most weird things. I bet it was nothing to do with you at all,' he added.

Carl told her that a good way to stop crying was to lie down flat on the ground, so that the tears drained back into your head. He was full of these random scraps of information. Along with his method of forestalling tears, he also maintained that if you ate fifteen apple pips in one sitting you would die, and that if you laid out all the blood vessels in your body they would stretch for 60,000 miles. They walked a little way across the West Hill and he took off his jacket and placed it on the ground so they could lie on the chilly grass, and he distracted her by seeing shapes in the clouds until Rora's tears slid away.

It was the fact that her mother hadn't written a letter that troubled Rora the most. It seemed to confirm her theory that she had been the cause of her mother's death. If Sandi didn't blame her, then surely she would have written something to say so. Or maybe Carl was right. Maybe her mother had just been so caught up in her feelings and sadness that she had forgotten.

Rora was still having dreams about it, still waking up and remembering with fresh disbelief and pain that she would never feel her mother's arms around her again or coax her to laugh or be able to luxuriate in the sound of it when she did. She thought over and over again about what her mother had looked like in the attic: the horrible colour of her skin, the way her arms hung down by her sides, the rose smell of the Turkish Delight crushed under Rora's frantic feet. Sometimes Rora felt angry about the way her wasteful mother had thrown herself away. On other days she thought that perhaps it was a good thing that she had escaped the blackness that had kept her trapped in her bed. During the nights she forced herself to summon up the happy pictures she had in her head – her mother peaceful in the garden or swirling round and round in a ridiculous Easter bonnet or lying close to her on the bed, whispering stories in her ear.

'Didn't your dad ask you to go with him to Yorkshire?' asked Carl on one of their Saturday afternoon walks shortly after her father had at last returned.

'No,' Rora said. 'He said he needed to be alone when he did it, and that I would be better off staying with my grandmother.'

Carl didn't reply, just moved his head slowly from side to side, a gesture intended to indicate disbelief and displeasure in equal measure.

'What a tosser!' he said.

She was aware he was looking at her and that his face would have adopted that soft, slightly slack gaze he sometimes had when he thought himself unobserved. She knew he wanted to touch her. Although there were times when she shared his longing, her natural caution exerted itself and she was stern, even a little strict with him. She thought that some of the other girls in her class let their boyfriends do more, but she wouldn't allow it for herself.

'We could do our own version of sprinkling ashes,' said Carl suddenly, as if inspired. 'It wouldn't be quite the same, since . . . obviously . . . it wouldn't actually be your mum or anything, but we could mark it.'

The following Saturday they walked along to the end of the pier and Carl handed her a cardboard box full of silk petals that he had begged from the woman at the Flower Makers' Museum. Rora scooped them up in handfuls and threw them as far as she could, though the breeze kept blowing them back so that her curls became littered with petals. Eventually the wind stilled for long enough to disperse them. Rora thought her mother would have liked the way they fell through the air and then floated on the water for quite a long time, pulled by the tide in ribbons of red and white.

'Say a few words,' Carl instructed, taking on the role of master of ceremonies with aplomb.

'I don't know what to say,' Rora replied.

'Imagine what you would say to her if she was still alive.'

Rora stood silently, wondering which words she should choose; there were so many.

'I've got the burgers and the pink water fixed in my mind, just like you told me to,' she said at last. 'I'll always remember.'

Carl stayed beside her until all the petals had drifted out of sight, and then he wiped the tears from her face. Afterwards, they went to Isobel's beach hut, which had become their favourite meeting place. Isobel was getting too old to go there as often as before; she had started to feel the cold keenly, and so they mostly had a free run of the place. Carl had found two chairs on a skip and polished them until they shone. He also got some curtains from somewhere – Rora had learned not to enquire too closely about where exactly he acquired the things he did. He hung them at the little window, tying them back with a length of blue fisherman's rope he had picked up on the beach. He often arrived at the hut with a new object to display in the cabinet of curiosities he had made of the wall cupboard that used to house the mugs. It became full of pilfered birds' eggs, blown and carefully labelled, fossils dug out of the cliff and plastic toys, which had been tumbled against the shingle until the colour had leached out of them. He would bring apples and bars of chocolate and packets of chicken-flavoured noodles that would take him ages to cook on the battered Primus stove.

'No one knows we're here,' he would say with great satisfaction. 'It's our secret home.'

The domestication of the beach hut had not gone unnoticed by Isobel, and had provoked an embarrassing conversation. Rora loved her grandmother dearly but she was much better at telling far-fetched stories than dealing with everyday issues. As if belatedly remembering that she should perhaps have furnished her granddaughter with more of a sex education than that provided by *The Book of Kisses*, and noticing a new brightness about the girl, Isobel had embarked upon a slightly confusing biology lesson.

'Now, I don't know what you understand of physical love,' she had said, with her mouth a little pursed, as if she had taken a bite of something unexpectedly sharp. 'It's wonderful, but you have to be ready.'

'I know about it, Gran,' Rora had said hastily. 'We've done it at school.'

'All I'll say to you, then,' said Isobel, 'is that they can take you by surprise, those feelings,' and Rora had nodded, keen to get Isobel off the subject of sex.

'It might be a good idea if you kept the beach hut door open when you are there with Carl,' she said.

'What, even when it's cold?' said Rora in an innocent tone of voice, although she knew full well what her grandmother was trying to say.

'My darling girl,' said Isobel, 'you haven't a mother and I fear I am a poor substitute.' Isobel adopted this rather grand turn of phrase because of the subject matter. 'It's my duty to keep you from harm.'

'Carl isn't harm,' said Rora.

'Harm sometimes comes very well disguised,' said Isobel. 'He's an interesting boy. Made for being loved, if only he would let himself, but all the same you are not yet fifteen, your whole life stretches away ahead of you.'

'I'm the sensible one in what's left of this family, remember,' said Rora.

'I know you are, my darling,' said Isobel, and put her arms around Rora, who inhaled her grandmother's comforting smell – a mixture of talcum powder and the musk of jumpers left a little too long in the back of wardrobes and the indigestion sweets she sucked continually.

'Being sensible isn't always much of a protection where love is concerned,' she said.

Carl and Rora sat together on the porch of the beach hut, their combined bodies making the canvas of the deck chair stretch all the way to the ground. They threaded bits of worn wood and shells with holes in them and made a mobile to hang over the window. The sea was a dull brown tipped with dirty-looking foam and the pools of water left by the retreating tide shuddered as the wind passed over them. Seagulls floated over the waves like flotsam and the tanker on the horizon moved so imperceptibly that it seemed fixed there. Carl took her hand and traced the lines on her palm with his finger.

'It says here that you are going to have a long and happy life,' he said, mimicking Sophie's spooky, fortune-teller voice. She laughed, even though she didn't feel like laughing, because she knew that he wanted to cheer her up.

'Do you think we'll know each other forever?' he asked with that sliding sideways look that she associated with his most serious moments.

'I can't imagine not knowing you,' she said, and pressed her lips hard against his and opened his mouth with her tongue, feeling her way into him, wanting the swell and rub of their mouths to blot out the pictures she could see.

'I would feel your kiss even if I was dead. I'm sure I would,' said Carl when they finally broke away.

'I'd kiss you back to life,' said Rora, and suddenly, despite everything, she was engulfed by happiness. It was the unstoppable, quivering feeling of being alive. Of being here, on this day, with him, in front of the churning sea, which somewhere – further out perhaps than the immobile tanker – was still traced with petals.

May 2010

'Would you like to sit in the garden?' Rora asked her father after she had given him a mug of tea and cleared away some of the mess of books and papers that always surrounded him. Since his illness he had brought the contents of his study to his bed and Rora often found him propped up, a thin board across his knees, reading and making notes.

'It's a lovely day.'

'You won't be able to get me down the stairs,' he said.

'I will,' said Rora.

Frank didn't say anything, just gave her a look through his smudged reading glasses and then returned to his book. Rora felt the usual irritation at his obstinacy. She wondered why she was even bothering to make him comfortable. What did it matter to her if he spent the rest of his life rotting away in the bedroom? She knew there was some combination of words that would penetrate the barrier between them, but she couldn't formulate them, nor did she know if she had the energy to make the effort. What was it she wanted from him now? It was too late, surely, for them to make a difference to each other. She knew nothing about him, and he wasn't going to put right the lack of understanding that had become a habit for them both. His hands lying on the sheet had begun to look redundant, the way sick people's hands always looked after too long spent in bed with other people doing the things for them that they used to do for themselves. His fingers were slightly bent and the nails were yellowed. They reminded Rora of the pale, thwarted shoots found underneath a moved flowerpot or stone and, despite herself, she was moved by the same compassion she had felt when she had found him helpless on the floor.

'Come on, it's so stuffy in here. Don't you want some air?' she said.

The unseasonably hot weather had continued and the heat had gathered here in this room with its bowed ceiling and heavy curtains. She had tried to open the window but it was stuck fast.

'Oh, all right,' Frank said irritably, 'if it stops you going on at me.'

She led him carefully down the stairs and settled him in a chair in the shade of the Japanese Snowbell tree she had liberated from the mass of weeds that had wrapped themselves around the trunk. It was covered in white flowers, despite the years of neglect that had caused the branches to droop almost to the ground.

'Sandi planted this tree when you were born,' said Frank, looking up through the branches.

'Did she?' asked Rora, feeling herself immediately tense at the sound of her mother's name. He hadn't mentioned her until now.

'We called it the Aurora Tree.'

'I don't remember that,' said Rora, and she had an image of her mother sitting under the tree in one of her fringed skirts. It must have been a good day because in her memory her mother was laughing at something Rora could no longer see.

'She loved this garden, didn't she?' said Rora.

'I think it was the only place where she was truly calm, pottering around, getting her hands dirty.'

'Was there a time when she wasn't ill? Did you know what she was like when you met her?' asked Rora.

She found she was holding her breath. She didn't want to snap this thin thread that had appeared between them.

'I met her at a party. I couldn't stop looking at her. She was brighter, more present than anyone else I had ever seen. I loved her straightaway. It took her longer to love me.'

Rora waited in silence for what he might say next. It was as if the garden had cast a spell on him – his voice was clearer and stronger than it had been since she had arrived.

'The sadness seemed to gather in her. It's hard to explain. At first it was just who she was, and then as time passed it seemed to get the better of her. She fought it. She never stopped trying to live.' He looked into the middle distance as if he could see Sandi in the garden, moving from flowerbed to flowerbed.

'Did she discover what you had been doing?' said Rora. She was surprised by her own words. She had not known they were coming. She thought perhaps she was being deliberately harsh to forestall the unwelcome emotion that was threatening to extinguish her. Frank looked at her quickly, just a darting glance, and turned his head away. Nothing had changed, she thought. He didn't let her off then and he didn't let her off now.

Just then the gate scraped and Ursula bounced round the corner and into the garden. Not for the first time Rora was struck by her resemblance to Sandi. She had something of her grandmother's fire and impatience, although Ursula often tried to damp down her own ebullience, as if she could tell that it made Rora uneasy. Now Ursula stopped short at the sight of her grandfather, as if she had remembered her mother's words of caution about being too noisy when he was around.

'I'm back,' she announced. 'Hannah would like a word.'

'Tell her to come round,' said Rora.

Ursula disappeared again, coming back with Hannah and her two daughters trailing behind her.

'Hello, Mr Raine,' Hannah said. 'How are you?'

'I'm dying,' said Frank. His earlier dreaminess had disappeared and he had reverted to his usual curt manner.

Hannah gave Rora one of her there-I-go-putting-my-big-foot-in-it glances and Rora smiled. Her friend was prone to saying the first thing that came into her head. Their friendship had endured despite the differences in their personalities.

'I'm from a seventies film about romance in a roller skating rink, all loud music and spangles, and you belong on a movie set in the forties with a heroine who has dark secrets and beautiful shoes,' Hannah had said once when they were younger, and it was an apt comparison. Rora hid what mattered most to her, and Hannah couldn't bear to hold back anything.

Hannah's two daughters shuffled forward shyly. Paloma, the youngest, was an eager, sweet child who seemed to attract debris like fluff attaching itself to Velcro. She would start the day neatly buttoned up in one of the bright dresses Hannah favoured, and by midday would look as if she had been rolling in a muddy field. Her elder sister, Robyn, who was two years younger than Ursula, was a disconcerting child who rarely spoke, and when she did it was only to utter what needed to be said in a quiet voice. Today, her habit of looking absolutely symmetrical was emphasised by the placing of two neat hair clips on either side of her head.

'Thanks so much for picking Ursula up from school,' Rora said. 'My turn tomorrow.'

'It's no problem,' said Hannah. 'Let's go out soon. Or let me cook you a meal.'

Rora winced inwardly at the thought of the meal. Hannah was fond of experimentation in the kitchen and some of her food combinations were startling. Rora remembered one particular dish of roast marrow stuffed with lamb mince and blackberries with a shudder. She thought it was no wonder that Hannah's husband, Richard, was a little on the slender side.

'Let's go out,' she said, and walked them back to the gate.

'How are you coping?' asked Hannah when they were out of Frank's earshot.

'I've got nothing to say to him,' said Rora. 'Most of the time it's like being with a stranger.'

'Maybe the words will come,' said Hannah.

'Maybe it's that I don't want them to,' Rora replied.

Hannah put her arms around her, and although Rora was undemonstrative as a rule and disliked being touched, she allowed her friend to hold her for a moment.

'I hope I didn't do the wrong thing, telling you to come back,' Hannah said.

After Pauline had settled Frank back into bed, Rora went in to check on him. She felt the responsibility of being alone with him in the house at night. She wondered if she would be able to cope if he took a sudden turn for the worse. Would she know what to do? What to say? It seemed strange to her that they were in this position of sudden intimacy after all the years of silence and indifference. Surely when you were dying, you wanted people around you who knew you well and with whom you were able to show your vulnerability. He never said he was in pain, although she suspected that sometimes he was.

He was dozing with his hand over his book when she came into the room. He opened his eyes and looked at her.

'I'll not finish it now, will I?' he said.

'Finish what?' Rora asked.

'My book,' he said. 'I've not got enough time.'

He indicated the spread of papers and notebooks that had crept back around his bed with a despairing air, as if he was contemplating spinning a hundred bales of hay into gold.

'How much more have you got left to do?' asked Rora.

'The last part. The section that covers the development of the town in the 19th century. I hate to leave it unfinished.'

Rora heard the plea in his words but resisted them. Why should she help him to finish his boring old book? What had he ever done for her? His pyjama top had become unbuttoned and she could see his chest – the fine white hairs, the curdled texture of his skin. He was changing shape, softening into his last version. Death was making him ready so that there would be no firmness, no muscle left to fight the pull.

'I'm not sure I will be up to the required standard,' said Rora, still holding on to her resistance – it was a useful shield.

'You are more than qualified for the task,' he said, 'and of course I will help.'

He looked eager. Something of the person she remembered as a child had animated him. It was only a fleeting resemblance, but it was there.

'I've read all your books, you know,' he said. 'You write well. Your stories are rich and detailed, like all the best stories.'

Rora was so surprised at the thought of her father taking the time to read her books that she didn't know how to reply. He had never mentioned her work and she had assumed he wasn't interested.

'We'll talk about it tomorrow,' was all she said.

She took a glass of wine out into the quiet garden and sat at the small wrought iron table by the shed. The trees were just beginning to darken and around her, over walls and from doorways, she could hear the Friday noise swelling in celebration. It felt strange to be disconnected from this weekly letting go – she had no routine to anchor her, other than this life she had temporarily taken on. The flowerbeds were humming still with desultory bees that stopped and sucked and moved on again as if they, too, were trying out the weekend. She heard the purposeful click of high-heeled shoes on the pavement beyond the hedge. The noise stopped suddenly and from behind her she heard a low laugh and a man saying something indistinct – against a shoulder or perhaps through hair. Rora imagined the unseen couple standing with their arms around each other, the days ahead full of unspent love, and for the first time for as long as she could remember she felt a ripple of longing moving through her as stealthily as water through the cracked base of a vase. Something was there, just out of reach, and the thought of it filled her with unexpected hope, but then the streetlights flickered on and the town, which had been covered in friendly darkness, rose up and turned itself towards the light, illuminating the familiar dread.

Kiss 5

'The train was going by them in a rush of light and hot air.'

14 June 1997

There were times when Carl scared Rora. It wasn't that she thought he would hurt her, it was more that she knew he wanted to hurt himself. Picking fights and attempting terrifying physical challenges seemed to be the only way he had of releasing tension. It was always the same pattern: he would become more and more restless, unable to sit still, devising schemes and inventing slights, until at last he would do something mad, something uncalled for, and then afterwards, free from the grip of whatever had him in its clutches, he would be briefly calm again. She knew he had chosen her because she could understand his constant drive to divert pain into a more immediate and obvious source. Someone had told her that women in labour alleviate their suffering by using a device that gives small electric shocks so that they trick themselves into focusing on this other, lesser hurt, and it seemed to her that this was what Carl did too, although she couldn't understand exactly what made him so angry and so sad.

Whenever Rora asked Carl questions about his family he would always change the subject, but she gathered he lived with someone called Mo. The name was short for Maureen but was the only thing diminutive about her, he said, since she was six foot one and had size ten feet. She was his mother's half-sister and they lived in a fourth-floor flat in St Leonards with a thin view of the sea if you hung over the balcony and twisted your neck at a 90-degree angle.

'What happened to your parents?' asked Rora.

'They died,' he answered, and then did what he always did when he didn't want to talk anymore, which was to do something showy and distracting, like swing from a branch or jump across a ditch.

The pair of them had created such a tight world of their own that it seemed no one else could get close to them, which made it all the more surprising when Carl developed an unlikely friendship with a boy who had joined their school halfway through the term. Unlike most people who come to a school long after friendship groups have been formed and then re-formed, Ian Silitoe was accepted almost instantly. It might have had something to do with his looks – he was improbably handsome. Whereas most of his contemporaries were suffering from spots and bodies that seemed to have stretched in alarming and awkward ways, he seemed to fit his skin seamlessly and his complexion had a peachy sheen that spoke of good meals and sporting activities and getting his own way. He wore his blond hair in a centre parting, long at either side, and he punctuated his sentences by raking it back off his face with a kind of stroking motion, as if he too couldn't quite believe how soft and golden it was. It wasn't just his looks that made him popular; it was also his easy manner and the way he made people feel important when he was talking to them. He had learned early on about the power of giving everyone, even those you are not particularly interested in, the full beam of your attention.

A few weeks after he arrived at the school rumours started to circulate that Ian had been expelled from four schools for various misdemeanours. This information, true or not, only served to add to his allure. All the girls were enraptured by him; they pretended not to look as he passed by and left him notes and sent their friends to find out if he was in a relationship. He reacted to these overtures with good humour, but remained indifferent. The boys admired his man of the world air. He gave the impression in lessons that he was vaguely bored. He would sit low in his chair with his legs stretched out and look into the middle distance. Miss Tarnish, the English Language teacher, who wore unbecoming headbands and never smiled, became almost skittish when he answered her questions, always correctly, even though he had given the impression he wasn't listening. He favoured a sarcastic tone of voice, as if he thought everything was a joke. It might have been something to do with the fact that, despite his apparent popularity, Ian was also an outsider that drew Carl to him. Rora would often find the pair of them talking and laughing, and sometimes they would stop talking when she approached, as if they had a secret.

'I think he's a bit of an arsehole,' said Rora to Carl, even though when she had dropped her pencil in class Ian had picked it up and given her such a dazzling smile as he handed it back that he reminded her of Sir Lancelot, an impression she didn't share with Carl.

'He's not so bad,' Carl said. 'He doesn't bullshit like some of the others.'

Meanwhile, Carl's reputation at school was getting progressively worse. There had been several altercations in the playground – an incident when Carl had thrown a book at a teacher, although he swore he hadn't intended to hit him – and endless hours spent in detention. Rora worried about him. She knew that something must have happened to make him behave the way he did. She recognised the way he shoved what he wanted to say so deep inside himself he couldn't get it out, because she did that too.

During break one day he charged out of the swing doors and ran up to the wall that separated the concrete playground from the sports field and smashed his fist hard against it. His hand was bleeding so badly Rora insisted on taking him to reception, where Miss Bundock pursed her lips and applied Germolene and a plaster covered by a stretchy bandage and made some comment about 'wildness' and 'learning discipline'. She looked at Rora as if she thought she might be contaminated. When Rora asked him why he had done it, he was vague. He said it was because one of the teachers had given him the 'evils', but then he said it wasn't only that, it was things piling up one on top of the other so that he couldn't breathe properly and sometimes smashing something made him feel better.

On the day Carl hurt his hand, he was waiting for Rora at the gates as she came out of school.

'Do you want to go for a walk?' he said, not looking at her and scuffing his already shabby shoes against the pavement.

'I'm supposed to go straight home after school during the week,' said Rora.

'Oh come on, you pussy. It'll only be for an hour, he said. 'They'll not even notice.'

Rora thought he was probably right. Isobel was having one of her bridge afternoons and her father would no doubt be secreted away in his study doing whatever it was he did in there.

'OK,' she said. 'As long as I can choose what we do.'

She had learned from a master how to persuade adults to do what they knew they shouldn't, and Carl stood back and watched smugly, like a teacher with a particularly adept pupil, while she convinced the man in the shop by the railway that she was buying the beer for her father. The shop smelled rich and spicy, like the beginning of an adventure, and Rora felt briefly ashamed of hoodwinking the man, who had sad eyes and a stacked shoe that looked like a Cornish pasty. But when she emerged victorious with four cans of Special Brew clutched to her chest, she quickly forgot the disappointed way the shopkeeper had looked at her. They made for a favourite spot in the woods above the railway line.

After drinking half a can Rora felt drunk, perhaps as intoxicated by the sense that she was behaving badly as by the beer. The day had been blisteringly hot and the evening felt heavy with incipient rain. Carl stood up and took her by the hand and pulled her along with him so that she was almost sliding down the bank towards the railway line. She knew him well enough by now to recognise this dangerous version of Carl that came out from time to time.

He took a length of string from the rucksack he always had clamped to his back. She was amazed at the variety of objects he had stored in there. It was as if he was never quite sure where he would find himself next and so he brought equipment for every eventuality. He tried to persuade her to tie him to the railway track, and when she refused he lay down anyway, his arms behind his head, his ankles crossed. She begged him to get up, and tugged at his legs in an effort to get him clear of the track.

'Lie down next to me,' he said, 'just for a moment.'

'I don't want to,' she said.

'You're either with me, or you're not,' said Carl.

And so Rora, with her keen grasp of the Highway Code and her almost pathological fear of house fires and incoming tides and other potential disasters, lay down between the tracks and waited for whatever it was that would happen. Carl looked at his watch.

'Put your hands flat on the ground on either side of you,' he said, and Rora raised her head and stretched her fingers out in the gravel.

'It'll start gentle,' he said 'just a little vibration.'

At first she couldn't feel anything at all, but then she began to detect the barest of tremors, as if someone was humming deep under the earth. Then it seemed to her that the sound she was feeling through her fingers, a kind of beating, was becoming louder, but still she didn't move and nor did he, and somewhere not too far away the train was coming. She could see it in her mind's eye – the birds rising up from the hedgerows as it advanced, puffing smoke and steam like the trains in films and books.

'FIVE. FOUR. THREE. TWO. ONE . . . NOW!' Carl shouted and pulled her up and off the track, and they fell back into the nettles and sticky weeds of the bank and in three heartbeats the train was going by them in a rush of light and hot air. It was as if the train's passage had punctured the skin holding back the rain because at that moment the sky opened and almost immediately they were both soaking wet and lying close together and Rora felt a kind of fluttering between her legs when she looked at Carl's eyes and mouth.

'That was scary,' she said.

'You were very brave,' he said tenderly, stroking the hair from her eyes and she felt the familiar rush of longing but at the same time a kind of exasperation at the way he continued to test her. Whatever she did it never seemed to be quite enough for him.

'Weren't you scared too?' she asked.

'That sort of thing never scares me,' he said.

'What does scare you then?' she asked.

'Being left,' he said, and then turned away from her as if he thought he had disclosed too much.

'Who left you?' she asked.

For a moment it seemed as if he would do what he usually did and employ a diversionary tactic. She was half expecting him to leap up and perform one of his stunts, but he didn't. Perhaps it was because they were lying so close together, or that she had accepted his challenge on the railway line, or perhaps it was simply the way the summer evening held them, heavy and sweet, but he turned back to her. She could feel the tension in his body.

'I lived with my dad and mum until I was about seven, and then my dad left,' said Carl and his face had an expression on it that Rora had never seen before – a kind of desperate resolution, part anger and part mortification. 'He sent me cards and letters at first, and then one day they stopped arriving. I tried looking for him once, but it was as if he had been vaporised. Nobody knew anything about him. After a while, I don't know how long exactly, Mum got a new boyfriend, a man called Steve, who used to hit me around the head when she wasn't watching and sometimes even when she was. She used to tell him to stop, but he never really listened to her. He once hung me by my jumper on a nail on the side of the shed and left me there.' Carl spoke quickly, as if he had to unburden himself before he changed his mind.

Rora took his hand and held it tightly, trying not to say or do anything that would stop this uncharacteristic volubility.

'I think I got in the way of his plans with my mother. I can't remember exactly what Mum looked like, but she had long red hair and a pale, round face. Pretty. She was kind too. She used to lie curled up around me on my bed when I couldn't sleep. She once sat up all night sewing felt numbers onto a pair of trousers for my costume for Maths Day. One morning she woke me up and said we were going away on holiday. I remember feeling really surprised because it was a school day and nobody had mentioned a holiday. Steve showed me a picture in a brochure of the place where we were going to be staying. It looked great, with a big pool and a bar with stools coming out of the water. I remember thinking the colours were brighter than any other colours I had ever seen.'

He stopped talking for a while. She thought that perhaps he was trying not to cry. She stayed very still so that she didn't interrupt his story.

'Mum told me to pack a bag, so I put my toy cars, a toothbrush and some pyjamas into my rucksack. Just before we were due to set off, Steve gave me some money to go and buy some sweets for the journey, and I went by myself to the shop nearby. I was used to going to pick up milk or a loaf of bread. I remember feeling happy because Steve had said we were going on a plane and I'd never been on a plane before. When I got back from the shop they'd gone. I'd only been away about ten minutes.'

'What do you mean gone?' asked Rora, her green eyes wide.

'Gone. Disappeared. Vanished,' said Carl. 'I waited for ages thinking that perhaps they'd gone to get something, you know, for the trip. Petrol perhaps. It was getting dark by the time a neighbour came out of her house and asked me what I was doing sitting on the pavement. When I told her, she made a noise as if I'd said something rude. She took me in like it was the last thing on earth she wanted to do, and gave me fish fingers and made some phone calls. In the morning someone came and asked me questions and then took me away. My strongest memory was that I had lost one of my toy cars. It had gone missing under the bed I had slept in. That's what made me cry, not so much that my mum had gone. I didn't really understand then what had happened.'

'They didn't leave a message or anything?' asked Rora.

'Nothing. In the end Mo agreed to have me, although she didn't have children of her own and didn't really want one at the age of forty-five.'

He told Rora that he couldn't recall the moment, the exact day when he understood that his mother wasn't ever coming back, but slowly the idea became a reality. Sometimes, in the early days, he would leave Mo's flat when she wasn't watching and go back to his old house and wait outside for a bit, just in case his mother had changed her mind and remembered she wanted him after all. Mo would come and find him and look angry all over again, though he soon learned that her anger was never directed at him. She never mentioned his mother, but she once said that her sister just didn't know any better and something about her only being someone if she had a man, which he didn't really understand at the time, but which he had come to see meant that his mother had chosen Steve over him.

'That is the single worst thing I ever heard,' said Rora. 'Why haven't you told me about this before?'

'I don't know really. I've never heard of it happening to anyone else. I felt ashamed that my mum had known me for eight years and then decided I wasn't worth keeping.'

'It wasn't that you were not worth keeping, Carl,' said Rora, 'it was that she wasn't worth having as a mother.'

They lay for a while and then he leaned over and kissed her softly. His lips were quiet, grateful, and she felt him pass something hard and cold into her mouth. She sat up and spat out whatever it was into her cupped hand.

'What's this for?' she asked, looking at the tiny silver key glinting up through the spit on her palm.

'It's the key to my heart,' he said, and then laughed like a drain in case she thought he was serious.

'No, Carl, seriously, what is it?'

Carl didn't reply, instead he took his rucksack off his back, unzipped it and took out a black tin box. He took a copy of the key he had given her from inside his jumper, where it hung on a length of thin string. He unlocked the box and placed it on the ground between them.

'The stuff my mum left me,' Carl said and took each object out carefully as if he was scared of damaging it and held it out for her inspection. There was a small bunch of hairpins tied together with peach-coloured ribbon; a faded photo of a young woman, her hair covering her face, bending over a baby who was swaddled tightly in a white blanket; a small, worn quilt made up of blue and red squares; and two teeth, still baring traces of blood at their roots. The things in the box didn't seem to Rora to be worthy of the reverence with which Carl was handling them, but she kept the thought to herself. She saw that this was the most private bit of Carl; the part he had never shown to anyone else. The knowledge made her feel tenderly towards him, but she also felt the weight of responsibility to react in the right way. His face was solemn and hopeful. She wasn't exactly sure why she felt a sudden tightness in her throat and chest. It was something about him and about her and about the lush fullness of summer and the way it smelled deep and green after the rain.

'It means something, doesn't it?' he asked. 'It means something that she kept these things . . . my teeth and everything.'

'It definitely does,' Rora said. 'It shows she loved you.'

'They found it under her bed when they cleared out the house,' said Carl. 'I think she left it for me as a sign.'

Rora couldn't help thinking that as signs go it wasn't particularly helpful. A forwarding address would have been more useful than a bunch of keepsakes. She felt a clutch of anger at the heedless, careless way adults behaved. She thought of her father's selfish mourning of her wasteful mother and of Carl's mother driving off in a van. Had she felt any regret at all as she turned the corner away from him? Did she ever think now about the boy she had left behind, who held onto these shreds of hope and invented a hundred ways of hurting himself?

'Why did you give me the other key to the box?' she asked him.

'It was the most valuable thing I have,' he said, and she laid her arm across his tense shoulders.

'Why don't you put some other things in there?' she asked after a while. 'Some new things.'

And so the box became a repository not only for the traces of Carl's mother, but for other treasures – some knapweed tied around with grass picked on their return home, the print-out from the 'Love Detective', the menu from a restaurant Carl took her to with enormous pride – the meal paid for with the earnings from half a summer of pavement drawings – and a felt bird that Rora had painstakingly embroidered with Carl's name as a Christmas present.

June 2010

Ursula trailed downstairs rubbing her eyes and then sat morosely at the kitchen table while Rora made toast and poured milk over cereal.

'Too much milk,' said Ursula gloomily.

Rora obediently took the bowl, tipped some of the milk down the sink and placed it back in front of her daughter.

'Not enough milk,' said Ursula, pushing her luck.

'Eat it,' said Rora. 'Talking of which, what's eating you this morning?'

'Nothing,' answered Ursula, kicking the leg of the table.

'Stop kicking' said Rora.

'I can't,' said Ursula. 'I've got restless legs syndrome.'

Rora ignored her and began spreading her toast with butter and some suspect-looking plum jam she had found at the back of one of the cupboards.

'When's Grandad going to get better?' asked Ursula.

'I don't know exactly,' said Rora wondering what she should tell her. 'It's hard to predict these things,' she said vaguely, knowing that she was simply postponing a conversation she was going to have to have at some point not too far in the future. 'We'll just have to do our best to make sure he's well looked after,' she said and emptied her toast crusts into the bin.

Rora had worried at first that the sights and smells of illness were something she should protect Ursula from, but her daughter seemed to enjoy her grandfather's company. He seemed to find a little life when she was around and the gaunt lines of his face softened as he listened to her improbable tales. Rora found herself wishing that she provoked the same feelings of tenderness in him as her daughter clearly did, and then told herself the time had passed for all that. She had managed without him for years and she could manage without him now.

Ursula always insisted that Rora drop her off outside the school, even though a lot of the other mothers walked their children all the way to their classrooms. This morning the ritual was the same. Through the gate Rora could see Robyn sitting on the buddy bench, a seat that was designed to encourage new friendships but only served, it seemed to Rora, to draw attention to loneliness.

'See you at going home time, Mum,' said Ursula taking her book bag from her mother and offering up her cheek to be kissed. Rora suspected that her daughter became so purposeful at this point in proceedings to forestall a lingering parting that the child would find much more difficult. It seemed to Rora that Ursula was too careful with her own and other people's feelings. Children as young as Ursula usually just reacted immediately, by turns blazingly exultant and then cast down in square-mouthed despair; but it was possible that what she had been through at her previous school had made her more cautious than other children. The idea that it might have changed her permanently made Rora feel sick. Rora watched through the gate as Ursula greeted another girl and they walked towards the entrance of the building chattering. Ursula seemed to have adapted remarkably well to her new school, and seeing her daughter's confidence Rora allowed herself to feel tentatively optimistic. It had been the right decision to bring her here and allow her to put the past behind her and start afresh.

When she got back from dropping Ursula off, Rora went to check on her father and finding him asleep, started to read some of the notes that he had made for the last chapter of his book. Hastings had expanded greatly during the period he had been writing about. The coming of the railway had made the town a fashionable seaside resort among well-heeled Londoners. They came to take the sea air and enjoy the invigorating water, emerging modestly from bathing machines that had been pushed into the shallows. Alexandra Park with its 100 acres of ponds and trees and well-tended lawns, the chapel on the seafront that later became the Fishermen's Museum and the pier had all become features of Hastings during this period.

Rora was soon immersed in what her father had written about the pier. She had always been fond of it. It had been the place where she had first seen Carl. She remembered his insouciant cockiness and the way, even then, she had known they were somehow linked together. At the time of the pier's construction some people in the town had thought it an arrogant notion to build a walkway out into the sea. There were squabbles, the money ran out and the weather turned foul. There were multiple injuries and two men suffered fatal falls. The work was back-breaking, as they had to drill down through submerged forests, through ancient tree trunks that were so hard despite all the time they had spent in the water that they broke the piles and set work back for weeks. She was astonished by how good his writing was. Perhaps she should help him with it after all. Maybe it would give them something to talk about other than the relative merits of fruit juices and whether his sheets needed changing or not.

Rora was so caught up in the stories that she forgot she was going out with Hannah and wasn't ready when she arrived.

'Where are we going?' asked Rora, taking her handbag off its hook in the hall and following her friend out.

'There's a Polish restaurant I've been meaning to try for ages,' Hannah said, taking charge of proceedings as always.

Zamek was situated off George Street in a narrow passage-way only just wide enough for the two small tables outside. It had an unassuming white frontage, window frames painted a deep red and a hanging basket overflowing with bright flowers by the door. Inside, the place was fresh and airy with simple wooden furniture and botanical drawings of herbs on the walls. They ordered Polish beer while they pored over the menu.

'I see you again!' said a familiar voice. Rora looked up into the face of the paddling man.

'It's me, Krystof,' he announced, perhaps thinking by Rora's slightly stunned expression that he hadn't been recognised.

'Eh, hello,' she said.

Hannah looked up at him with interest.

'Do you two know each other?' she enquired.

'Not really . . . ' Rora began, only to be interrupted by Krystof.

'Of course we know each other,' he said, which Rora felt was overstating the facts. He didn't even know her name.

'Well, we met once,' she corrected and then thought she was being unnecessarily pedantic.

'Ignore Aurora. She's a terrible grump,' said her friend and extended her hand. 'I'm Hannah.'

'Nice to meet you,' said Krystof and then turned once again to Rora.

'Aurora . . .' he said, 'what a wonderful name. Like the aurora borealis.'

At rest his features had a rather morose cast. He had a square face with a downward slanting mouth, but he was completely transformed when he smiled. His slightly cartoonish features were made handsome by the goodwill he clearly extended to the world around him.

'It's Rora, actually,' she said.

'She doesn't really like being called Aurora,' said Hannah conspiratorially. 'Thinks it makes her sound a bit up herself.'

Rora ignored both of them and bent over the menu.

'Well . . . what can I get you?' asked Krystof. 'You must have a feast. I suggest pierogi, which are dumplings stuffed with pork. I've just made them fresh. Then perhaps rabbit served with mustard sauce? Or maybe some beef with beetroot and fresh horseradish? Moist, with the fire from the horseradish and then the earthiness of the beetroot and the meat you can cut with a spoon. Some fresh cod perhaps, I bought today, with sweet chilli sauce on a bed of tender spinach, wild boar sausages with sauce of juniper berry, tangy and rich.'

Krystof had become quite flushed with enthusiasm and eagerness, and to forestall further descriptions of the menu Rora said, 'Why don't you decide what we should have?' This sent Krystof away rubbing his hands.

The food when it arrived was delicious, with fresh, punchy flavours and hardly a vestige of the cabbage that Rora had been expecting. Krystof hovered over proceedings, darting backwards and forwards from the kitchen with extra sauces and seasonings and keeping their beer glasses well topped up. Rora noticed that he moved fluidly, like a dancer, his athletic physique at odds with his slightly lumpy face. They finished off their meal with some almond biscuits and strong, sweet coffee.

'You must come back,' said Krystof after he had deliberately added up their bill wrongly and excluded most of the dishes.

'We will,' said Hannah. 'Next time I'm going to bring my husband.'

'You'll bring Rora too, won't you?' said Krystof.

'You've got a bit of a fan there,' whispered Hannah as he went off to fetch their coats.

'Don't start,' said Rora warningly.

They had lingered so long over their lunch that it was time to pick up the girls, so they decided to go together to the school. Their progress was hampered by the quantity of food they had consumed.

'I don't think I am going to want to eat again for a week,' Hannah groaned. 'In retrospect those last three biscuits were probably a mistake.'

They walked along in companionable silence for a while, but Hannah was always trying to provoke Rora into disclosing her feelings. It was ironic that despite being so open herself, she seemed to be surrounded by secretive, silent types. Robyn barely said anything at all, her husband, Richard, was a man who chose his words carefully, and she had never been able to get Rora to properly confide in her.

'What's happening in your love life?' Hannah asked.

'Nothing,' said Rora.

'I just don't understand why not,' Hannah said.

'I've not met anyone since . . . since Nick that I really wanted to be with for more than a couple of months.'

'What are you looking for?' asked Hannah, who had noticed and wondered at the slight hesitation before Nick's name.

'I'm not looking for anything,' said Rora. 'I'm fine on my own.'

'Of course you are. I don't think I've ever met anyone as self-sufficient as you, but all the same . . .' Hannah trailed off.

Even after ten years together Hannah still looked forward to the moment when Richard walked back into the house from wherever he had been. It wasn't that he made her feel safer, she could more than look after herself – she had once thwarted a mugging on the Tube by poking the hapless thief in the eye with the heel of a court shoe – it was more that when he was there everything was better. He made the unbearable days bearable and the good days glorious. She wished Rora had someone who would do the same for her.

At bedtime Ursula developed a stomach ache and insisted that Rora lie beside her on the bed.

'What sort of a pain is it?' asked Rora.

'It's like when I caught my finger in the door, but in my tummy,' said Ursula.

'How horrible,' said Rora. 'I'll lie here and you try and sleep, but tell me if the pain gets worse.'

'Keep the light on,' said Ursula. 'It hurts more in the dark.'

'Is there something worrying you, Ursula?' asked Rora. 'Are you worried about Grandad?'

'He's going to die before I've even got to know him,' said Ursula.

'He's very ill,' said Rora softly, holding Ursula's somewhat clammy hand in her own and stroking it with her thumb.

'He's getting weaker and weaker and sometime soon he will be too worn out to stay with us. It will be sad, but he will be ready to go.'

'I'm going to get him to tell me his life story,' said Ursula.

'He's often too tired to talk, darling,' said Rora.

'I'm going to get a notebook and do it bit by bit,' said Ursula firmly. 'Will you read me another chapter?'

After two chapters of *Prince Caspian*, Ursula's eyelids at last began to droop.

'I think things would be clearer if I had a daddy,' Ursula said with her eyes shut, as if this was a conversation she could only have if she couldn't see her mother's face.

'Clearer in what way?' asked Rora, her heart sinking.

'I'd know all of me if I had a daddy, not just half,' said Ursula.

'You are a complete and whole Ursula. You are not a half of anything,' said Rora gently.

When Ursula's breathing was regular Rora carefully extracted her hand and turned on the pillow to look at her sleeping daughter. Tiny curls had attached themselves to her hot forehead and one fist was clenched up against her chin. In the half-light the skin of her daughter's face gleamed with a pearly sheen, her chest rising and falling gently. Rora was so overwhelmed by love that she felt it as a kind of pain – as if something was wrapped tightly around her heart and was squeezing it. She wondered if she had done the right thing over the years, not telling Ursula who her father was. At first she hadn't been absolutely sure herself, but by the time it had become obvious, she had already made the decision to keep Ursula a secret from him. She told herself that it was best that Ursula should not know about her father. Rora would protect her from anything that hurt or diminished her so that she would grow strong and resilient. She vowed that no one would make Ursula feel small and ashamed and full of terror about the thought of the coming morning, the way Rora had.

Kiss 6

'Although she didn't completely recognise the moment for what it was, it was when he kissed his mother that Rora fell in love with him.'

25 May 1999

It was Rora's idea to try and find Carl's mother. When she first suggested it he stopped and stared at her as if he hadn't quite heard what she had said, and then his face rippled like the reflection of water on a wall. It was so fleeting this look of almost-hope that she would have missed it if she hadn't been so acutely aware of all his moods and the way his countenance changed from moment to moment. She thought he had the most 'speaking' face of anyone she had ever met, although he had told her more than once to stop scrutinising him the way she did.

'You see things that are not actually there,' he had said to her once. 'Most of the time I'm not thinking of anything at all . . . I'm a blank.'

Carl didn't immediately respond to her suggestion and she didn't push the idea, knowing that he always needed time to think things through. He was a curious mixture of a boy; impulsive and cautious, tender and wild. He threw his body around in indiscriminate ways, seldom giving a thought for the damage he might sustain, but he was far more careful with his heart, as if he knew where the real risk lay.

Rora had stayed on at sixth form to do A-levels, but Carl, who had barely made it through his last year at secondary school, turning up for only three of his final exams, had taken a job at a bakery in the centre of town. Despite the way their paths seemed to be parting and Isobel's anxious remarks about whether it might not be better if she went out with one of her classmates, or preferably eschewed all boys until her exams were safely over, they had stayed together. She met him after work and they went to their old haunts, Carl's jacket pockets full of pilfered sausage rolls and the sticky Chelsea buns that were Rora's favourite. Sometimes she would watch him while he chalked out his pictures on the tarmacked walkway – huge seascapes with diffused, lemony skies – and then 'bottle' for him, walking among the tourists holding out his cap, persuading them to give money.

Sometimes Ian, who had stayed on to do A-levels too, joined them, even though Rora didn't really want him there. She disliked the way that Carl seemed to hang on his every word, even when he was saying things that made Rora angry – like giving passing girls marks out of ten and making comments about their breasts and legs. She thought perhaps Carl liked Ian so much because he wasn't used to male attention, and Ian continually littered his conversation with phrases like 'You're so right, mate' and 'I've never thought of it that way before' that made Carl puff out a bit and look pleased.

Rora's lack of interest in Ian stood out among the other girls, who hung round-eyed on his every word and who followed his progress down the corridors with a murmuring, collective breath of thwarted desire. He had sought Rora out a few days before when she was working in the library at lunchtime; trying desperately to complete some course work that Carl had distracted her from the night before. She was so absorbed that she didn't notice when Ian sat down opposite her at the table and so she jumped slightly when he spoke.

'I think there could be an earthquake and you wouldn't notice,' Ian said.

Rora looked at him and then made a kind of shrugging motion as if to excuse herself.

'Yes. Got to get this done in half an hour,' she said, and put her head down again.

'What is it you're doing? Can I help?' he asked.

'No thanks, better if I just get on with it,' she said dismissively, wishing that he would go away and leave her in peace.

'Suit yourself,' he said, and got up and pushed his chair into the table so that it banged loudly. She wondered vaguely why he seemed so cross and then forgot about him.

Carl's slightly delinquent reputation gave Rora a kind of cachet among her contemporaries, particularly since he sometimes picked her up from school on his motorcycle, looking dishevelled and firm-shanked, with his helmet-tousled hair and beaten-up jeans. Even Hannah, who still harboured a soft spot for men on motorbikes, had warmed to him but she still had her doubts about his reliability.

'There's something heedless about him,' she said. 'He always seems to be on the edge of doing something he really shouldn't.'

'He knows me,' said Rora, as if that was explanation enough.

'He's completely obsessed with you. I don't know if that's the same thing,' Hannah said.

Hannah's family background in counselling had given her an unhealthy preoccupation with the importance of communication and encouraged her to be quite observant. She had noticed the way that Carl seemed to focus on Rora to the exclusion of all else.

'You're the only person he has,' she said.

'All the more reason to be with him,' Rora replied.

She didn't say that being with him felt essential to her. As necessary as breathing and the sun and the way the grass moved in the wind. Nor did she say that when he touched her with hands that had become rough from taking bread from the ovens, she felt her skin leap and tighten. They had almost made love a couple of times in snatched half-hours at her house when everyone was out, when the feeling was overwhelming and his fingers on her breasts made her tremble, but she had resisted him so far and despite the ardour in his eyes and the way his breath became ragged when she pressed herself against him, he was tentative too. He regularly leaped from the end of the pier with his legs tucked beneath him and made great burned rubber smears across the car park with his bike, but when they were together he was different. He always checked her responses and gentled his own to match.

A few days after she had first made the suggestion about finding his mother, he brought it up again. They were on the beach and Carl was throwing stones into the sea, making them bounce across the waves, and Rora was writing an essay about Yeats that was due in the next day.

'I don't have that much to go on,' he said.

'For what?' she asked, her mind on a young man in a plane, trying to work out exactly what was meant by the phrase 'a lonely impulse of delight'.

'Where my mother might be,' he said, looking firmly out to sea.

'Surely you have a bit of information,' said Rora, putting aside her book. 'Doesn't your aunt know anything?'

'I don't really want to tell Mo that I'm thinking of looking for her. She might be hurt,' said Carl. 'I know my mum had a friend called Frances, because Mo has mentioned her a few times and

I sort of remember going to visit her when I was little. She lived in a house in Bexhill. It was by a big, strange building that looked like a ship.'

The following Saturday they took the bus to Bexhill. The 'strange' building of Carl's memory was the De La Warr Pavilion, a once-glorious edifice that now looked tired, its previously crisp edges bitten, worn down by the wind and neglect. Right next door, exactly as Carl had remembered, was a row of houses with onion-shaped roofs. After knocking on four doors, the fifth one was opened by an elderly woman who peered closely at Carl after he had introduced himself, and somewhat reluctantly let the pair of them in. She took them through to a living room crammed on every surface with ships in bottles of all shapes and sizes.

'I don't remember you having all of these,' said Carl, indicating the rows of bottles.

'Only started collecting them four years ago,' she said. 'Can't seem to stop now.'

She had a surprisingly deep voice for someone with such a slight frame. She was dressed in a brown polo neck tucked into brown drawstring trousers, which showed her masculine body with its almost flat chest and sturdy legs.

'What do you want?' Frances asked Carl bluntly. 'You haven't changed much. Still that same cocky look.'

'I'm looking for my mother,' he said.

'Thought you might be,' she said. 'You're wasting your time with me. I don't know where Gloria is. Haven't seen her for years.'

'We thought she might have been in touch with you,' said Rora.

'Nope,' said Frances, picking up one of her bottles and giving it a polish with the cuff of her sweater. 'All I know about her is that she was a selfish old cow who upped and left. Mo called me to tell me just after you moved in with her.'

She stopped polishing and fixed him with a sharp stare. 'Mo is a bloody saint and I hope you know what sacrifices she's made for you,' she said.

'I wouldn't have survived without her,' said Carl quietly.

'Everyone goes,' said Frances, and the sun came out and blazed through the net curtain onto her so that she suddenly looked ancient, her face marked with a hundred tiny grooves.

'People go one by one, until you are on your own,' she said sadly. 'I think that's why I've taken to collecting these. Ships caught in bottles, going nowhere.'

'Did you ever know anything about the man Mum went off with? Steve, his name was,' Carl asked.

'Not much, other than he had a pet shop in Eastbourne.'

'I don't suppose you remember what the shop was called?' asked Rora.

'Heck no,' said Frances. 'It's all I can do to remember to tie my shoelaces, let alone remember things like that.'

By mid-afternoon Rora and Carl were in Eastbourne, making their way along the carefully maintained seafront where old people sitting on cane chairs looked out of the conservatory windows of identical hotels and watched the tide go out. They drew a blank at three pet shops, but at the fourth, they found Steve's son, a reticent young man called Colin with a tattoo of a tiger on his neck. He was suspicious and his eyes continually flickered between them as if he was trying to work out how he was to be tricked and if he could get the better of them before it happened.

'Dad died three years ago,' he said. He spoke as if the words had to be dragged out of him.

'I'm sorry to hear that,' said Carl.

'I don't remember him mentioning a Carl, or a Gloria,' said Colin, and he moved from behind the counter and opened the door of a large cage in which a brown snake was coiled tightly around a piece of wood. He unwound the creature and took it out and began to stroke it hand over hand as it twisted around his arms, as if by doing so he was comforting himself rather than petting the reptile. A man came into the shop with a bale of straw and Colin greeted him and indicated that he should put it in the storeroom.

'My mother had red hair,' said Carl. 'Did you ever see him with a woman with red hair? Did he mention a girlfriend with a child?'

Colin shook his head. 'He wasn't an angel where women were concerned,' he said and his face twitched a little in what might have been an attempt at a smile. 'There were so many of them. Redheads, brunettes, blondes. He wasn't that fussy. They lasted as long as they didn't cause complications.'

'So the name Gloria Richards doesn't mean anything to you at all?' asked Rora.

'Never even heard the name before,' said Colin, and the snake raised its head and flickered out a thin tongue as if suddenly irritated by Colin's ministrations.

They were walking back to the bus stop when the man who had been delivering straw approached them.

'I couldn't help overhearing,' he said. 'I've been supplying the shop for years, right back when Steve first went into business. He introduced me to a Gloria once. What you said about her red

107

hair rang a bell. I bumped into him at the pub once and he was with her. This is going back a while now, mind, at least six years.'

'Did you see them again?' asked Carl.

'I never saw her again. He mentioned her once or twice and I used to ask after her occasionally when I came into the shop. I do remember they used to live together in a flat above the old cinema in Seaside.'

The cinema he described had become a bingo hall, had given up that incarnation and now lay empty, the walls plastered with layers of peeling posters. They rang on the only bell they could find, and presently an indistinct voice over the intercom denied all knowledge of Gloria or Steve.

'To be honest, mate,' said the voice, 'me and my girlfriend have only lived here for four months and I haven't a clue who lived here before us.'

By this time despondency and hunger had taken over, and Carl and Rora entered the first café they could find. Although unprepossessing from the outside, with windows that needed a clean, they had a surprisingly good meal of fish and chips.

'I don't think we're going to find her,' said Carl.

'She could be anywhere,' said Rora.

'With Steve dead and with no other leads, I can't think what to do next,' said Carl, and she could tell he was crushingly disappointed. He had spent so long thinking about the possibility of finding his mother, now that he had embarked on the quest it seemed that he might have left it too late. While they were talking about whether they should abandon the project for the time being and go back to Hastings, Rora noticed a curtain in the window of the house just across the street from the cinema being held aside and a face peering out at them.

'It's a bit unlikely,' said Rora, 'but I'm going to knock on that woman's door. She looks old enough to have been here for some time.'

At first the door remained unanswered, but finally a woman opened it. Her face was like a mask and her eyes were lined with glittery green kohl that extended in wavering but coquettish lines half way to her ears.

'Who are you?' she asked and her voice was tremulous and scared.

Carl explained why they had knocked on the door and apologised for disturbing her. She looked at Carl through eyelashes so weighed down with mascara that it was a wonder she could see at all. 'You're her boy, aren't you?' she said. 'I did wonder if you would ever come looking for her. She used to talk about you sometimes when she got pissed.'

'You don't know where she is now do you?' asked Carl.

'We stayed in touch for a while. She'd come and see me from time to time, but I haven't seen her for at least four years. She's living in The Heights. I don't know the address, but it's just out of town.'

'I don't know what I'm going to feel when I see her,' Carl said. Footsore and unable to walk any further, they had succumbed to the luxury of a taxi. They were on the narrow road above Eastbourne that curved across the Downs. The fields were a cold green, the trees permanently scalped and bent into cowering shapes by the merciless wind. Rora felt unsafe – the grass was spread out to the very edges of the cliff, as if to lure the unwary.

'Do you think you'll recognise her?' Rora asked, and she could tell by the expression on his face that he hadn't really thought about how she might have changed. In his mind she was still the woman who had driven away from him; still the person who had the solution to the puzzle of what had happened.

'Don't expect too much of her,' Rora said, sensing his eagerness and wanting suddenly to protect him from disappointment or further sorrow, or even humiliation if she rejected him again. To her mind a woman who could leave a child behind in the way that she had was unlikely, despite the passing of the years, to have changed into a decent human being.

'I'll probably just feel angry with her,' said Carl. 'That's if I feel anything at all. It might be like meeting a stranger.'

The Heights wasn't an apartment block as they had imagined, but some sort of a care home with a neglected look about it; terracotta pots had cracked over the winter and had been left with their soil and roots spilling over the driveway, and the windows were obscured by yellowing curtains.

Carl was puzzled. 'Why is she living here? She can only be in her mid-fifties,' he said.

The young woman at the reception had a head that seemed out of proportion with her too slender body. Everything she said sounded like a question, because she ended statements and queries alike with an upward cadence.

'We've got all sorts here?' she said when Rora asked her. 'We look after people who can't look after themselves?'

'Does a Mrs Richards live here?' Carl asked, still sure that there must have been some mistake. Perhaps the woman who lived opposite the old cinema had got the name of the place wrong.

'Mrs Richards?' the young woman said. 'It's been a while since anyone has visited her? I'll show you the way?'

She took them through to a large open space, ringed around the edges with high-backed chairs. Small tables were dotted about the room, but since there were no chairs around them it was clear that this wasn't a place for conversation. The people in the room were distinguishable one from the other in ways that seemed too subtle to define; the colour of a sweater, a head held down or up, hands clasped across the body, or held loosely by the sides.

'Here she is?' said the receptionist. 'I'll leave you to chat?'

She had stopped in front of a woman who had the same slumped look as many of the others. There seemed to be nothing remarkable about her; her hair was cut short, she was wearing a shapeless dress on which there were traces of food. Carl started to say that he thought there must have been some mistake, but then the woman in the chair lifted her head and looked at them and the likeness was unmistakable. She had her son's dark, almond-shaped eyes. Carl froze. Rora heard him make a small noise, a kind of swallowed breath. His face had an expression that was halfway between fear and astonishment.

'Mum?' he said, his voice low.

Rora was surprised that he had called her that. He had told her he didn't ever think of her as his mother. She thought that some sort of instinct must have kicked in when he saw her. It was only then that she realised quite how much this meant to him.

'Gloria?' he said, and this time Rora could hear something that sounded almost like a plea in his voice. 'Do you recognise me?' he asked, and his eyes scanned his mother as if trying to see the woman with the pale, oval face of his memory in the grey fleshy folds.

'Hello. Who are you?' she said, and her voice sounded rough, as if it didn't often get used.

'It's Carl,' he said, and Rora could hear what she thought was anger hardening his voice, or it may simply have been shock.

'Are you a friendly face?' she asked.

'It's Carl,' he said again.

There was no flicker of recognition, no animation in her face at all, just a sense that she was clinging to a dimly remembered reflex.

'Would you like a cup of tea?' she asked.

'I don't want a bloody cup of tea,' Carl said.

He had raised his voice and several of the people sitting in the room turned their heads towards him.

'I haven't come all this way just to drink tea,' Carl shouted, and Rora could see that his hands were clenched into tight fists. This time his voice was loud enough to catch the attention of the receptionist, who came back into the room and approached with a wary yet purposeful air, as if she was accustomed to dealing with furious relatives.

'She'll not know who you are? She's suffering from early onset dementia?' she said, putting her hand on Gloria's shoulder.

'I'm sorry,' she said then, her voice low and sincere, as if this was not a matter of conjecture but something she could be certain of.

They had come too late after all. Whoever Gloria had been, whatever mistakes she had made and whatever cruelties she had demonstrated, they were no longer part of her. She had been wiped clean. Rora thought about saying that he had never really had her, but she knew it would be no comfort to him just then.

They stayed a while and tried to tell her things, but the words had no purchase. It was like throwing objects into a bowl with no bottom. Nothing stayed with her. Just before they left, Carl bent down to her and looked carefully into her eyes. Rora wondered if he would at last express a little of what it had been like to be left on a pavement at the age of eight. His mother wouldn't have understood what he was saying to her, but it might perhaps have given him some sort of release. Instead, he touched her cheek with his lips as tenderly as if he was kissing a child. Although she didn't completely recognise the moment for what it was, it was when he kissed his mother that Rora fell in love with him.

June 2010

Rora looked out of her father's bedroom window at the red interlocking roofs studded with acid-yellow moss and streaked here and there with seagull droppings, the sycamores with their hanging golden-green clusters, and just visible, the tops of the tall oaks fringing the park. As far as her father was concerned, Hastings with its mixture of new and old, raw and age-smoothed, no longer existed anywhere other than in his memory. His world had become smaller and smaller; first he was limited to a slow perambulation around the garden, then restricted to the house, and now, finally, his world had shrunk to this one room, this one bed. Now he had to rely on what he remembered of this view he loved so dearly.

She thought he was asleep until he suddenly spoke.

'Hattie Jacques has trussed me up like a kipper,' he said. 'She's tucked me in so tightly I can't move my arms.'

Rora went over to the bed and loosened his sheets.

'I've been reading your book,' she said, and felt a quickening in him, a kind of alertness she hadn't seen for some time.

'What do you think?' he asked in a carefully neutral voice as if he didn't care, but she wasn't fooled. She recognised his desire to be told he had made something good, that the hours spent, the sentences arranged and rearranged had been worth the effort.

'It's not bad,' she said, still finding it hard to say what she knew would make him happy. In fact, she had been impressed by what she had read so far. His telling of the history of Hastings was both deeply personal and well informed. Some parts of it had caught her up and carried her along and made her want to see the town as he saw it. She wondered at her own hardness. Even now she couldn't let go of her animosity; even now, when a few words from her could make things better for him. For the first time she wondered at her part in the failure of their relationship. He might have set the direction for them, but she had done nothing to try and turn off that path; she had run down it away from him, refusing to look back or to stop and consider where she was going.

'It's better than not bad, actually,' she said. He smiled at her and although she resisted it still, she allowed herself, just for a moment, to be warmed by it.

'What bits did you like best?' he asked eagerly, pushing himself up against his pillow so that he could look at her.

'I like a lot of it . . . I love the parts about the pier and the history of fishing, and the chapter about the America Ground and how people made a whole town on a stretch of shingle, and the stories about smuggling are really good. There are parts that need trimming though,' she said, wanting him to know that she had looked at it carefully, that she was someone who knew how books were put together. She found to her surprise that she wanted him to think her clever.

'You have a tendency to drift off at times. I really don't think we need for instance to know quite so much about how many bricks were used in the construction of parts of the town or exactly how the fishing boats were made.'

'Trimming. Yes. It needs trimming,' he said. 'We could trim it together.'

'We'll make a start tomorrow,' she said, moving around the room, fussing with the curtains, the water jug by his bed, so that he wouldn't take her decision to help him as a softening.

'I still miss her every single day,' Frank said quietly.

Rora had spent so long shoring herself up against feeling that she was astonished by the emotion her father's words evoked in her. It was as if his slow slide away from life was taking a layer of her skin with it. It was in order to hide this new rawness from him that she spoke more harshly than she intended.

'You let missing her become your life and mine,' said Rora.

'I wish it had been different. I wish I had been stronger,' Frank said wearily.

'You don't have a monopoly on grief,' said Rora, aware that her voice was too loud in the still atmosphere of the sick room. The fan she had set up for Frank at the end of the bed seemed not to be cooling the room at all, just blowing the hot air and their hopeless words round and round.

'I'm too tired for this now,' said Frank, and turned away from her.

She sat for a while by the opened window and persisted with her embroidery, a cross-stitched cat lying curled up on a chair, her first attempt at such a project. The sewing was intended to calm her, but she had a tendency to tug at the thread too tightly and her cat was developing a lopsided air. She pricked her finger for about the fifteenth time and set the material aside impatiently. She wanted to get out of this room, this house, away from her diminished father and get some proper air, not just the faint breeze that strayed through the window. She was still nervous that she might bump into Carl, although as time had passed this anxiety had changed shape. It felt now as if she was readying herself for the possibility that they might meet. She had taken to formulating sentences in her mind, things she might say to him if they were suddenly face to face. She wondered if she would get any words out at all.

She decided to walk to the Fishermen's Museum. Her father had started making some notes about the life of the people who had lived in increasingly cramped conditions in the Old Town. Nineteenth-century Hastings had been divided by class and by the Bourne Stream, which snaked its gassy way down to the sea and marked the border between the more affluent residents of the west of the town and those living cheek by jowl in the east.

The museum was housed in a former church on the front next to the fishing huts. The walls displayed grainy photographs of boats and grizzled-looking men in sou'westers and thick polo necks. There was an albatross and a white pelican, both in glass cases, and a ghoulish effigy of a member of the Winkle Club dressed in full winkle-adorned regalia who looked like Tony Blackburn. She was also interested in an exhibit about the sand-scratchers, artists who had used metal forks to score pictures in the damp sand left by the retreating tide. She thought of Carl and the way he had laboured over his pavement drawings with the same disregard of their impermanence.

A case on the other wall contained some clothes worn by fishermen and their families – a threadbare smock, a single satin wedding shoe, a small blanket made up of scraps of material sewn together with rough stitches. Rora thought how strange it would have been for the person who had made the blanket almost 200 years ago to know that it would end up in this place for strangers to look at. It was often the most random things that survived to illuminate the past and perhaps told quite another tale from the one that was intended. It was ironic, given her relationship with her father, that she too had become a historian. She resisted the notion that she was in any way similar to him and yet she knew that it was from him and from her mother and grandmother that she had inherited her love of stories. History's allure for her was the infinite ways there were to understand what had happened. The explanations for the triumphs and shames of the past depended on who was telling the tale.

Rora sat for a couple of hours looking through some papers and books. Once he had discovered that Rora was Frank's daughter, the museum attendant had ushered her to a table and given her access to any documentation she required. She was a special guest, since her father had volunteered at the museum for many years, helping out with the exhibits, even selling the museum's souvenirs and books. After making as many notes as she could on the tablet she always carried with her, Rora took some photocopies of the archived material to make notes on when she got home. It would be something to do after Ursula had gone to bed and Frank was asleep. She decided she wanted to write a whole section about what women who lived in the

Old Town did while their husbands were away at sea, apart from gossiping in the washhouse on the high street and waiting for their men to return.

On her way home Rora decided to cheer Ursula up with a gift. The toyshop didn't have a wide selection, being a wooden trucks and improving books sort of a place, but after some indecision she settled on a baby doll with a cloth torso and plastic limbs that lay flat, like a boned chicken. She thought its round head and rosy cheeks and natty striped outfit would appeal to Ursula. She was standing at the till waiting to pay when a familiar voice addressed her.

'We meet again!' said Krystof.

Rora's heart sank.

'Hello,' she said, paying for the doll and hoping she might be able to make a quick getaway, but he stood beside her until she had completed the transaction.

'You look tired,' he said, bringing his face close to her own and scrutinising her so minutely, she drew back.

'The matter is settled,' he announced. 'You are coming with me to the restaurant for a restorative snack.'

'Oh no. I really couldn't,' said Rora. 'I'm expected at home.'

'An hour here and there won't make a big difference,' he said, and it was clear that he wasn't going to let her escape. She waited while he debated the merits of a pull-along caterpillar versus a pull-along donkey as a present for a newborn nephew in Poland. He tried both toys out by walking them back and forth across the shop floor, commenting on their relative merits.

'The caterpillar makes a good clacking noise, but I think the donkey sound is better,' he said and walked back and forth some more until Rora thought he would never stop.

'I'd go for the donkey,' she said at last in desperation.

'What's your reason?' asked Krystof.

'Umm, I suppose because a donkey can be pulled along in real life, but no one pulls along a caterpillar,' she replied.

'Quite right! Good logic!' he exclaimed. 'The donkey it is. I also like the little red saddle.'

He took her through to the back of the restaurant and settled her down at a table hidden behind a wide pillar well away from the paying customers.

'I will bring you a small selection,' he said, and disappeared into the kitchen for ten minutes. He re-emerged with a large, flat platter on which there was a variety of small, beautifully formed pastry parcels stuffed with smoked cheese and pickled cucumber, chestnuts with spiced beef and sweet sausage mixed with slivers of a sharp, green apple. Krystof sat opposite her and poured both of them a glass of chilled, flowery white wine.

'Are you not eating too?' Rora asked.

'I will graze with you,' he replied. 'In truth, I get a little sick of Polish food. I often crave Yorkshire pudding with lashings of onion gravy.'

'Did the bank manager say yes?' asked Rora between mouthfuls.

'He did!' said Krystof, looking delighted by her question. 'You remembered!'

'What did you want the money for? If you don't mind me asking.'

'To buy the building next door and make Zamek twice the size,' said Krystof.

'You must be doing well, then,' said Rora. 'I can tell you are. This is all delicious.'

'So tell me,' he said, looking complacent as she devoured the food, 'what are you doing here in Hastings?'

'I'm from here. I've come back because my father is very ill. He is dying actually.'

'I'm sorry,' said Krystof, and his comedy face became quite stricken with gloom.

'I think he has probably only a few weeks left. It's hard to know exactly.'

'And you are looking after him?' asked Krystof.

'Well, not really,' she said, 'he has a nurse . . . I'm not really sure that he even wants me here.'

Krystof's face became even more downcast. 'Surely he does,' he said. 'At the end you want people around you that you know. Not strangers.'

'We haven't got on so well over the years,' she said, and then wondered why she was confiding in him. She was not given to blurting out personal information to relative strangers.

'What happened between you?' he asked. He rested his face on his hands as if settling down for a long narrative.

'He did something he was ashamed of and I did something I was ashamed of and we stopped being able to talk to each other. My mother died and he didn't cope very well. He kind of removed himself from me.'

'Have you talked to him about what you feel?' asked Krystof, and as he lifted his head up towards the light Rora noticed what a strange colour his eyes were. They were a kind of golden brown, flecked with yellow.

'He isn't easy to talk to. I know I should say something about what happened between us before it's too late, but it's hard to find a way in.'

'You just tell him you love him,' said Krystof. 'Job done. That's what I want said to me when I come to be dying. I want people to tell me they love me, and I want to tell them that I found in my life everything that I ever wanted.'

'You make it all sound so neat and tidy,' said Rora, irritated by Krystof's certainty. 'I don't love him. There is no use pretending. There's no point making speeches now. Anyway,' she said, pushing her plate away from her. 'Thank you for lunch, it was delicious. I must pay you for it.'

'Lunch is of course on me,' he said. 'Maybe one night I can take you to dinner?'

He made the request with an old-fashioned incline of his head that half annoyed Rora and half made her want to laugh.

'I'm not really looking for a relationship,' she said. 'I'm only here for a short time.'

'We are all here for only a short time,' said Krystof and then smiled his watchful, joyful smile. The one that made her think that he wasn't perhaps quite as much of a sap as he appeared.

'Well, anyway, I'll write my number here on this very nice napkin and you ring it if you want anything,' he said.

She accepted the proffered napkin reluctantly and slipped it into her bag. It really wouldn't be polite to roll it into a ball in front of him.

'Goodbye, Aurora,' he said. 'Until the next time.'

She thought him surprisingly confident, even perhaps a little arrogant. He had seemed so self-deprecating at first, but now she wondered if her initial assessment of him had been the right one. She thought maybe he was tougher, more resilient than she had thought. She left without noticing that she had forgotten the bag containing Ursula's doll.

Her father was asleep, lying on his back, his mouth slightly open, his skin pale. It looked as if another man was pushing through his old, familiar shape, some stranger who had been lying in wait until the time was right to take possession of his body. She touched his forehead, which felt slightly warm, and smoothed his hair back from his face. This was the first time in years that she had touched him without a practical purpose. In recent days she had helped to sit him up on propped pillows and moved him from bed to chair and back again, but she hadn't touched him with tenderness for as long as she could remember, perhaps not since she was a child. He woke and for a few moments lay still, halfway between sleep and waking. It was as if something had been tugging at him and had let him go reluctantly.

'Hello Aurora,' he said, and her given name on his lips after such a long time sounded like an endearment. 'What have you done today?'

'I went to the museum and they pulled out all sorts of bits and pieces for me. I was treated like an honoured guest, being your daughter,' she said. 'Then I ate Polish food at the restaurant belonging to someone I keep bumping into.'

'Is he nice?' asked Frank.

'Why do you assume it was a man?' asked Rora. 'Nice enough I suppose.'

'Boyfriend material?' he asked.

'I'm not looking for a boyfriend,' said Rora, disconcerted by the line the conversation had taken. Her father never asked her about personal matters.

'I don't like to think of you alone,' Frank said in a quiet voice. Rora was concerned about his breathing, which seemed more laboured this evening than it had before. She also wondered if his dose of morphine needed to be raised. She resolved to speak to the doctor about it when he came the next day.

'I'm not alone. I've got Ursula. And anyway, you were alone for years,' she said accusingly.

'I just didn't find anyone that would suit,' said Frank.

'Would anyone have suited? After Mum I mean,' she asked.

'She was certainly hard to replace,' said Frank, looking down at his hands.

'That's what I mean,' said Rora. 'And even if you could find someone else, why put yourself through all that pain again?'

'Just because I didn't manage it, Rora, doesn't mean you can't,' said Frank.

'I don't want to,' said Rora, and she found her eyes were filling with tears. She hastily rubbed away the moisture. She knew her father had never been good when it came to displays of emotion. She remembered one occasion, years ago, when he had come into her room and found her weeping. She had been looking though an album of photos of her mother. He had come in too quietly for her to have time to hide her distress in the way she usually did. He had taken one stricken look at her and then turned round and left the room.

'There is more than one way of loving and more than one person to love,' said Frank.

'You didn't love anyone else after Mum, did you?' she asked.

'No, but I don't have as much capacity for love as you do, Rora,' he said, and he looked through the window. The sky had traces of gold in it and a bat traversed the glass with a sudden swoop. It moved so quickly it was almost as if she had imagined seeing it. Rora felt again that slow peeling back of the caul she had grown over her heart. Was it true what he said? Is that how he saw her? For a moment she saw herself as if through his eyes – his Ursula.

'I would give anything to see her again,' he said. 'I could bear anything, being old and sick, even dying, if I could see her again for five minutes.'

'Maybe you will,' said Rora.

'The first thing she will ask me is how you are,' said Frank.

'And what will you tell her?'

'I'll tell her that you are managing admirably, but that you think your story is over, and that makes me sadder than anything else.'

'This family has always set too much store by stories.'

'You've got to make yours as good as it can be.'

Kiss 7

*'He put his hands on either side of her head and held her tightly,
like he thought she might be trying to escape.'*

30 July 2000

Carl and Rora's it's-us-two-against-the-world attitude worried
Isobel, who thought her granddaughter was too young to have
become so attached. In fact, she considered, being fixated on
one person was bad news at any age and she wanted more for
Rora than what she considered to be a wanton narrowing of
expectations.

'There's a whole world out there,' she said to Rora, who was
standing impatiently in the kitchen waiting for Isobel to finish
talking so that she could go out.

'It's just waiting for you to claim it.'

'I *am* claiming it,' said Rora who loved her grandmother, but
who seldom listened to her these days. It seemed that Isobel
always chose the least convenient moment to start one of her
lectures. Her grandmother had slowed considerably over the last
year or so and Rora had noticed a new frailty and a querulous-
ness about her that both irritated her and smote her to the heart.
Without her grandmother she would have been lost, but this
knowledge felt like a burden rather than a blessing. The close-
ness they had shared in the years when Isobel was the teacher
and Rora the willing pupil had to a large extent gone. Now Rora
wondered how Isobel could possibly understand the things that
preoccupied her grandchild. It was years and years since her

grandmother had been young and things were no longer as she imagined them. Could she even remember how it felt to have a boy's eyes darken when he looked at you? Or how it was to feel beautiful one day – gloriously triumphant in her silky skin – and then wretchedly scratchy and lumpy the next? Or how the whole of life seemed misty and difficult to grasp, and everything, each thought, each action seemed precariously balanced, ready to tip at any moment one way or the other?

When Rora finally got away from the house and went to meet Carl at the café on the West Cliff, she was surprised to see that Ian was with him. Carl hadn't mentioned that he would be joining them. The West Cliff Café was one of their places and she didn't like the idea of Ian knowing where they went together. When she arrived, Carl got up and went to the counter to get her a drink. She was uncomfortably aware that Ian was staring at her.

'You're very beautiful. Do you know how lovely you are?' he said, and reached out to touch her hand, not seeming to care if Carl saw him. Rora pulled away, but was aware of a traitorous feeling of excitement. He was looking at her in a strange, intense way – his eyes passing over her face and resting on her mouth. She knew Carl thought she was beautiful too, but he never said it. When Carl returned to the table, Ian leaned back and started to talk about other matters and he didn't look at her again, but Rora remembered the way his eyes had grazed her lips, and despite the fact she didn't want him she felt a thrill at the thought he seemed to want her.

Later, after Ian had gone, she and Carl walked home together. She sensed a shift in his mood – he was talking loudly, walking fast. She wondered if he had seen Ian touch her, even though he had made no mention of it. For some reason she couldn't quite understand, she hadn't told him about what Ian had said to her. It felt strange to be keeping a secret from him – they had always told each other everything. When they got to the car park at Rock-a-Nore she was alarmed to see that Carl was checking the doors of the cars, trying the handles and peering at the dashboards. He stopped in front of a blue Mini, and before she could see what he was doing, he had taken a length of flat metal out of the pocket of his coat and had slipped it down the edge of the car window.

'What're you doing?' she asked aghast. Don't do that.' But he got the door open and within seconds was inside, fiddling with the wheel. The engine sprang to life.

'Get in,' he said. He was smiling, his face full of a kind of restless joy.

'No. Don't be mad, Carl,' she begged.

'Come on, get in,' he said again. And then there was a shout from the other side of the car park.

'You have to come now. We have to go.' Carl reversed out of the car park and turned onto the seafront and then there was wind through the open window and some music on the radio that made it feel as if they were going very fast.

For a while Rora was caught up in the glamour of it; the stolen car, the road out of town made unfamiliar by the speed they were travelling, the seafront illuminations smeared by a sudden, violent downpour. She almost said aloud what she had been thinking – that she wanted to stay sitting next to him and to drive on through the night, taking roads at random – a holiday route. She imagined the long, dark, intimate journey down roads arched by overhanging trees, arriving in the morning at some perfect, bright place. Despite the dazzle of the passing road and the danger of what might lie ahead she felt strangely safe, as if his tough invincibility was contagious. She sometimes wondered over the years how it would have been if she had said those words out loud, because, of course, she didn't. She had seen where holiday routes ended up.

'You've got to stop,' Rora said, 'stop now Carl. We can leave the car and run.'

But he didn't even slow down and they carried on past the bottle alley and the rock pools and the white marble statue of a dying king in West Marina Gardens. Carl was exultant. She could feel the life rippling through him.

'I'll stop in a bit,' he said, 'let's just get a little way out of town,' and she held on to the door handle and prayed that it would be over soon. In the end it was over quicker than either of them expected. Carl swerved to avoid an elderly man crossing the road, briefly lost control and mounted the pavement. There was a dreadful screeching noise of metal on concrete as the car hit a bollard and then they finally came to a halt. There was a moment's muffled silence like that following a heavy fall of snow and then Rora came to life and opened the door. The man they had almost knocked over seemed to be OK, although he was shouting at them.

'We've got to get away,' she said. 'Come on Carl.'

She dragged him out of the car and they ran, stopping occasionally to catch their breath, all the way to Carl's flat in St Leonards. They were relieved to find that Mo was out and they locked the door and drew the curtains over the window and hid, giggling with a kind of hysterical relief on the floor behind the sofa. It was unlikely that anyone had seen the way they had gone, but they still hunkered down, whispering and shaking, tormenting each other with the possibility that the old man had seen their faces and might, right this moment, be describing them at the police station.

'He didn't look like he could see a foot in front of himself, let alone see us clearly,' said Carl, with more bravado than she knew he felt.

'You could have killed me,' she said angrily when they finally stopped their trembling laughter, as if she hadn't realised until then that they had been in danger. It was what he had always done – tested her resolve, made her prove over and over again that she belonged to him, that they belonged to each other.

'We're immortal,' he said and looked at her with shining, sad eyes.

He put his hands on either side of her head and held her tightly, like he thought she might be trying to escape. His lips were soft and tentative at first and then the sliding stroke of them became more urgent. He pressed his mouth hard against hers. She could still feel the rush of the car moving through her body and the sensation of being taken somewhere she wasn't sure she wanted to go, and for a while it became part of what she was feeling now. She looked into his face for the comfort of its familiarity. He looked awestruck, soft-mouthed, lost, but she knew every line of him. Then the sweet heat of his body on hers blotted everything else out. He took off her shirt, undoing each button with solemn care, and touched her neck and shoulders with his scratchy palms and she knew she was where she wanted to be.

June 2010

Although Frank pretended to be grumpy with her because bad-tempered was his default position, Rora knew he had a secret soft spot for Hannah. He liked her practicality and the way that she was never thrown by what he said, even when he was being provocative.

'Who said you could come in?' he said as a greeting when Hannah walked into the bedroom, where Rora and he were sketching out the contents for the last section of the book.

'The nurse said it was OK to come up,' said Hannah unapologetically.

Always high coloured, today her face glowed with an even ruddier hue after a couple of afternoons sunbathing on the beach. She was holding an enormous bunch of pink and blue larkspur in a vase in one arm and a toolbox in the other.

'I've come to unstick the window,' Hannah announced.

'The flowers are beautiful,' Frank said. 'Put them on the table there where I can see them.'

'Don't let me interrupt your work,' Hannah said, sweeping clear a side table near Frank's bed and putting down the flowers.

'We've almost finished for the day, actually,' said Frank. 'I was just telling Rora that I didn't want the book to become some sort of treatise on the downtrodden lives of the wives of fishermen.'

Rora rolled her eyes behind her father's back.

'I know you're making faces, Rora,' he said. 'I may be ill but I'm not blind yet and I can still see your reflection in the mirror.'

'The women weren't downtrodden. They were amazingly resourceful and they made up two-thirds of the population. By all accounts they were a feisty lot, and when the fishing trade wasn't booming they took up all sort of jobs like running lodging houses and as shopkeepers. The Caves, the Castle and the bathing machines all had female proprietors.'

'Hmm . . . some of them were fond of a brawl or two,' said Frank, 'and considering the size of Hastings and the fact there wasn't a big port there were a surprising number of prostitutes,' said Frank.

'That's what I said, resourceful,' said Rora.

'If you've finished work, I thought I might be able to drag you out for a coffee or something,' said Hannah, picking up Rora's sorry attempt at a cross-stitched cat. 'I've never seen such a puckered creature!' she exclaimed laughing.

'Rora takes out her fury on that bit of fabric,' said Frank wryly.

'It's quite soothing actually,' said Rora with dignity, taking the offending item away from Hannah and stowing it in its sewing bag.

'I've just joined an embroidery class,' said Hannah. 'Why don't you come with me next time?'

'I'm not sure I'm the stitch and bitch type,' said Rora. 'I suspect I'm beyond help.'

Hannah quickly set about loosening the paint around the stuck window, and within a few minutes she had managed to open it and a cooling breeze sprang up.

'I can smell the sea,' said Frank breathing deeply. 'You're a resourceful woman Hannah. Thank you.'

'I get it from my ancestors,' said Hannah and winked at Rora.

'Stop your winking and leave me alone,' said Frank. 'All this chatter has tired me out.'

'I bumped into that Krystof again,' said Rora a little later when they were sitting in the garden. Rora had propped up a faded beach umbrella against the rickety table so that they could shelter from the sun.

'Oh yes,' said Hannah. 'Bumped into as in accidently met again or was it more a case of accidentally on purpose?'

'I met him in the toyshop when I was buying Ursula a present,' said Rora, 'and then he invited me back to the restaurant for lunch.'

'Did he?' said Hannah speculatively. 'I wouldn't have thought he was quite your type.'

'What's my type?' asked Rora.

'I thought you preferred men who didn't really give a toss. It strikes me that our Polish friend is a feeling sort of a chap,' said Hannah.

'I'm not looking to have a relationship with him,' said Rora.

'Just as well. He's lovely, but you would eat him up, along with all those delicious dumplings he keeps feeding you.'

'You make me sound horrible.'

'You're not horrible. You're just a hard nut to crack. I never know what you are thinking and I've known you for ages. I wish you did tell me more.'

'I'll try,' said Rora, and Hannah was surprised to see her eyes fill with tears. 'I think I've lost the habit,' she said. 'If I ever had it. It's been so long, I can't really remember.'

'What would make you happier than you are now?' asked Hannah gently, disconcerted by Rora's uncharacteristic display of emotion.

'It's like I've forgotten what it is I want,' said Rora. 'I think I'm still waiting for my life to get going, and while I do that it's just trickling away.'

Hannah got up and put her arms around Rora's shoulders and rocked her gently, the way she did her children when they needed consoling. Rora felt herself tense up and then made a deliberate attempt to relax in her friend's arms and accept the consolation that was being offered. Only she knew what a battle it was to let herself be loved.

Getting Ursula to sleep was a protracted business. At ten o'clock, thinking that she had at last capitulated, Rora crept away, made herself a cup of tea and settled gratefully in front of the TV. Ten minutes into a chat show in which an actress was sitting curled up on the sofa attempting to look relaxed and failing, Rora heard Ursula's voice calling her and her heart sank. She hoped that Ursula had not reverted to her previous, unhappy, unsettled self. She went back into the bedroom to find her daughter sitting bolt upright, her eyes wide and her mouth trembling.

'I've got a stomach ache again Mummy,' she said.

'It's bad to make things up,' said Rora crossly, straightening Ursula's bedclothes that she had pulled into disarray. 'Remember that story about Matilda. She kept pretending there was a fire and people got fed up with her and didn't come when there really was a fire. It's the same with stomach aches.'

Ursula's face crumpled and Rora instantly felt guilty.

'It's all right, darling,' she said. 'I'll lie down next to you like I did last time.'

Ursula's sobs gradually subsided.

133

'Did you know that when Grandad was a boy he had an out-side toilet and toilet paper that was scratchy like cardboard and smelled of medicine?' asked Ursula.

'No, I didn't know that,' said Rora.

'And did you know that he had a dog called Fetters and that he used to steal food from the kitchen to feed it and that he once broke his arm in three different places?'

'I didn't know those things either,' said Rora. 'You're finding out a lot about your grandfather.'

'He's old but interesting,' said Ursula, 'and I can talk to him and he seems to understand.'

'I'm glad,' said Rora, wondering at her father's previously well-hidden empathy. 'You can talk to me too, you know.'

Ursula seemed for a moment as if she might say something. She turned her face towards her mother and then almost imme-diately turned away again.

'I'm fine,' she said. 'You can turn out the light now.'

As she settled herself back down on the sofa Rora wondered if she should be worried about Ursula's behaviour. It was prob-ably just her age. Rora too used to combat sleep when she was a child. Unable to bear the thought that she might be absenting herself from something good, she would lie in bed, holding her-self fast, her eyes firmly open against the tide of darkness. Ursula was no doubt fighting the same battle, while upstairs her grand-father was letting the wave roll over him, unable or unwilling to fight any longer for what he might be missing.

Kiss 8

'She felt the smooth slide of her dress across her thighs as she stretched and turned.'

25 August 2000

The kiss on the night of the party at the sea cadets hut was one Rora regretted all her life. It changed everything, including the way Rora thought about herself. It wasn't a kiss she wanted to put under tissue paper, nor would she choose to have it illustrated in the beautiful colours of Isobel's book, but it was, in her grandmother's words, one of the beads that made up the string of her story and the necklace wouldn't be complete without it.

Rora's exam results had been very good, despite the distraction of Carl. Good enough to do history at the university of her choice in London, and Carl was adamant that she should go straightaway rather than have the gap year she was contemplating.

'It's only London, not the other side of the world. I'll come and see you all the time,' he said. 'I might even move to London myself. It's not as if there's much keeping me here.'

Although he talked a good talk, telling her there was no point in delaying embarking on something she really wanted to do, she knew that the thought of her going was difficult for him and that he occasionally lapsed into gloominess. Sometimes he couldn't prevent himself from revealing his feelings, although she knew he was trying not to say anything that might dissuade her.

'You'll meet better, more interesting people,' he said.

'I'll not meet anyone better than you.'

'You'll all be in it together,' said Carl, ignoring her attempts to console him. 'Before long you'll meet some bloke with a fuzzy little moustache and a wide forehead bursting with brains, who will take you out for a coffee and you will be so impressed that you'll forget all about me.'

'You're bursting with brains too. It's just that you don't seem to want to use them,' said Rora.

'I'm going to be a late bloomer,' Carl told her.

'Or a cottage loaf,' said Rora a little unkindly. She didn't understand why he didn't want to do more than work in a bakery. She was always trying to persuade him to use his artistic talents and apply to art college.

'I don't think they'd be that impressed by someone who just does pavement drawings,' he said when she brought it up.

'So do something on paper or canvas,' she said.

'I like pavement drawings because they don't last,' was all he would say before the stubborn look she so disliked came across his face and he clammed up. She suspected that for all his vigour and the brightness that shone through him when he talked about the things that mattered to him, he didn't really believe in his own abilities. She thought there was nothing she would change about him except this tendency he had to denigrate himself and his prospects. He believed she could do anything she wanted, but he wasn't able to feel any confidence about himself.

Rora had invited Carl to the end of sixth form party as her plus one, although he wasn't keen on the idea of going.

'It'll just be a bunch of losers drinking vodka from Coke cans,' he said. 'Let's go somewhere else, just the two of us.'

But Rora had been looking forward to it. She was sentimental about occasions that marked events and she wanted to commemorate the transition from this part of her life to the next.

'It's a way of saying goodbye,' she explained to Carl.

'Why do you want to say goodbye to a load of people you didn't even want to say hello to?' Carl muttered, knowing he wasn't going to change her mind.

The boys were wearing black tie, or some version of it, hired if they had the money, or if not, making do with what they could cobble together from their fathers' and elder brothers' wardrobes. Rora had deliberated long and hard over what she was going to wear. Isobel had given her enough money to get something special and she had spent several Saturdays leading up to the event trawling the town's shops.

'Buy something green to match your eyes,' said Isobel. 'And remember, the more you have on show the less of a mystery you will be.'

Rora wasn't at all sure she wanted to be a mystery and settled at last for a short, silky slip dress in dark plum and shoes with a small heel and an ankle strap. She gathered her wild hair back in a loose ponytail. Just before she was due to leave Rora came to show her grandmother the finished product. Isobel clasped her hands to her heart.

'My darling girl, you look so beautiful. I'm going to get your father to come and see you.'

Frank came reluctantly out of his study and stood looking at Rora without saying anything.

'Doesn't she look grown up?' asked Isobel, her eyes dewy with emotion.

'She looks great,' said Frank without smiling and he turned and left the room.

Isobel could see the disappointment in Rora's face.

'He's not one to gush,' she said. 'It's not his style.'

Rora remembered the way he used to twirl her mother around the kitchen.

'Isn't she a rare beauty? Isn't she?' he had said, his face full of awe and surprise, as if he couldn't quite believe his luck.

'He doesn't gush about me, that's for sure,' she said quietly, and then put her shoulders back and tightened the ribbon in her hair and resolved to have a good time, despite her father's lack of enthusiasm. Hannah knocked on the door to pick her up, wearing a red Chinese-style dress that made her look fabulously sexy.

It was a perfect evening. The sky was a silvery blue and the sea was still and beautiful. Rora felt a great swell of feeling. It filled her up and carried her along past the groups of girls walking in bright dresses and past the people sitting outside bars catching the last of the day's sunshine. It was one of those rare times when she felt anything was possible and that simply wanting it would make it so. Although Rora would have preferred to go straight to the party with Hannah, Carl had insisted that they meet up at the beach hut first, and so she and Hannah parted at the top of the road leading down to the beach.

Carl was sitting on the step outside waiting for her as she approached, looking a little awkward in his defiant checked shirt and jeans. When he saw her he gave one of his rare, radiant smiles.

'You look . . . . different . . . amazing,' was all he managed, but she could see him giving her surreptitious looks, as if he was checking it was really her.

'And you look like Carl,' she said laughing.

He had placed a bottle of white wine in a plastic bucket of ice and two glasses she had never seen before on the little table on the porch. He poured her a glass of wine very carefully, making sure not to spill a drop and then wiped the neck of the bottle with a piece of kitchen towel. They toasted the end of Rora's schooldays and the beginning of whatever would come next, and Rora fixed the taste of the wine and the feeling of the sun and the expression on Carl's face when he looked at her, tight in her mind so that she would remember it.

The scuffed lino floor and sticky walls of the sea cadets hut had been transformed with lights and streamers and the dented metal tables were covered with silver cloths and candles in glass holders. Carl and Rora parted to chat to other people for a while, but they always found each other again. The music was loud, the floor slippery and Rora danced as if she would never stop. At one point she noticed that Ian had arrived. He was wearing an immaculate black suit and his hair had been combed back from his face, but she looked away and when she looked back he had disappeared. Later, she saw him sitting at one of the tables. He was staring at her, and without really being conscious of what she was doing, she increased the sway of her hips and the curve of her arms. She felt the smooth slide of her dress across her thighs as she stretched and turned. She wasn't dancing for him, she was dancing for herself, but the heat of his regard made her feel more sensuous, more delighted with the evening and with herself. This is what it's like to be beautiful and desired, she thought.

Rora looked around the room for Carl, but couldn't see him. She had danced herself out and thought she would sit by the sea and cool down. It was dark but the beach was lit up enough by the lights on the promenade to see where she was going. She walked a little way from the hut, her heeled shoes slipping on the loose pebbles, and sat down on one of the steps leading up to the walkway. The sea shifted slowly, all in one piece, like the flank of some great animal. She heard the crunch of stones underfoot and she looked up thinking Carl had come out to find her, but it was Ian standing there.

'Had enough of dancing?' he asked and sat down beside her on the step. He smelled warm and aromatic, like a Christmas orange.

'It's hot in there,' she said, conscious of his leg next to hers and of his breathing.

'You made me hot watching you,' he said, and put out his hand and caught one of her curls that had come loose from the ribbon. He twisted his finger through it. She turned away from him and got to her feet. He rose too.

'Let's walk a little,' he said, and she was relieved that they were moving. He was too close, too attentive. There was something avid about him.

They walked along the promenade for a while and then Rora said she ought to go back.

'Carl will be wondering where I've got to,' she said.

'Let's walk back on the beach,' he said.

They went down the next flight of steps. This bit of the beach was further away from the lights. He stopped and pulled her to him so that they were leaning against the wall, out of sight of anyone that might pass above.

'Can I kiss you?' he asked, and without waiting for her to reply he put his mouth on hers. She froze for a moment, and then she kissed him back. In all the agonising, terrible days that followed she tried to understand what it was that had made her open her mouth to him. It was curiosity perhaps, and something about the way he had made her feel when she was dancing, but greater than all of that was the desire to be polite. She felt she had made this happen and should therefore go along with it. His lips were soft, his tongue searching. He pushed her harder against the wall and too late, much too late, she felt the anger in him.

June 2010

Using Ursula's need for summer clothes as motivation, Rora took a deep breath and hit the shopping centre on Saturday. Her daughter, always particular about what she wore, rejected various dresses that Rora held up for her inspection, but finally graciously allowed her mother to buy her a couple of neon-coloured shorts, a handful of T-shirts, a new swimsuit and some denim overalls. For herself she bought a white shirt-dress, a navy A-line skirt, a cream silk blouse and a pair of leather flip-flops. She chose the sort of easy things she had worn before because it meant she didn't have to think too much. She didn't even try them on, simply took them straight to the counter.

'What about this one, Mum?' asked Ursula, disappointed by Rora's dull choices. She held up a long, red dress with thin straps. It had so much material that she couldn't hold it up far enough and most of it dragged on the ground.

'I don't think I'd ever have the chance to wear that, darling,' said Rora.

'Why not? You could wear it anywhere. It's a classic!' said Ursula. Rora didn't know where she got the phrase from but recently she kept referring to everything as being classic or not classic.

'Put it back carefully,' said Rora.

'Can we have an ice cream? It's a long time to lunch.' Ursula was no slouch when it came to timing her ice cream breaks. She knew when her requests were most likely to be granted. They bought flake-topped cones and walked home licking quickly, trying to catch the drips.

They had been invited to Hannah's house that evening for supper and Ursula was to have a sleepover with monosyllabic Robyn.

'How do you get on with Robyn?' asked Rora, trying to plait Ursula's hair.

'She's OK. She's a lot younger than me,' said Ursula, wriggling away from her mother's attempts to tame her locks.

'Only OK?' said Rora, wondering at the little frown that had appeared on Ursula's forehead. She was usually more enthusiastic about her friends.

'She's not very popular at school,' said Ursula.

'Is that because she doesn't talk much?'

'She sticks out a bit.'

'Well, it's very nice of you to be her friend, especially since she isn't the most open of children,' said Rora.

'She's not so quiet when the grown-ups aren't there. She's a bit bossy actually. She chooses the best dressing-up clothes. I always have to be the lion,' said Ursula with resignation but no rancour.

'What does she dress up as?' asked Rora.

'She's always God. She gets to wear the white robe,' she said.

Rora couldn't persuade Ursula out of her shorts and into a dress, and she gave up the fight and started to get ready herself.

While Ursula watched *Calamity Jane* on DVD for about the hundredth time, Rora had a leisurely bath and put some much needed cream on her wintered body. As she rubbed the lotion on her scaly legs she could hear Ursula singing along to the movie. Rora smiled. Ursula was very taken with the idea of herself as a cowgirl, flicking whips and marching around in chaps giving as good as she got. She surely couldn't be too miserable if she was able to join in with Doris Day. Rora put on her new skirt and shirt and carelessly twisted her hair into a knot and fastened it at the nape of her neck.

It was a balmy evening and as Rora and Ursula walked down the passageway towards Hannah and Richard's house Ursula took her mother's hand and squeezed it in her own.

'Are you happy yet?' she asked her mother, and Rora felt the guilt she always felt when it was clear her daughter worried about her. You shouldn't have to be anxious when you were nine years old. Parents were supposed to absorb worry and not pass it on.

'I'm fine, darling. How could I not be on an evening like this and with the thought of Hannah's cooking in store?'

The two of them giggled conspiratorially at this.

Rora's heart sank when they entered the living room and Richard introduced her to the single male who had been invited along for her benefit. Rora had been half expecting this since Hannah had made a few sly comments, but she still felt embarrassed and sorry for this person who had been hoodwinked by Hannah into imagining that Rora might be interested. He had an unpromising little beard and a deliberately firm handshake, as if an interview coach had told him once that he had to improve upon his limp grasp. Ursula was whisked away by Robyn, who had a godly gleam in her eye, and Hannah settled Rora down on the sofa next to her intended, whose name was Lionel.

Supper was a surprisingly conventional roast chicken, although Rora discreetly moved the anchovy paste it was served with to the edge of her plate. She drank several glasses of red wine very quickly. Lionel was perfectly nice and talked just enough about his work as an engineer without becoming boring or forgetting to ask Rora about herself. He was clever, had a dry sense of humour, didn't speak with food in his mouth and despite the facial hair had no other apparent physical defects, but she felt nothing for him other than some sympathy for the way he had been tricked into spending an evening with her. She stayed long enough for a post-dinner cup of coffee and to see Ursula into the bottom bunk in Robyn's bedroom, and then she made her excuses and left. Lionel looked relieved and did another of his firm handshakes. In the hall Hannah cocked her head questioningly in his direction and looked crestfallen when Rora shook her head vigorously.

'Stop matchmaking, Hannah,' Rora hissed under her breath, then felt bad and gave her friend a hug of thanks.

'I'm not giving up,' Hannah whispered into her ear.

'That's what I am afraid of,' said Rora with a groan.

Even though it was late and the streets had emptied, she didn't feel like going home. Frank was getting weaker and Rora had requested more nursing hours to cover the nights, and she knew Pauline was with him now. She had got over her initial horror at his illness and the diminishment of his body but it was the transition she dreaded now. When she was alone in the house with him she was torn between the fear that she would miss his slipping away and the fear of witnessing it. A couple of weeks ago she would have predicted feeling nothing at all when he died, but now she wasn't so sure. All these years she had thought them so different, despising his coldness, his inability to speak about anything that mattered, but being with him had made her see just how similar they were.

She had a memory of walking with him somewhere, a park or a garden that was full of snowdrops.

'You think they are all the same, don't you?' he had said, indicating the snowy expanse. To her they had looked like nothing much at all, besides, it was cold and she was keen to get back into the car. 'Just look inside them,' he said, bending down and turning the head of one flower up so that she could see. 'There are actually hundreds of different kinds. Each marked with green in a special way.'

The cold forgotten, they had stayed for some time trying to find as many species as possible. Some had extra frills, some little spots and dashes and others even had what looked like faces. Rora had taken her gloves off and recorded them all in a little note-book, painstakingly documenting the way each snowdrop hid its expression away beneath its icy petals.

As she walked along the front Rora saw a couple lying on the beach next to each other. There was a hazy, full moon made for lovers and for a moment Rora felt the beauty of the night. The feeling in the air of a day finished and another to come brought with it an irrepressible hope. It was there despite everything. It curled itself around her, murmured in her ear. She thought maybe she could be happy. Then something shifted. She wasn't sure why. Perhaps it was the way the moon touched the edges of things, changing them. Perhaps it was the ambiguous sound the woman on the beach made – somewhere halfway between laughter and protest, perhaps it was the way the man held her arms above her head securing her to the shingle as he bent over her, but Rora was sent hurtling back. She saw in a beat how small the distance was that she had travelled between then and now. She had forgotten none of it . . .

On the night of the party Ian had become someone different. The boy with the entitled, nonchalant manner and silky skin was gone. She saw that it wasn't a transformation, only the shedding of a disguise. She had pushed him away, but he took hold of her again, and when she tried to run he caught her around her waist and pushed her to the ground. She landed awkwardly against the hard stones. Her shoulder had twisted. He got on top of her and the weight of his body crushed her. Some moisture fell from his face onto hers. She wasn't sure if he was sweating or crying. She screamed again, as loud and as wide as she could, but the sea and the music from the party and the cars passing heedlessly above and the sound of her heart beating up through her throat were louder than her voice. Above all, she still remembered the look in Carl's eyes when he found them.

'Are you all right?' a man had stopped and was looking at her with concern.

'I'm fine,' she managed to say and walked on, although her legs felt weak beneath her and her breathing was loud and fast. She thought she might be having a panic attack. She had had them before, but not since she had been back in Hastings. She sat on a bench and tried the techniques she had been taught, slowing her breathing, visualising a place where she felt safe, but this time the loosening of the terrible clutch of fear didn't happen as it had before. She needed to get away from the beach and the sea and go somewhere light and free. To her surprise the person she thought of first was Krystof. She hadn't been aware he was so near the surface of her mind. It was only a quarter past eleven, surely his restaurant would still be open and it was only a five-minute walk away.

There was one couple left in the restaurant when Rora got there. They were sitting at the table in the window, deep in the kind of conversation that people have when they don't know each other very well yet. Krystof was behind the bar, bent over some papers. He looked up as the doorbell went and his face went through one of its endearing transformations – his features changing in seconds from melancholy to beamingly pleased. Rora stopped at the threshold, suddenly embarrassed that she had come here so late. Her panic had subsided and now she only thought about what he would think about her motive for coming.

'Hello Rora! How lovely!' he said.

'I've come for the doll,' she said, thinking that having this as an excuse might make her appear less strange, although when she thought about it, coming to recover the doll at this hour was not exactly normal behaviour. She couldn't even explain to herself now why seeing Krystof had seemed such a good idea.

'I think I left it here the other day.'

'You did. You did. I was worried about how to return it to you. I was waiting for you or your friend to come in. It's safe here behind the bar.'

'Thank you so much,' she said taking the bag from him and turning to go out again.

'Stay for a quick drink, why don't you?' he said, and she wavered at the door.

He took out a bottle of Chopin vodka and put it on the bar with two glasses.

'Have you tried this? It's made from potatoes, but don't let that put you off. I drink it just with ice.'

She sat on the stool he indicated and he came round to sit beside her. The vodka had a smoky, creamy taste and after a couple of gulps Rora could feel its restorative powers swirling round in her throat and head.

'It's magic potion!' she said.

'How come you are walking by yourself by night, even with this splendid moon?' Krystof asked.

'I've been out and I didn't want to go back straightaway,' said Rora.

'Because of your tricky father?' Krystof asked.

Rora smiled to hear her father referred to as tricky. It was a good word for him and for their odd, awkward relationship.

'Well, not so much him tonight,' she said. 'I think it was partly indigestion caused by roast chicken with anchovy paste, and a blind date with a bad beard and my past catching up with me.'

Krystof made a scandalised face, which Rora assumed was due to her mention of her unorthodox supper. She rather hoped he might offer her a snack now. She hadn't eaten much at Hannah's and the smell coming from the kitchen made her mouth fill with saliva. It was so intensely aromatic, sweet and savoury at the same time, that she imagined it as a swirl, something visible that was coloured burnt orange tinged at the edges with a citrusy green. She was usually largely indifferent to food, frequently skipping meals altogether, but something about Krystof's food affected her eyes and nose and made her suddenly ravenously hungry.

'Facial hair needs to be bountiful or totally absent,' said Krystof and Rora realised that he had focused on her mention of her blind date rather than the chicken.

'This was of the mean and scratchy variety,' she said.

'Poor man,' said Krystof shaking his head with mock sadness. 'He loses his heart and all you can do is comment on his teeny, tiny, miserable, shameful beard.'

Rora laughed. 'I don't think he lost his heart. He looked very relieved when I left.'

'Then he is a fool as well as the owner of shabby facial hair,' said Krystof. He held Rora's glance for just a moment longer than was necessary and she found herself tracing his features, lingering a little on his merry, yellow flecked eyes. He wasn't handsome, she thought, but his face was restful and coura-geous, and she then realised that she was getting drunk. She had already had quite a lot of wine at Hannah's house and Krystof had filled her glass again without her noticing.

'He just very sensibly recognised hard work when he saw it,' she said.

'When did you decide you are hard work?' asked Krystof. 'You strike me as easy work.'

'Oh I do, do I?' said Rora, raising her eyebrows at him and laughing.

'I didn't mean . . . my English lets me down sometimes,' said Krystof and Rora was amused to see him blushing.

'You speak it very well,' she said. 'How long have you been here?'

149

'I came ten years ago for a woman. I loved her but I loved Hastings longer, and anyway by that time I had opened this restaurant and this town became my place to be.'

'I used to like it when I was a child,' said Rora 'and then it got tainted and now I find it hard to see the beauty.'

'I wish I could show you its beauty again,' said Krystof and put out his hand to touch hers as it rested on the bar.

'What's to like?' she said, taking her hand away, although she had almost wanted to leave it resting under his. No plane would crash with Krystof on it, she found herself thinking. No plane would crash and the storm would blow its way around him keeping him safe. 'A decrepit old pier, ugly houses and it closes down at half past five.'

'The pier will be splendid again one day, mark my words,' Krystof said, 'and there are ugly houses everywhere, but not everywhere are they bathed in the special golden light. As for closing down at 5.30, excuse me, am I not open?' he said and made an expansive gesture to indicate his kingdom, as if he owned all this and the sea and the cliffs too.

'It's time for me to go. It's late,' said Rora. 'Thank you so much for the drink. I seem always to be taking your hospitality.'

'Let me walk you home,' said Krystof. 'I will tell the chef to finish off here and lock up.'

At Pilgrim Street he watched until she had let herself in and then made that odd little incline of his head she had noticed before.

'Sweet dreams, Aurora,' he said.

When she closed the door behind her Pauline was coming down the stairs.

'I'm glad you are back,' the nurse said. 'I am afraid your father's a little worse. I've had to increase his morphine dose and his breathing isn't good. He's been asking for you.'

'He has?' said Rora, astonished.

'Yes. On the hour every hour,' said Pauline.

Rora went straight to her father's room and sat on the end of his bed.

'You're back,' he said, opening his eyes, and Rora could see he had stepped a little further from her and she felt a new, sharp grief for what they had lost, what they had allowed to fall into the deep hollow between them.

'I was worried,' he said.

'Whatever for?' she said. 'I'm twenty-eight, old enough to find my way home.'

'Parents never stop worrying,' he said.

Rora bit back the reply that came immediately to her lips. She wanted to try and be softer to him now.

'Do you remember the night you went to your end of school party?' he said, and Rora's heart skipped a beat. She had relived that night many times.

'You were wearing a dark red dress and you had your hair tied back and you looked so beautiful.'

'I'm surprised you remember,' she said.

'I remember that I didn't tell you how lovely you looked. I couldn't tell you. You looked so much like your mother it broke my heart.'

His voice trailed off in a fit of coughing that seemed to shake his whole frame. It went on for so long that Rora became worried. She poured him a glass of water.

'Try and drink this,' she said when he finally stopped and lay back exhausted on his pillow, but he waved her offer away as if he was shooing away a fly.

'I never really had her,' he said. 'I never felt I saw into the secret bit of her. She always kept a part of herself away from me.'

'I'm not sure we ever really know anyone,' said Rora.

'I couldn't make her happy. It made me so terribly sad not to be able to make her happy.'

'It's all right now, Dad,' Rora said. Frank was becoming very agitated. 'I think you should rest.'

'I'll be resting soon enough,' he said with a touch of the old spite, but nevertheless he settled back at her command and closed his eyes. Rora sat with him a while and wondered if it would have made a difference if her father had told her she was beautiful that night. Would she have been more confident? Was it her neediness Ian had seen? It was impossible to untangle the threads so that she could see clearly where the first stitch was made, and maybe, after all, it didn't matter when the thing was done.

Kiss 9

'Rora kissed her on her tiny, puckered mouth.'

7 April 2001

Isobel was surprised and a little hurt when Rora said she was leaving Hastings and going to London several weeks before her university term was due to start.

'What's the rush?' she asked Rora. 'You've got the whole summer to do what you want. I thought we might go on a little holiday together. Dorset perhaps.'

'I want to find somewhere to live and get settled in,' Rora said.

Isobel had sold several of her precious paintings and almost all her jewellery to top up the grant that Rora had managed to secure. Rora had felt bad about the sacrifices her grandmother had made on her behalf, but feeling guilty was such a continuous state for her that this extra debt she now owed Isobel barely registered. She knew her grandmother was desperately worried about her. She had tried every one of her ruses to encourage Rora to talk – she had bought bottles of tonic and suggested picnics at the beach hut, she had sat on the end of Rora's bed late at night telling her stories that used to comfort and divert her but which now simply served to lock her deeper inside herself. Anything that reminded Rora of her life before made her feel worse because it only emphasised what had changed. No tonic and no stories would ever restore what she had lost. She felt as if sharp teeth were tearing away inside her, and at night she couldn't sleep because her head was full of images and sensations that wouldn't leave her.

On the night of the party she had waited outside the house until Isobel's light went off. She couldn't let her grandmother see the state she was in, her dress torn, blood on her face and hands. She felt cold, detached from what she was doing. She watched herself take off her ruined dress and hide it under the bed. She stood in front of the mirror in the bathroom and looked at her face as if she had never seen it before. Her face had settled into new, unfamiliar lines. She realised that she was shaking in a strange juddering rhythm. She held onto her wrist to try and still the leaping, but there was no stopping it. She felt as if she no longer had any control over her body or her thoughts that skittered from one blurred, frantic impression to another, like film footage that froze and disintegrated and then came into focus briefly. She wondered what the fortune-teller had seen. They had thought that part of the beach was deserted, but when Rora ran up the steps desperate to get away, Sophie was on the walkway above. Rora had no idea how long she had been there, and she put her head down and tried to get past the woman without being recognised, but Sophie put out a hand to stop her.

'Can I help?' she had asked in her strange, otherworldly voice.

'No. I'm fine,' said Rora walking away, her handbag held up in front of her torn dress, her head low so that it didn't catch the light. She carried on past the woman, walking fast, aware of her breathing catching in her chest. She was crying although she wasn't aware of it until she got home and saw the marks of tears on her face.

She had seen Carl just one more time. He came to Pilgrim Street the day after the party with his new, stiff, blank face and told her not to tell anyone what had happened.

'I want you to forget it,' he said, his hands restless, his eyes dark and bruised looking. 'Forget it. OK? Rora, OK?'

'How can I?' she said.

'Go to university. Go now. Leave it behind you.'

'But what will you do?' she asked, crying so hard she felt she would never stop.

'I'll sort it, Rora,' he said, and tried to wipe away the tears that kept coming.

'How can you?' she asked holding onto him, feeling the banging of his heart under her hands.

'I love you Rora,' he said. 'I love you more than anything.'

She couldn't answer him as she wanted to. The words stuck in her throat. She thought she wasn't worth loving and that meant she couldn't love him. He didn't stay long. She could tell that it had taken everything he had left to come. He looked at her for a long moment, as if he was learning his way back home. She watched him from the window as he walked away, his arms rigid by his sides and she felt as though something was tearing inside her.

In the terrible days that followed she hid the bruises on her body with long sleeves and skirts and brushed her hair with a new parting that covered the wound on her forehead. Harder to hide was the fear that had lodged itself deep inside her. Every time the doorbell went or the phone rang her stomach lurched, and on two occasions the reaction was so strong she ran to the toilet and was violently sick. She was terrified in case Sophie might bump into her grandmother and mention that she had seen her in a state of distress. The new person she had become had learned how to lie with a shuttered face and fake animation. To her own ears she sounded like an advertisement for something hard to sell. She told Isobel that the party had been the best she had ever been to. She said that everyone had admired her dress, that she had danced until she was out of breath. She described the streamers and the tablecloths, going into a mass of detail to prevent Isobel from asking any questions. She carried the feelings of helplessness and the fear of discovery everywhere she went. Her skin was sore and her body hunched as if she had inhaled something sharp that had caused her to pucker and shrivel. She was plagued by flashbacks and a kind of auditory haunting – the music from the party playing heedlessly on in the distance, the sea's swelling, sucking noise as the wind picked up, the sound of struggle and her own whimpering breath.

She knew she looked dreadful. She could see the evidence of that in the mirror every morning – she had lost weight and her hair had started falling out. She plucked it off her brush in great, sticky, nauseating chunks and wrapped it in toilet paper and flushed it away. She thought the only solution to her torment was to leave Hastings as quickly as possible. She didn't know then that moving away would not be enough. She would not be saved by new geography – the erosion would simply deepen as time passed.

'I know it's been hard for you, with Carl . . . and everything,' Isobel said, 'and I can understand you wanting to get away, but I don't think you're in a fit state.'

'I'm fine. I'll be fine,' said Rora, resisting her grandmother's attempts to hold her. She could not be comforted. She couldn't bear to be touched, even by Isobel. Her body recoiled from the smallest of contacts. She packed her clothes and one of her mother's wooden boats – Rora knew it would not be missed from the flotilla on the mantelpiece – and one plate, mug and set of cutlery, as if she was setting out on what she expected to be the most solitary of journeys.

On the day of her departure Isobel pressed the soft skin of her face against Rora's cheek and a lizard-skin clutch bag into her hands. Rora discovered later when she was on the train that the bag contained ten £10 notes and a stick of what her grandmother called the 'universally flattering' pale rose lipstick. Frank waved goodbye from the living room window, turning aside before she had even got into the taxi. She looked down at her lap as the train took her away. She didn't want to see any of it again – the shabby, half-arsed entertainments, her indifferent father and the ghost of her dead mother or the ever-present sea. It had been a witness to what had happened and she thought of it now as something watchful and malevolent. The only person she would miss would be Isobel, but her grandmother had promised to come and visit her in London.

'We'll have tea in Fortnum and Mason,' Isobel had said, 'and you can tell me about all the young men who are queuing up for you.'

Rora smiled and nodded even though she knew there would be no young men.

She found a room in a converted nunnery in King's Cross, with bars on the window and a book at the entrance for signing visitors in and out. She put a blanket from home on the bed and her books on the narrow windowsill, including *The Book of Kisses* that Isobel had slipped into her bag without her noticing.

Every week she wrote to Carl and every week the letter was returned unopened. She wasn't sure whether he was sending them back or someone else was.

'You are never to be in touch with me again. Do you understand? Rora, do you understand? I don't want to see you ever again,' he had said, his face grey, his fists tight.

She kept the letters and they became an account of her sorrow and of her gratitude and of all the ways she was falling apart because she was not with him. Writing them helped to calm her because it was a way of talking to him. Slowly, she became acclimatised; she joined the university literary society and the film society and seldom went to either gathering. She got a weekend job in a pizza restaurant on Tottenham Court Road, where she learned to deal with men who thought the alpine-style corset she was obliged to wear was a licence to flirt with her. One day a customer pinched her bottom as she passed by and she turned on him with a savagery that surprised both of them.

'What gives you the right to touch me?' she said to him, shaking and furious. 'What is it about me that makes you think I want your filthy hands on me?'

She was so angry that she burst into tears and the restaurant manager sent her home for the day, but not before he had offered his gospel according to the world of pizza restaurants.

'It's best just to smile,' he said to an incredulous Rora. 'It doesn't mean anything.'

The next time it happened, she remembered to smile as she dropped a piping-hot deep pan into the offender's lap.

The days passed and she sometimes managed, for an hour or so, to not remember. She thought she might, after all, be able to survive. She took to running in the early morning when sleep was elusive. She enjoyed the punishing pound of the pavement against her shoes and the fact that her struggle was a solitary one. She ran all the way to the park with its dark trees and frost-hardened grass, the benches still littered with the detritus of teenage gatherings, and stopped and caught her breath for her return.

One morning she was running towards the gates of the park, willing herself not to stop until she had reached the finishing post, which was just inside the park entrance. Then she saw him. He was standing just a little way from her, under a tree, his head turned in the opposite direction. She stopped short, hope rising in her, as if some sweet substance was replacing her blood. It was him – the tilt of his dear head, the way he stood with his legs wide apart as if he was getting a better grip on the earth. He was waiting for her. She ran towards him, her heart leaping and fluttering with joy. She must have made a sound because he turned, and she saw with a punch of breath-stopping anguish that it wasn't him after all. Of course it couldn't be. What had she been thinking? This man was nothing like Carl. He stared and moved towards her as if he had indeed been waiting for her and she turned and ran.

The incident in the park made Rora see that she had been fooling herself to think she could live like this. How had she imagined that she would be able to move on with her life? Pretend nothing had happened? With a feeling of sickening dread she understood that she had to go back to Hastings. She had to face whatever was waiting for her there, even though he had forbidden her to.

She had packed up the contents of her room, even written a letter to the university to notify them of her departure, when she fainted in the corridor. A young woman called Judy who lived next door to her in the nunnery (who spent her days threading beads and twisting metal into jewellery no one would ever want to wear and who labelled all her many pots of yoghurt before putting them in the communal fridge) found Rora lying on the floor and made a great production of putting her across her plump knees and fanning her with a newspaper.

Rora thought at first her collapse was due to the fact she had been rushing around and had skipped a few meals, but then she tried to remember when she had had her last period and realised that she must have missed at least two. She had been so focused on trying to keep herself together enough to walk around and talk and act as if there was nothing troubling her that she had lost touch with her body. It had become something she had to shuttle from one point to the next, nothing more. She had learned to smile, choose food from a menu, match jumpers to skirts, she had even summoned up enough enthusiasm to concentrate in lectures, but all the time she had merely been going through the necessary motions. She went to the chemist, bought three tests and then sat in the park for an hour trying to pluck up the courage to go home and use them.

Three out of three were positive. At first she felt almost nothing. She treated the discovery as she had treated everything else over the last few weeks – with a kind of nervous lethargy. This was simply one more thing that she would have to deal with, but at least this time she could do something about it. She would have an abortion and then stick to her plan of going back to Hastings. It made no difference. She would have it scraped out of her and in twenty-four hours all that would be left would be another scar, another wound to hide.

She made an appointment at the clinic, and in the meantime lived out of her packed suitcase. On the third day after she had discovered her pregnancy she was overwhelmed by a nausea that made her retch, crouched helplessly across the toilet bowl. The sickness came almost as a relief since it gave her something to react to, to fight against. She cancelled her first clinic appointment; she was too ill to get there, and stayed in her room, the curtains drawn, ignoring the knocks of her neighbour, who seemed to have made Rora her latest project.

When she finally ventured out, everything was too loud, too bright – she could feel the sound of a spade scraping against the road and the crack of a lorry shutter as it was rolled up as if the noises were coming from inside her. She was assaulted by smells of burned rubber and perfume and smoke and pizza. A globule of spit on the pavement in front of her made her stomach lurch and rise and she thought she might be sick there in front of the crowds hustling their way to the station. In the throng of quick-stepping, frowning people she felt as if she was floating on waves. She was invisible. She thought that if she lay down on the pavement people would simply step over her. She deserved their indifference and their blame because she was culpable. She put her hand on her stomach and felt the first flutter of life. It was a tiny, hopeful tremble. Under her fingers, deep beneath her sore skin and her ailing heart, an undamaged life lay coiled, floating in its own sea. She stood still while she felt it and people tutted and parted around her. She walked to the clinic and stood outside for a while, and then turned round and went back to her room.

She didn't tell anyone about her pregnancy and as time passed her secret took on a life of its own. She looked at pictures of embryos at four, five, six weeks and scrutinised the developing shapes – the stealthy growth of the bean-like mass, the slow unfurling of the bud limbs and the strange ridged back, anchored safely by the translucent cord – the line by which she imagined her baby would find its way up to the surface. From the very first moment of conception through to the burdensome bearing down of the head, she began to feel as if she was seeing images of her own child's story.

She unpacked her suitcase and resumed her classes. The college said she could complete as much of the course as she was able and then take it up again after the birth on a part-time basis. She found a way of caring for herself that wasn't about her own survival but about the child inside her. She had to look after the alien thing her body had become so that it did the work it had to do. She drank smoothies, rubbed cream on her stomach and attended a class where she learned to breathe for her child.

Her waters broke all over her suede boots when she was shopping in the Co-op. She sat on a chair in the manager's office and waited for the ambulance. She rang Judy, who had a key to her room, and asked her if she would come with the bag Rora had left ready by the door. Judy became almost incoherent with excitement at the prospect of playing a starring role in the drama.

'Should I notify someone else?' she asked Rora. 'The father, perhaps?'

Throughout Rora's pregnancy Judy had made subtle and not so subtle attempts to establish the baby's parentage, but had been frustrated at every turn.

'It's as if she has cut herself off from whatever it was that happened to her before,' Judy said to her ailing mother, who she visited three times a week in a home in Milton Keynes to read the *Telegraph* aloud and feed her cottage pie.

'There's no one to notify,' said Rora, and wondered if what she was saying was true. It didn't matter anyway. This baby was going to be hers.

The birth was swift and painful. Ursula was born at three minutes to midnight. She had a long, bluish torso and scaly, starfish hands and her navy eyes were already wide open. Rora kissed her on her tiny, puckered mouth and inhaled the malty smell of her. She was hers and yet she was completely and perfectly herself. For the first time in months, Rora experienced a kind of easing. She was not the end of the story after all. The best of her would live on. She felt her heart contract and then loosen as she let the love in.

June 2010

Rora woke in the night and lay for a while wondering what it was she had heard. She thought at first it might be her father calling out for her or that a book had fallen from his bed, but when she went up to check he was sleeping soundly. In Ursula's room the bed was empty, the sheet thrown off onto the floor. Rora felt a clutch of panic.

'Ursula where are you?'

She wasn't in the bathroom, nor had she gone downstairs to the kitchen to get a drink. Rora ran back upstairs to check in case Ursula was there after all and had perhaps decided to creep into a corner – there had been times she had decided on a whim that she wanted to sleep on the floor wrapped in a duvet, but the room was still empty.

Rora had just about given in to sheer panic when she heard footsteps on the attic floor, which was directly above Ursula's bedroom. She went out onto the landing and saw that the previously locked door was wide open. Heart in mouth, she went up the stairs, trying not to remember what she had last seen up there, and turned on the light. Ursula was standing still in the middle of the room.

'Ursula! What are you doing here?' she asked, astonished. 'How did you get in?'

Ursula didn't reply and as Rora crouched down beside her she seemed to look beyond her mother at a spot somewhere in the middle distance. Her face was slack but absorbed and Rora could see that she was fast asleep. She led Ursula carefully back to bed and tucked her in. Ursula made a small noise of acquiescence and then put her arms around her mother's neck and held her for a moment. Afterwards Rora went back up to the attic and stood where Ursula had stood moments before. After all her dread of coming back to this place, now that she was standing there she saw there had been nothing to fear after all. It was just an empty room. Nothing of Sandi had been left behind in the plaster or in the cracks between the floorboards. What remained had been taken along in Rora's heart and in the hearts of those who had known and loved her.

Rora heard Frank's voice calling for her from his bedroom. It seemed no one was sleeping restfully tonight.

'What's going on?' he asked when she went in. 'I heard voices.'

'I found Ursula in the attic,' she said. 'I think she was sleep-walking.

'Sandi used to do that from time to time,' said Frank.

'Did she?' said Rora. 'I don't remember that.'

'I once found her sitting on the sill by an open window,' said Frank. 'Frightened the life out of me.'

If Ursula was like Sandi in this particular habit, what else might she have inherited from her grandmother? Rora thought of the way Sandi had lain helplessly on her bed, unable to banish the monster that held her by the throat in its terrible grip. She didn't want that for Ursula. She wanted her to have long happy days without shadows, free to be exactly who she wanted to be.

'How did Ursula even get in there? I thought it was locked,' said Rora.

'I gave her an old bunch of keys I had in my bedside table the other day,' Frank said. 'They were all different shapes and sizes and she was making up stories about the doors they might have belonged to. Maybe she went and tried them out for real.'

'But why should she have gone up there? Surely she couldn't have opened the door while she was asleep.'

'Maybe she opened it earlier on in the day,' said Frank. 'People do all sorts of things when they're asleep. Sandi once ate half a meat pie when she was sleepwalking.'

'It's just odd that she chose to go up there,' said Rora.

'Children are very sensitive to things. Maybe she picked up on our reluctance to go into the room and she was curious.'

'She's so like Mum, isn't she?' said Rora.

'In all the good ways, not the bad,' said Frank and caught hold of her hand.

'Will you do me a favour?' he asked.

'Of course,' said Rora.

'I put Sandi's ashes in the river near a tree in a village in Yorkshire. It was special to us. It was the place she first told me she loved me.'

'Yes, I remember,' said Rora. 'I also remember you not coming back for months.'

'I was a mess,' said Frank.

'So was I,' said Rora, taking her hand away from his and getting up.

'I want you to take my ashes to the river,' he said, 'so that I can be with her.'

'Let's not talk about this now,' she said and pulled aside the curtain to look out of the window. The sky was just beginning to relinquish the darkness. In a nearby street a milk float vibrated into life with a strange moaning noise. It sounded like an echo of the past.

'We have to talk about it. There's not much time left,' said Frank.

'Write the name of the place down for me.'

'Promise me you'll do it,' said Frank, 'although I don't really deserve to lie next to her.'

Rora thought of the afternoon a few weeks before her mother had died when she had come home from school early. She couldn't remember why now; some club had been cancelled or a teacher absent. Her mother had gone away with Isobel to a spa; it had been another of her grandmother's efforts to cheer Sandi up. Rora had been surprised to see her father's study was empty, he was almost always there behind the closed door when she came back from school. She heard a noise coming from her parents' bedroom and thought that her mother and grandmother must have returned earlier than expected. She had no reason not to walk straight into the room. She always sought her mother out as soon as she came home. The shapes in front of her were so surprising, so not what she had been expecting, that at first she couldn't understand what she was looking at. Her father was spread out on the bed. She noticed his legs and thought that they looked strange – so white, and one of them had a bumpy, purplish varicose vein running along all the way from his ankle to his thigh. Someone was sitting on top of him moving forward and back the way Rora's old rocking horse moved on its metal hinges. Her father was making a noise she hadn't heard before. It sounded as if he was crying. The room smelled of perfume. Not her mother's jasmine but a dark, meaty scent, like hedges in early summer. She stood watching. There didn't seem anywhere else to go and after a while her father opened his eyes and saw her. The worst part by far was the way his face changed, tightened into shock, and then his eyes went wide as if, for a moment, he was trying to convince her of something. He made a noise like he had been punched and pushed the woman away, gathering the sheets around them.

'Rora –' he said, and he sounded like a stranger.

And she had left the room at last and walked then run all the way back to school. There was no point being there, her lessons were over, but she thought if she could walk the route again, next time she arrived at home it wouldn't have happened.

'Did she know?' Rora asked her father.

'She found out a month or so before she died. I told her about it because I was so scared you would mention it to her first,' said Frank. His voice had dropped to a whisper and Rora could see by the way the sinews in his neck were knotted what it was costing him to tell her this.

'I think it may have been why she killed herself.'

'I wouldn't have told her,' said Rora.

'Why not?'

'She was so full of unhappiness already. Who was the woman?'

'She was someone from work. She was married too. It didn't last long. She slept with me out of revenge because her husband had been unfaithful. I slept with her because I just wanted something uncomplicated. Loving Sandi could be exhausting. I knew this woman didn't want anything from me. It was nothing. That's what people always say about affairs, isn't it? But it really was nothing.'

Rora looked at her father, lying exhausted with the effort of telling her what he had lived with for so long. Now in his final days it was still what tormented him. It had been nothing really – people committed graver misdemeanors every day, but she understood, how could she not, how the things that shame us touch everything and turn ugly what was once beautiful.

'I don't think it was just what you did,' Rora said. 'I thought she killed herself partly because I told her that I might as well not have a mother.' She could feel her sudden, unstoppable tears gathering in the collar of her shirt.

'Did you say that to her?' asked Frank, looking sadly at his daughter. 'I didn't know.'

'I thought she took me at my word,' said Rora, twisting the edge of the sheet with her hands as if wringing something from it.

'She would have known you didn't mean it. You were just a child. Children say things like that all the time,' said Frank. 'No one really knows why she did what she did. She loved me despite my weaknesses and I loved her despite hers. That is the way it works. I think. I don't know . . .' Frank's voice trailed off. 'We all blunder through,' he said and closed his eyes.

'Did you think I was a toll, Dad?' she asked, not really believing he would hear her.

'What do you mean, toll?' he said.

'You once called me that,' said Rora. 'You said I had been a toll on Mum.'

'Not you, you daft girl,' he said faintly, putting out his hand to her. 'It was the other baby. The one we lost.'

Rora fell asleep straightaway when she eventually went back to bed, but was woken two hours later by Ursula coming into her room.

'Are you awake, Mum?' she asked, leaning over so that Rora could feel her earnest breath on her face, sweet with the smell of milk and cereal.

'I am now,' she said without rancour. 'Why don't you get in to my bed for a snuggle. Give me a chance to wake up properly.'

Ursula complied eagerly and Rora winced at the sensation of Ursula's little feet sliding down her leg.

'Why is it that even in this boiling weather your feet are icy?'

'I have poor circulation,' said Ursula with dignity.

'Do you remember anything odd about last night?' asked Rora, carefully keeping her voice neutral.

'No,' said Ursula, 'but I think I had a dream. And Mummy, look, something strange . . . the bottoms of my feet are all sooty.'

She sat up and withdrew herself from the bed and sat cross-legged so she could show her mother the soles of her feet.

'You little grub!' said Rora, tickling her until she half laughed and half cried herself off the bed onto the floor.

'Why is it that with tickling you really, really want it to end and then when it does you want it to start again?' she asked.

'It's one of life's great mysteries,' said Rora. 'You can talk to me about anything, Ursula, you know that, don't you?'

'Can I Mum?' asked Ursula, suddenly serious.

'Of course.'

'Well, today, we don't have time,' said Ursula bossily. 'We are going to the beach with Hannah and Robyn and Paloma.'

When they arrived at the surprisingly crowded beach, Hannah took off her dress to reveal a typically sensible one-piece and elegant thighs and took the girls in for a swim while Rora stayed chatting to Richard, who was very easy company, particularly when he had an ice box full of beer and no prospect of a picnic devised by Hannah. After a while she began to feel hot, and plucking at her own rather elderly swimsuit, which had lost a bit of its elasticity around the legs, she hobbled over the stones to the sea, wishing she had had the foresight to wear her sandals up to the water's edge. She sat down in the shallows and allowed herself to be pushed gently from side to side as the waves came in and then slid out. She saw Krystof coming towards her from some distance. He was deliberately churning up the water as he walked in great big splashing strides. She wondered if he ever did anything quietly.

'Hannah told me you were here,' he said. 'You look like a mermaid that has been washed up in the tide.'

'Um, yes ... Don't swim as well as a mermaid though,' said Rora, feeling cross with her meddlesome friend. She noticed that

170

even though Krystof was wearing ridiculous, oversized swimming trunks adorned with grinning sharks, and some rather lurid sea shoes, he had strong, well-shaped legs and broad shoulders. He walked a little way further out and with a small sound of protest against the coldness of the water threw himself backwards over a small wave and then began swimming a fast front crawl backwards and forwards in front of her. Rora wished he would carry on swimming in the other direction and leave her to sit bobbing in the shallows quietly, but Krystof had other ideas. He indicated to her that she should swim out to where he was now floating on his back, his large feet sticking up comically above the water.

'Come and join me,' he shouted. 'It's better than lovely!'

Rora shook her head. 'I'm fine here thanks. I don't really swim all that well.'

Krystof stopped floating and swam back towards her with a look of astonishment on his face.

'You don't swim?' he said. 'And you lived by the ocean? You are missing so much, to say nothing of the fact that you are exposing yourself to possible danger.'

'It's fine, really,' said Rora weakly, who could already see where this conversation was going.

'I am a master swimmer,' said Krystof, shaking the water off him like a dog as he stood in front of her in the shallows. 'I will offer my services as your instructor.'

'No, really . . . I'm happy enough here,' she protested, looking around to see if Richard or Hannah might come and rescue her, but Richard had lain down flat on his beach mat, balancing a can of beer on his stomach. Hannah was some distance away, still cavorting in the waves with the girls and no doubt keeping half an eye on this scene. Rora stood up reluctantly and allowed herself to be led out until the water was up to her waist.

'It's cold,' she shivered.

'You just need to start moving,' said Krystof, and so she let herself down into the water and did a few frantic paddling snatches with her hands before getting to her feet again.

'You don't need to create such a big motion,' said Krystof. 'The sea will hold you. Just allow yourself to lie back.'

Rora looked doubtful. 'Come on, just lie back,' he repeated. 'I will be here.'

She gingerly put her head back in the water, feeling the clutch of the cold around her skull. For a couple of moments, it seemed as if she was doing it. She could feel the swell of the sea beneath her, carrying her, rocking her gently, but then she turned her head out to sea and panicked at the sight of a large wave coming towards her. She felt herself taken up by it and pulled under and for a terrifying moment was unable to breathe or to get her footing on the shifting shingle. Krystof's arms held her upright, and as she stood gasping and choking he patted her on the back.

'You almost did it,' he said. 'A little more practice and you will be able to float to France.'

He left his hand on her back and Rora found that she liked the heavy, protective feel of it against her skin.

'I like you Rora,' he said. She was aware his face was set in its most lugubrious lines. He had little glittering drops of water on his eyelashes. He was a shining sort of a person, she decided, and much too kind to be exposed to her particular brand of indifference.

'I like you too,' she said lightly.

'No, I mean I really like you,' he said. 'You have started up my heart again.'

Despite his serious expression, Rora couldn't help smiling at the quaint turn of phrase.

'You make yourself sound like an old banger with a flat battery,' she said.

'That's it exactly,' he said. 'I am an old banger and my heart has been flat for the longest time. You have made it swell again.'

'I'm glad to have had such a remarkable effect on your ... organs,' she said laughing, surprised to find herself flirting with this earnest man. He was as far from her type as it was possible to be. He didn't so much wear his heart on his sleeve as wrapped around his body.

'Is there a chance for me?' he asked her, taking hold of her hands, and despite herself she was disarmed by his candour.

'I'm so tied up with my father and what is happening . . .' she started. 'I'm really much better on my own at the moment.'

'There's no rush,' he said. 'I'll take it so slowly you won't notice I am making progress at all! I'm an extremely patient man. I can move with stealth.'

'I'm not sure I'm that keen on the idea of you being stealthy,' Rora said. 'Sounds a bit creepy.'

'I only mean I will be gentle with you,' he said. 'You need gentleness.' He put a hand up to her cheek and traced the outline of it. 'You really are the most beautiful woman I have ever seen.'

On the lips of another man the words would have felt like a line, but coming from Krystof they sounded as if he really meant it.

'I'll take you out for a picnic,' she said, and then was slightly aghast at her words, not least because he would surely expect a higher standard than the Marmite sandwiches and scotch eggs she usually provided.

He smiled widely. 'That for me is the best treat I can be offered,' he said. 'Not to cook is my ultimate luxury.'

'I wouldn't get your hopes up,' said Rora and watched while he ran back along the beach to get a pen and paper to write down his phone number, since she had left her phone at home.

Kiss 10

*'As he kissed her she took herself away and it was Carl's face
she saw beneath her closed eyes.'*

5 October 2007

After Ursula was born Rora finally stopped writing letters to
Carl. She thought of the stubborn, uncompromising way he
had always stuck to his decisions, and she knew he would never
contact her now. Although there were still days when the sun
was a certain diffused, lemony colour, or when the rain fell in
oily dimples on the windows when she yearned for him, but she
knew she had to protect Ursula now. She had to try and move on
with this version of life that had presented itself. She didn't even
go back to Hastings when her father rang her to tell her about
her grandmother.

'Isobel's dead,' he had said without any preamble. It was typi-
cal of him, she thought, not to bother to prepare her for the news.
He had never made any attempt to protect her from anything.

'She died in her sleep last night.'

The first image that came into Rora's head when he said the
words was of her grandmother, her face lit by the light from one
of her shrouded lamps, her eyes shining, talking about her hus-
band, Jack. Thinking about this helped Rora to cope with the
sudden pain she felt, which was a much bigger, more physical
sensation than she expected. It came upon her as if she had sud-
denly slammed into a wall. There had never been any point in
expressing any kind of sorrow to her father and she wasn't going

to start trying now. After she had put the phone down, she went out into the little garden at the back of her flat and cried the kind of tears she hadn't cried since the nights when she used to weep for her mother. Isobel had been the only constant in Rora's life after she left Hastings. When she came to London to take Rora out for the grand tea she had been promising since she had left home, Rora broke the news of her pregnancy to her. Isobel was unable to hide her shock and worry.

'Oh my darling girl,' she said, her face troubled over the pile of perfectly executed sandwiches. 'Can you cope on your own?'

'I have no choice,' Rora said, and Isobel laid her hand over her granddaughter's.

'If anyone can do it, you can. And you always have me,' she said.

Isobel made the journey to London on a regular basis, and she had fallen in love with Ursula at first sight. The three of them would have lunch or visit a gallery, where Isobel would position herself in front of a favourite painting and point out things that Rora would never have noticed otherwise. Rora knew her grandmother would have understood her decision not to attend the funeral. She sent Hannah in her stead, who reported back that there had been pink champagne and camellias and a portrait of Isobel at twenty-one propped up against the coffin. Rora remembered the picture. Isobel claimed it had been painted with an unsteady hand by one of her many doting suitors.

Rora had managed, after taking a year out, to get her degree, and by a stroke of good fortune had been recommended by her tutor to an editor who was looking for writers of historical books for children. The solitary nature of the work suited her. She compartmentalised her life firmly. There was work and there was Ursula, and then sometimes, when loneliness got the better of her or when she felt the need to be touched by someone who didn't care enough about her to hurt her, she went out with a certain kind of man.

Nick was in the same mould as Rora's previous boyfriend, and the one before that – handsome, confident, solvent and quite clear that he wasn't going to be around indefinitely. Two of her previous lovers were married and another lived abroad and met up with her every third weekend in hotel rooms without much of a view – having a view from a hotel room only mattered if you intended to go out into it. Their pattern for the nine months they were together was one that Rora recognised as banal, even as it was happening. The knicker-less meal in a hotel restaurant, the trip in the lift when he looked at himself in the mirror as he put his fingers inside her, and then sex that was urgent at first, and then a little showy, as if they were watching each other.

She and Nick had met on an online dating site. She had been attracted to his narrow, clever-looking face and the way that he put his work as a surgeon at the top of his list of priorities in life. He didn't view the fact that she had Ursula as an asset, but neither was it a deal breaker, and in any case Rora was rigorous about keeping the life that she had with her daughter separate from everything else.

Rora had always assumed that Nick shared her view that they were OK together until something bigger and better came along. She didn't for one minute imagine that what they had would turn into anything permanent, and so she was astonished when one evening he took her to a favourite restaurant in Greenwich and then for a walk by the river during which he stopped abruptly, fell to his knees on an almost certainly predetermined patch of grass (he was a man who liked a plan) and presented her with a diamond that was big enough to catch the street lights in a convincing way. She was even more astonished when she found herself saying yes. It wasn't so much that it felt right, more that it didn't feel wrong and it seemed senseless to spoil something that was working so smoothly. Her relationship with Nick was the longest she had ever had and she cared about him just enough for it all to seem easy to her. There were no messy extremes of emotion, no worries about who loved the other more. Above all, she knew that whatever happened Nick would never break her heart, since it had already been broken.

She reassured herself that once she was fully immersed in details of menus and wedding dresses, when she had actually embarked on the business of getting married, she would stop thinking about Carl; but he was hard to dislodge. He tended to stray across her mind when she was least expecting it. Someone walking down the street with his loose, rangy stride, or a hunched schoolboy waiting at a bus stop with a frayed collar would remind her of him, but she would push the memory aside.

Any doubts about her engagement were sublimated into renewed efforts with her work, regular punishing gym sessions, with two yoga classes a week thrown in, and dedication to the research and arrangements for what she resolved would be the most elegant wedding ever. She took her bridesmaids – Hannah, Nick's sister, Emma, and Ursula – dress shopping, but even though she spent all day trying on a variety of confections, she couldn't really decide what sort of bride she wanted to be. She tried grand dresses with trailing hems, flirty versions with knee-length skirts and laced bodices, modest vintage lace, high-necked and long sleeved, gowns dusted with crystals and ones that were simple and unadorned. She toyed with ivory, with beige, with the palest of pink. She modelled full-veiled and sacrificial and jaunty and feathered. But none of them seemed quite right, and so she postponed the decision and bought sexy purple dresses and scarlet stilettos for Hannah and Emma and a puffy party dress and patent shoes in the same colours for Ursula so that the shopping expedition would not be a complete waste of time.

Rora and Nick had their first major row in bed on a Saturday morning. It was unusual because although Rora was sometimes prickly and spoiling for a fight, Nick's good humour, or what she sometimes took to be his lack of deep feeling, usually swerved them away from potential confrontation. She was aware that he used his doctor's soothing bedside manner on her when she got tetchy and the notion always managed to annoy her even more than she was already. Rora had voiced her misgivings about making her family and friends travel to the Cotswolds for the wedding, but Nick was adamant that they should get married in the village where he had been brought up. What he wanted was a proper service in the family church followed by a reception at his parents' home.

'You were happy enough when I suggested it when we first got engaged,' said Nick. 'What's changed?'

'I've thought about it some more,' she said, 'and I think it would be better to get married in London. I don't even know the Cotswolds. It doesn't mean anything to me.'

'Well, it means a great deal to me,' said Nick, stroking her thigh under the duvet, trying to dislodge her bad mood, but she pushed his hand off.

'I won't feel like it's my wedding with your family doing everything,' she complained.

'At least I have a family who are up to the task,' said Nick. 'Imagine getting married in Hatings with your dad in charge of proceedings!' He was joking, but she felt suddenly incandescent with anger. It just came at her like the felling of a tree.

'Don't call it Hatings, you fucking moron,' she hissed. 'It's not bloody funny.' She couldn't look at him. It was one thing when she complained about her father's lack of interest, it was quite another when someone else talked about him in a derogatory fashion.

'At least my father doesn't think it's the pinnacle of achievement to have a workshop with all his tools hung on the wall with their silhouettes drawn around them, like a . . . like a . . . fucking crime scene for murdered hammers.'

She knew she was overreacting but she had temporarily lost all sense of proportion. She couldn't be in the same room as him and she threw herself out of bed, dressed furiously and went to her friend Sasha's house. When she arrived she was still shaking and her skirt was on back to front. Sasha, a woman who dressed in pastel tones and who had a weakness for men who treated her badly – would have denied it vehemently, but Rora knew she took a secret delight in the relationship breakdowns and traumas of her friends, since it meant that her exclusion from their coupled lives would be postponed for a while. She gleefully fed Rora cocktails, persuaded her flatmate to babysit Ursula for the night, and took Rora to a club where Rora undid most of her shirt, danced with drunken abandon and allowed herself to be groped outside the toilet by a bloke who had the paunched and pallid look of a man who spent his working week in his car and his weekends eating ready meals for one.

The next day, contrite and hung-over, she phoned Nick and he came and picked her up from Sasha's house. Sasha watched sourly from the window as Nick stowed Rora tenderly into the passenger seat of the car.

'I'm so sorry,' said Rora, wondering what had come over her. She had behaved like a complete idiot and Nick was being kind and forgiving and grown up. 'I don't deserve you.'

'Of course you deserve me,' said Nick, and drove her back and administered white wine and chicken casserole and solicitous sex. Rora was so grateful to be forgiven that she didn't even wince when he made the strange bleating sound he always made when he came.

Nick took care of the routes to their destinations and filled in all the cracks. He made things so smooth and so easy for Rora that she developed a habit of not thinking about anything difficult at all. On the few occasions when they had all spent time together he had treated Ursula with vague kindness. They were supportive of each other's work. They had regular, though unspectacular sex – what more, after all, did she need? Her life was in any case too busy to spend too much time musing. Any opportunity actually to examine why they were together was successfully sublimated into purposeful activity. Nick was very good at motivating them out of bed at the weekend with improving activities and excursions. She sometimes had the traitorous and quickly banished thought that it wasn't so much curiosity that propelled him out of the house, more a sense that his bedside manner was wearing thin.

It was Nick's idea to go to Kew Gardens. They had worked their way through a long list of 'good places to visit' and this was one of the few recommended destinations they hadn't yet been to. Ursula was staying the night with a friend and so they were free to go wherever they wanted. It was a bitterly cold day and most people had taken shelter in the greenhouses for a fix of tropical weather. Rora took a great gulp of air when she went inside the Palm House and it felt to her like the first breath you take when you get out of a plane on holiday; aromatic and full of promise. She loved the beautiful structure of the building, which looked like an upturned boat from a distance but had real grandeur when you were inside. The delicate wrought iron balcony and staircases provided the perfect foil for the towering palms with their oddly distended trunks that looked as if they had consumed something without digesting it and the comical, outsized banana leaves.

Nick and Rora would sometimes pretend they didn't know each other. It was a joke that started at a party when they had only been together for a few weeks, and every now and again they slipped back into it. Nick had been the instigator of the game. He went to get Rora a drink at the party and when he came back he acted like he had just met her. He kept it up all evening, flirting with her, asking her questions he knew the answers to, and when they got home they had hasty sex in the hallway with the door barely closed behind them. He seemed to want Rora to be resistant, even disdainful of him, as if the real satisfaction for him lay in the overcoming of her, the persuading. At first she liked the game, too; it seemed to show an unexpected, creative side to him that she didn't know he possessed, but the longer they were together the more forced the game became, and as the pleasure of it increased for him it lessened for her.

She was never quite sure what the trigger for playing strangers was and was surprised when he responded to her question about whether her coat was coming down at the back with mock bewilderment, as if he thought she might be addressing someone else.

'Sorry, are you talking to me?' he said, and he stood and surveyed the back of her legs as she twisted round to show him. He looked her up and down slowly.

'It all appears to be perfectly in order.'

He had started speaking in the slightly avuncular manner he always adopted when he imagined himself a seducer. Rora rolled her eyes and walked on, and he followed her through a sheaf of slipper orchids with tendrils that hung at eye level and on past a brown pond in which bright carp flashed in and out of hollow stones. She stopped by a strange palm with roots that grew out of the middle of the trunk and descended in thick fingers to the floor. He came up to her, all pretend nonchalant, looking around him, his hands balled up in the pockets of his trousers.

'Hem's still intact,' he said, 'in case you were wondering.'

His eyes were on her, assessing. They grazed her cheek, her throat and then moved lower. It was as if he was drawing an outline of her with his eyes – the swell of her breasts under her opened coat, the curve of her hip. His mouth was slightly open and his skin had a faint sheen as if the steam in the air had moistened him too.

'Marvellous great trees,' he said.

She had a sudden impulse to get away from him, and without replying she moved swiftly on, the soles of her shoes making a sharp clatter on the iron floor. She could hear him behind her, trying to keep up.

'Where's the fire?' he said. 'Hang on a minute,' and then when she didn't stop he laughed, the sound high and delighted.

When she got to the end of the greenhouse she looked back, but she couldn't see him. She went up the spiral staircase to the balcony where there was a view of the tops of the trees and of the garden outside. Perhaps it was the height and the altered perspective up there among the canopy of the mini-rainforest, but she started to feel a little sick. She leaned on the iron railing in an attempt to stop her head from spinning. As she looked down she caught a glimpse of Nick through the vegetation. He was looking upwards, scanning the balcony, presumably searching for her. Seeing him from this angle was odd and disorientating. The top of his head had an unfamiliar white parting and his arms swung out as he walked in a strange, uncoordinated way. It was as if she was seeing him for the very first time. Rora dropped behind the shelter of the leaves, but he must have seen her, because a few moments later he appeared beside her.

'Where did you get to?' he asked. 'I was wondering if we might go somewhere . . . get a drink.'

'Why not?' she said and it was all she could do not to move away from him as he leaned into her, his breath hot and fast, his arms around her waist. As his mouth touched hers, the hair above his upper lip grazed her lips, which were already sore and wind chapped. He smelled faintly of the 'naughty bacon sandwich' they had had before they left the house, fat cut through with the sharp vinegar of ketchup. She felt fingers on her breasts, a feeling at once familiar and disgusting. As he kissed her she took herself away and it was Carl's face she saw beneath her closed eyes.

June 2010

Frank was finding it increasingly hard to stay awake and the periods of time he was alert enough to work on the book with Rora were getting shorter and shorter. They would talk in the mornings when he had just woken up, and then Rora would sit by his side while he slept, typing up what they had just discussed. Despite the urgency she felt to do as much as she could as quickly as possible, she was enjoying their collaboration. They argued about the finer points of language and emphasis, but their discussions felt purposeful and equal, as if they were each learning something from the other.

Frank had dozed off again, but opened his eyes suddenly as if he had remembered something he had to tell her.

'Ursula is having a tough time at school,' he said.

'Is she?' asked Rora, surprised. 'I thought she had settled in pretty well.'

'It's that friend of hers . . . you know, Hannah's girl.'

'Robyn? What about her?'

'She's getting picked on at school and Ursula has got involved . . .' Frank broke off as a coughing fit took hold of him and made his thin shoulders shake. Rora poured a glass of water and held it to his lips. He drank a little and finally the coughing stopped, but Frank's voice was even weaker than it had been before.

'They wait in the toilet for Robyn, these girls – they sound like horrors – so she wouldn't go in and she wet herself, poor little thing. Ursula went into the toilet with her to confront the girls. Felt like she couldn't leave Robyn to face them by herself. They seem to have transferred their attention to Ursula now and apparently some of the other people in her class have been join-ing in. She has been condemned by association.'

'How do you know all this?' asked Rora.

'She told me this morning. She often sits and tells me things. I think sometimes she thinks I'm asleep and that I won't be able to hear what she's saying. She said she thought it must be some-thing about her that makes people hate her.'

'I feel terrible that she hasn't talked to me about what's going on,' said Rora.

'She told me that she doesn't ever want to tell you anything sad,' said Frank, 'said you are filled to the brim with sadness already.'

Although she wanted to rush straight to the school and scoop Ursula up in protective arms, Rora knew that it was probably more sensible and less dramatic if she waited until going home time. She filled the time until then by clearing up the kitchen, which had been left in its post-breakfast state. As she scraped soggy Cheerios down the sink she felt a despairing sense of her own failure. Once again she had left Ursula vulnerable. Once again she had failed to notice what was going on. Ursula noticed more than she did. Nothing escaped her gimlet gaze. She had even seen the way Rora averted her head when they drove past the beach huts.

'Why do you always look away when we go past this bit of the beach?' she had asked.

'I don't know what you mean,' Rora said. If Ursula found out that she owned a beach hut they would never hear the end of it. She would be relentless in her desire for the ultimate seaside accessory, but Rora knew she could never go there again.

On the way back from school Rora bought Ursula an ice cream and they sat on a bench on the seafront next to a border of regimented blooms and a fountain from which water, dyed an unearthly blue, spilled in erratic bursts.

'That water looks like toilet cleaner,' said Ursula.

'It does a bit,' said Rora. 'I gather you've been having a hard time at school.'

'How come you know?' asked Ursula, looking at her in surprise.

'Frank told me, darling.'

'I TOLD him not to say anything,' said Ursula.

'It's my job to know these things,' said Rora. 'I'm supposed to protect you.'

'The girls are horrible,' said Ursula tremulously. Now that she felt able to speak of it, the words came tumbling out. 'They kept waiting for Robyn everywhere, and in the toilet at break time. They said she was a freak and snatched the bands out of her hair.'

'Frank says you got involved because you were trying to help her,' said Rora.

'She didn't have any other friends. I didn't want to, but I had to,' said Ursula, who already looked as if a weight had been taken off her.

'They pinched me underneath my arms,' she said pulling up the sleeve of her shirt and showing her mother a series of purplish bruises, 'and they poured some sticky stuff into my hair, and I didn't notice at first and then they pointed it out to the other people in the class and everyone said I was dirty. The worst one is called Mia. She tells the others what to do.'

'Why didn't you tell someone straightaway?' Rora asked, aghast at the sight of the bruises.

'Mia said she would come round to my house and tell you that I had been cheating in my tests.'

'And have you been cheating?' asked Rora.

'I do change some of my spellings when I'm supposed to be marking my test,' Ursula admitted. 'It's hard not to just slip in a letter when you've left one out,' she said dolefully. 'And when you get ten out of ten, you get a star on your chart. I hate having gaps. I want a solid line of stars.'

'I'm so glad you were able to tell your grandfather about it,' said Rora, thinking how ironic it was that the man who had never been able to face her troubles when she was a child was now the one to uncover what had been worrying Ursula.

'We'll go in to the school tomorrow and talk to the head teacher,' she said.

'Do we have to?' Ursula asked, the worried frown back in place.

'I think we really do. Those girls mustn't be allowed to behave like this,' said Rora.

'They will only get worse,' said Ursula, starting to cry.

When Ursula's sobs finally subsided, leaving her red-faced and hiccuping, Rora suggested a visit to the aquarium, which was a short walk from where they were sitting. At first Ursula shook her head, unwilling to relinquish her misery even with the prospect of such a treat.

'Oh go on,' said Rora. 'It's got sharks and an octopus and lots of jellyfish.'

'Has it got sea horses?' Ursula asked, raising her head at last, as if scenting something promising in the air.

'It has,' said Rora.

'OK, then,' Ursula said grudgingly and took a wet wipe from her school bag and gave her sticky fingers a clean.

'You are the neatest neat nick that ever was,' said Rora laughing.

'There are lots of tanks in the aquarium,' said Ursula primly. 'I wouldn't want to get marks on the glass.'

It was impossible to tell whether it was day or night. With no windows and with barely a breath of air, except that which was artificially generated and maintained, the fish moved endlessly through their small sealed world, through the unchanging light and space. Rora wondered if they knew what they were missing and dreamed about the unpredictable sea where their ancestors had started all of life. She thought that the aquarium was a place that provoked dreaming, even prayer. It had the same muffled quality as a church. She passed a tank in which fish glided by with markings so clear and fresh they looked as if they had been applied with a careful brush only a few moments before. In another, a school of herrings shimmered round and round, propelled forward in an endless silvery rush by a non-existent threat – safety in numbers. Ursula was quickly entranced, rushing from tank to tank, pointing and exclaiming.

'Don't go so quickly,' Rora said, 'we've all the time in the world.'

But it was impossible to stop her, and she went on ahead, drawn from one exhibit to the next as if she couldn't help herself. Rora noticed that all the children were behaving in the same way. A party of them came in dressed in blue uniforms and they moved en masse in an excited wave, their teacher unable to keep them in one place long enough to tell them about the ancient looking octopus which had just unfurled itself from its dark corner and had put one slow-moving tentacle against the side of the tank, as if trying to make contact with the outside world. They had the attention span of goldfish or perhaps one of the strange pufferfish, which was presently fixing Rora with exceedingly beady eyes.

In the shark tank a diver was rearranging some weed that had become twisted round a fallen plaster statue contrived to look like ancient remains. Rora watched as he came to the surface, small sharks drifting by him unconcerned. A few moments later a door a little distance from the tank opened and the diver came out, still dripping with water, his mask on his head and his diving suit rolled down to his waist. He had a deep, golden tan and the stomach emerging from the rubber suit was toned. With a sudden shock that stopped her dead in her tracks, she saw that it was Carl. With her heart jumping in her chest as if it was trying to get out, Rora turned and started walking away before he could catch sight of her.

PART TWO

Kiss 11

'She knew she would always remember the way he had held on to her as if he was holding on to life.'

21 June 2010

Her father's breathing changed in the night. Pauline came to her room and woke her and they both sat with him for a while. The doctor was called and he spent some time with Frank before coming down and asking Rora for a cup of tea. She knew that this was doctor-speak for wanting to tell her something bad. She also knew what he was going to say, so she delayed sitting down at the kitchen table with him by fiddling with the teapot and the cups. She found herself searching hopelessly for a milk jug at the back of the cupboard when she knew that it had been broken years ago, simply to put off the moment when she would have to look into his face.

The doctor drank a large mouthful of boiling hot tea as if he really needed it, and then cleared his throat. He looked young, younger than her, and a little panicked. She wondered how many times he had done this before and whether as a student he had participated in role-plays to practise the conveying of bad news. She could imagine him in a room with a circle of chairs, perhaps having his endeavours filmed on video so that it could be played back later and analysed, eager to get it right, holding eye contact as he had been told he should. His eyes were rather lovely, she thought, an unusual pale grey, and she helped him hold her gaze.

'You father is very much worse,' he said, and she nodded because she felt that she should show that she knew. She didn't want him to think that she was going to be ambushed by this death.

'It's extremely hard to predict these things,' he said, 'but I think it can only now be a matter of days.'

She was expecting it. Of course she was expecting it, and yet on the grey-eyed doctor's lips the fact of it sounded outrageous.

After the doctor had gone, she went upstairs and told Pauline she would take over. She sat by her father's side and watched the rise and fall of his chest. It seemed to Rora that her own breathing had changed to keep time with his. She remembered the game she had played with him when she was a little girl. They would take it in turns to time how long each of them could hold their breath. Rora would be purple in the face and bent double, whereas her father would sit, not breathing, for an extraordinary length of time, looking completely serene and unruffled. She never managed to win the breathing battle; he won every game they played, and it seemed that he was playing the game with her now. Each of his breaths felt as if it was a little longer coming than the one before.

She thought about seeing Carl at the aquarium and how her heart had begun beating so loudly she thought the people around her could hear the sound. She had hustled Ursula out of the building. She didn't want Carl to see them. Despite the way she had prepared what she might say to him, and despite the fact that deep down she knew she wanted to see him again, when confronted with the reality, she had panicked. How would it have been between them after all these years? What do you say to someone who had done what he had done for her? The thought of standing there with Ursula making small talk was inconceivable.

Ursula read from her schoolbook while Rora made supper. She felt jittery, and kept dropping things. When a mug skittered across the floor and ended up breaking into fragments against the table leg, Ursula broke off her reading and told Rora to stop being clumsy.

'You're making so much noise, I can't hear myself read,' she said indignantly.

'I'm sorry, darling. I'm all over the place,' said Rora.

'Grandad is getting ready to go, isn't he?' asked Ursula, and Rora found herself suddenly close to tears.

'I'm afraid it won't be long now,' she said, turning back to the sink to hide her emotion.

'I thought you didn't really like him,' said Ursula.

'I've got to know him a bit more over the last few weeks and I've changed a bit,' she said, feeling ashamed that she had made her resentment so apparent.

'I think he's very nice,' said Ursula in her firmest voice.

'What do you like most about him?' asked Rora. She loved the way that Ursula was so definite about things. She wished she too could feel the same certainty. It seemed that for as long as she could remember she had been blown this way and that, unable to get a proper purchase. Ursula wouldn't be like that. Whatever sorrows and joys her life would deal her, Rora was sure that her daughter would hold fast, keep true.

'I like the way he's interested in me,' said Ursula. 'He makes me feel like I'm the most important person. It's like being in the sun.'

Later, as Rora sat by her father's bed, she told him what Ursula had said and he smiled.

'I'm so glad I've had the chance to get to know her,' he said, and then slid away from Rora again into the kind of sleep that was so deep she feared there was no coming back from it. The doctor had been in again earlier and had patted her on the shoulder as if reassuring a small child.

'I think you should prepare yourself,' he said, and she wondered why this expression was always used in the context of an imminent death. Preparing yourself suggested there was some equipment to adjust, a bag to pack, a bracing movement to be made against a landing, but there was no getting ready for this outlandish thing. No straightening of the shoulders, no deep breath could possibly make you ready for the sheer unlikeliness of presence and then absence in a single heartbeat. Pauline had left for the day, telling Rora that she was on standby if she was needed.

'Just call any time,' she said and put a meaty hand to Rora's face and patted it. Sometime in the last few weeks she must have decided that Rora was OK, because she was now very kind. Rora had even grown used to her strange face and the way she stomped around the house. It was clear that death held no fear for the woman – she didn't feel the need to creep around talking in a hushed voice – she was too used to marshalling the exit to feel any reverence.

While her father slept Rora resumed her embroidery. The stitches were so tight that the poor cat now looked less as if it was enjoying the warmth of the open fire and more as if it was slowly roasting in front of it. She lost track of time and thought she might have dozed off, because she woke with a start to the sound of the seagull tapping on the window. It persisted until she got up and opened the window and dislodged the bird into squawking flight.

'Bloody rat with wings,' she muttered.

'They are actually very clever creatures,' Frank said, startling Rora, who hadn't realised he was awake. 'They stamp on the ground to imitate rainfall to trick earthworms up to the surface.'

'They are creepy and greedy,' said Rora. 'Can't find a corner in my heart for the wretches. Can I get you anything?'

'Come and sit with me,' Frank said, and Rora settled on the end of his bed. She didn't know if it was her imagination but it seemed to her that he was taking up less space under his sheet than he did before, as if he was performing a disappearing act in front of her.

'I was a terrible father,' he said. 'I got lost in my own misery and guilt and I forgot you.'

'It doesn't matter now,' said Rora. 'Please don't get upset.'

Nothing seemed to matter much anymore now that this last bit of him was slipping away from her.

'I wasn't a very good daughter,' she said.

'I didn't give you the chance. I'm so sorry Aurora. It's the thing I regret the most.'

'Don't be sorry,' she said, 'I can't bear you to be sorry now.'

She felt a great wave of anguish. She had tricked herself into believing that this would not matter, but it mattered more than anything.

'These last few weeks have been such a gift,' he said. 'It's as if I have been given another chance. You are going to be all right. You just need to live, my darling girl.'

'I'm going to miss you so much,' she said and the tears came at last. She could feel them falling on her hands and his. She kissed him on his cheek, and he held her to him for a long moment. She could feel the effort it was costing him in the shaking of his arm around her neck and the tremble in his face. His skin was warm and feverish and he breathed as if he had been running. Even as she drew away from him she fixed the kiss in her mind. She knew she would always remember the way he had held on to her as if he was holding on to life.

Frank died during the night. Rora had fallen asleep beside him and so had missed the transition she had been so dreading. She knew he had gone the moment she opened her eyes and saw his hand hanging over the edge of the bed. She was glad she had opened the bedroom window when she had scared away the seagull, because he would have had an easy route out and up the hill, along the cliff paths to the place he liked best, just above the nesting cormorants. She smoothed the sheet around him, touched his hand and looked with wonder at his emptied face.

She was anxious about whether or not to let Ursula see her dead grandfather, but the doctor said that it often helps children to be able to see the ending so that they too can make an accommodation for it, and so Rora took his advice. Ursula looked at Frank gravely. She made an odd little gesture with her hand – she passed it over his body, as if she was waving goodbye to the whole of him. She went downstairs and came back with some flowers that she tucked in to the top of his sheet. Pauline made him ready; she sponged skin and straightened clothes and freed his body at last from its tethering of sheets and tubes. Rora thought that from above the scene would look like a dance; the way they moved silently around the bed, to and fro, touching and then withdrawing and then approaching the centre point again, which was now nothing but an absence. A little later, with what seemed like obscene efficiency, two young men chosen for the task Rora thought because of their shuttered expressions took him away in a black plastic bag, his face hidden forever with the slide of a zip.

Kiss 12

'It was almost as if neither of them had kissed before.'

27 June 2010

Rora was glad to have her father's funeral arrangements to focus on. She still found solace in imposing a clear shape on chaos. After a lot of digging about through random documents and ancient letters she found Frank's address book shoved up against the back of his desk – it had clearly been some time since he had communicated with anyone much at all. She made a list of people who needed to be informed of his death and then a second list, which largely replicated the first, of people who needed to be told when and where the funeral would be. She had been told by the funeral director that the vicar who would conduct the cremation would find it useful to have some notes jotted down about her father's life and she found this task much more difficult than the planning of the order of service or thinking about what food she should provide for the wake. How should she choose which memories to share? How do you tell the story of someone's life in a way that has any real meaning? A five-minute summary from the mouth of a stranger was all it would inevitably amount to. There was the work that he had done as a historian, the book that he had laboured over endlessly, his years volunteering at the museum, but how to tell of the way he had loved her mother and of the years spent afterwards grieving her loss? How to explain the way he had kept the pain in so that it curdled his love? And how to find the words to say how much she had loved him despite that and because of that. It seemed to Rora that as time passed each funeral became the sum of all the others that had come before. She reflected that very old people must approach such occasions burdened by their multiple losses.

Feeling unable to be still, her body fired up with a terrible restlessness, Rora made a start on sorting out Frank's room. She avoided looking at the empty bed that still bore the indentation left by her father's body. By the bed was a glass of water he had drunk from, under the bed the slippers that he had stopped wearing only a month or so ago, although it seemed to Rora as if much more time had passed since she had come home to look after him. She felt overwhelmingly tired. The kind of tired that fells you in your tracks and prevents you doing anything other than collapsing onto the nearest available surface. Just then the doorbell went and Rora ran down the stairs expecting to see Hannah, who had said she was going to come round, but instead Carl was standing on the top step so close to the open door she suspected he had been peering through the letterbox.

'Hello, Rora,' he said.

For a moment she was speechless. Frank's death had absorbed her completely and driven out any other thoughts and so seeing Carl again felt like a new shock.

'What are you doing here?' she asked, so panicked by the sight of him she was almost ready to shut the door in his face.

'I heard about Frank's death. They put a sign outside the museum with his photograph and I saw it as I was passing, you know . . . "We regret to announce the death of long-term volunteer Frank Raine . . ." It was a nice tribute actually,' he said. 'I wondered if you'd come back.'

'I came back a few weeks ago,' Rora said.

Beneath the defined angles of his face and a short haircut he looked just the same, despite what he must have been through.

'Was it terrible?' she asked, her voice catching.

'I don't want to talk about it. Really I don't,' he said. 'It's over.'

'I left you,' she said.

'It was what I wanted,' he said.

They looked at each other for a few moments. It felt too much for Rora seeing him suddenly like this without being able to prepare herself.

'It's really not a good time,' she said, taking refuge in the conventions of the situation. She could hear Ursula moving around in the living room and hoped that she wouldn't come and see who was at the door.

'I've a lot to do,' Rora said.

'I'm sure you have. I'll leave you to it,' he said, turning away.

She almost let him go but something about his quiet resignation, his lack of presumption, smote her heart. She owed him so much. She couldn't just let him walk away as if they had never meant anything to each other.

'I didn't know you were back,' Rora said.

'I wasn't sure whether to let you know or not . . . I almost got in touch with Hannah to ask where you were, but in the end I thought it was better not to . . .' His voice trailed off.

'I would have liked to have known,' Rora said, biting her lip to forestall the tears that were threatening to come.

'I didn't know if it was what you wanted,' he said.

'Of course it is,' she said, although she wasn't sure she was telling the truth. Not allowing herself to think about him and what he had done had become so habitual that having him standing in front of her was unreal. It was as if he had come back to life.

'You look just the same,' he said and his severe mouth broke into the old, wide smile and she felt her stomach clench like a fist, the way it had always done since their very first kiss in the woods.

'So do you,' she said, and although she had thought so a few moments before, it wasn't quite true. There was a wariness about him now that she didn't remember from before. He had always been self-sufficient, but now he seemed more remote, even tougher than the boy who had punched walls in order to feel a more manageable pain. Part of her wanted to throw her arms around him, the other part wanted to hide herself away from him. Why had he come? What did he feel about her now? Perhaps he just wanted to see the person who had ruined his life.

'All these years I have imagined what you were doing,' he said. 'I thought of you perhaps married with children by now. Living in a nice house. Being happy.'

Rora didn't answer. She wasn't sure what to say. She couldn't tell him that she had spent her time trying not to think of him at all.

'Are you married, Rora?' he asked.

'No, I'm not,' she said.

He looked at her intently then, as if he was searching for something in her face that he had expected but couldn't see. It was perhaps this look of his that she read as disappointment that made her suggest they should meet again. Although she thought it was inevitable that in the flesh she would appear less than the images of her he had created over the years, she found she wanted him to look at her the way he used to as a boy – as if she held all the answers. It was unreasonable of her, selfish even, but she couldn't help herself.

'After the funeral's over and everything . . . let's meet up and talk,' she said.

'I'd like that very much,' he said, with something of his old swagger and that familiar sliding sideways look. She gave him her number to put into his phone and went back into the house, her skin fizzing the way it did when she almost fell or when her ankle turned at the edge of a pavement – the effect of a sudden jolt, or a near miss.

The day after her father's funeral she rang Krystof and invited him out for the picnic she had promised him. She wasn't entirely sure, if she was honest with herself, that her desire to see him was completely unconnected to Carl's reappearance. After the immediate impact of seeing him had abated she began to regret the fact she had given him her number. It would have been better to let things be. It was not possible to go back and make right all the things that had gone wrong and it was a mistake to try. She wanted the balm of the obvious admiration that Krystof offered – it was uncomplicated and reassuring.

He sounded delighted to hear her voice, but was immediately concerned that it might be too much for her so soon. He had come to the house on the day after Frank's death, bearing chicken and noodle soup. She was touched by the thought of him walking all the way from the restaurant, holding the cling-filmed dish out in front of him as carefully as if he was carrying live ammunition.

'It's the best cure for heartache I know,' he had said solemnly, handing it to her and refusing her invitation to come in.

'Just eat and rest,' he said.

On the phone he took some persuading that she really wanted to go to all the bother on his behalf.

'Wouldn't you prefer to postpone for a while?' he asked. 'Not that I am not eager to see you,' he said hastily, in case she might imagine that he was putting her off.

'I promised you a picnic and a picnic is what you will have,' she said. 'Besides, I haven't been anywhere for days. I need the fresh air.'

He was waiting for her at the appointed spot on the West Hill. He was stretched out on the grass with his hands behind his head, and so she had the opportunity of seeing him before he saw her. He looked completely himself, she thought, relaxed, not watchful and jumpy as Carl always was. Then she wondered why she was comparing the two men. They were as different as it was possible to be. He heard her approach and sat up with a wide smile.

'I'm afraid I chickened out and went to M&S,' she confessed, sitting down beside him and spreading out the blanket she had brought with her.

'The delight is being here with you,' he said. 'I love this view over the town. It makes the place look old-fashioned. Like a child's view of a seaside town.'

'Yes, you can't see the litter, or the globs of chewing gum or the spitting boys on bikes hassling you off the pavements from here,' said Rora, unpacking the sausage rolls and ready-made sandwiches she had bought.

'You keep your true soul well hidden,' said Krystof, smiling at her.

'I'm afraid that's not true,' said Rora. 'I'm a noticing-the-chewing-gum kind of a girl.'

'I don't believe it,' said Krystof. 'I think it's just a thing you do to make people think you are tougher then you are.'

'Believe what you want,' said Rora, 'you'll soon discover you are mistaken.'

'How are you feeling about your father?' asked Krystof as Rora poured some wine into plastic glasses.

'It's so strange. I didn't see him properly for years and hardly thought about him from day to day, but now I really miss him and I regret all the time we didn't spend together. I wish I'd had more of him.'

'I'm so glad you found him before it was too late. It's good you feel sad now. It would be much worse if you didn't feel anything,' said Krystof, munching contentedly on a smoked salmon sandwich and tipping his head back to drink from the narrow glass.

'Imagine dying and no one missing you at all. You would just disappear into the ground as if you had never been,' he said and shuddered.

'I'm going to finish his book. I really want to do it as a tribute to him. Even if it means we have to stay for longer in Hastings than I had intended. I have to go to London to see about some other work-related things, but it will only be for a day or so,' said Rora.

'This is good news all round,' said Krystof. 'You have a project and I get to have you near me for longer.'

Rora was still not used to the forthright way he came out with his feelings. She was accustomed to men who spun themselves stupid trying to create the right impression. Not Carl, of course. He didn't care about how he was perceived, but that was less about being honest and more about the fact he really didn't seem to give a toss. She shrugged the thought of him off.

'There's no point keeping hidden what I feel,' said Krystof, as if he had read her mind. 'It's a waste of time.'

'There is a middle ground, you know,' said Rora.

'I'm sorry. I told you I would creep, and here I am being pushy again,' he said. He ran his hand over the top of his head with a rueful expression that made Rora laugh.

'You look like a boy who has been told off for putting his fingers in his food,' she said.

'I often have my fingers in food,' said Krystof, 'It's the best place for them.'

'How are your plans for extending the restaurant going?' she asked.

'Moving at the pace of a geriatric snail,' he said. 'Everything needs permissions and forms, and then just when you think you might be about to move ahead something else will crop up. It's exasperating. I just want to knock down walls and get on with it.'

'You surprise me,' said Rora in a teasing tone of voice.

He did one of his searching looks, the one that made her feel as if he was trying to memorise her features in case he would have to describe them to a third party.

'Let's leave the basket here, no one will pinch it, and if they do they're welcome to what's left of the food,' she said, jumping up. 'I want to have a look at the castle. I haven't seen it for a while and I want to include a description of it in the book.'

All that remained of the Norman castle were fragments. A wall here, an arch there, an edge of what might once have been a room, but Rora had always loved the sketchiness of the ruins. It allowed her to imagine the towers and the keeps and to guess what the views from the battlements would have looked like when the building was intact. The sandstone walls outside the castle bore the marks of hundreds of names, some linked with a heart, some scratched hastily into the stone, others deeply gouged. Just outside the main entrance to the castle was a small cave made up of two passageways, one bearing left to a small chamber and the other ending in a circular space.

'I seem to remember that if you whisper something in one part of the cave,' Rora said, 'it can be heard in the other. It's quite spooky. Shall we go in?'

The cave was dark and cool and smelled of the earth and the whispered breath of a hundred tourists. Rora took the left turn and pointed Krystof to the other chamber.

'I'm not sure I totally like it in here,' said Krystof. 'I'm fonder of wide open spaces.'

'Go on, it won't take a minute,' said Rora.

When she got to the end of the tunnel she stood still and waited, but she couldn't hear anything at all.

'Can you hear me?' she whispered, feeling a little foolish. 'Krystof, answer me if you can hear me.'

There was a pause and then just as she was about to give up and go and find him, she heard his whisper, a faint and curling noise that sounded as if it was coming from the centre of the earth or from the top of a mountain.

'I hear you, Aurora,' he said. 'Will you marry me?'

'You're a crazy man,' she whispered. 'I'll see you at the entrance.'

'Interesting acoustics,' she said smiling at him when they emerged back into the light. 'There is a theory that the sound is conducted by the ironstone in the walls.'

She made no mention of what he had said and neither did he and she wondered if she had perhaps misheard him. They retrieved the basket and walked down the steps back into town.

'My turn next,' said Krystof, just before they parted. 'I will plan the next outing and ring you. That is, if you want to see me again ...' he stopped and turned to her, waiting for her response.

'I would like that very much,' she said, and she held his gaze.

'Am I in with a chance?' he asked.

'A slim chance,' she said and then, disarmed by the way his face lit up at her words, she kissed him.

She was intending just to kiss him on his cheek as a thank you for the afternoon, but their lips met. As kisses go it was rather a clumsy one. It was almost as if neither of them had kissed before. He kissed the side of her mouth then her top lip and then his mouth found the shape of hers and lingered there. He was warm, as if all the heat of the day had gathered in him, and the lashes over his closed eyes trembled like the edge of a butterfly's wing. It might only have lasted a short time and been the most chaste of kisses, but she had felt his strength and his tenderness and her reaction to the embrace was more emotional than she had expected.

Hannah rang her as she was walking back to Pilgrim Street.

'Where have you been? I've been phoning you all day,' she said.

'Oh sorry, I didn't hear my phone. I've been out.'

'Bring Ursula to our house this evening. Rich will look after the girls. We're going out.'

'I don't really feel up to it.'

'Oh come on, it'll do you good. A bottle of wine, fish and chips and me. What could be better? We'll leave the flamenco dancing class until next week.'

'OK,' said Rora, who knew that Hannah wasn't going to relent and relieved that at least she wasn't being asked to swivel her wrists and click castanets. 'I'll be there at seven.'

They took their wrapped packets of fish and chips and the bottle of wine they had bought from the supermarket to the beach and settled down with their backs to the still-warm harbour wall. The light was soft and the cliffs gleamed with a honey sheen. The nearby fishing boats gave off a smell of hot paint and cracking wood. They looked dry and spent, as if they would never touch the sea again, and their ropes lay curled beside them like sleeping snakes.

The beach slowly changed its aspect at this time of the evening, the colourful towels and umbrellas were folded up and put away and the families drifted off with rubbish bags hanging from their fingers, walking heavily across the stones as if the sun and the sea had exhausted them. The fishermen were gathering in green anoraks, the evening army ready to claim the edges of the sea now that the ski jets and splashing children no longer held sway, to take up their solitary positions with stools, bags and tin boxes full of wriggling bait. There was just a hint of a coming chill, as if the heat wave might be about to pass and leave the town panting and blistered in its wake. At their feet were a dozen or so tiny herrings that had fallen from a net and lay perfectly silvered, their tails curled up like paper mood fish on a giant palm.

'When are you thinking of going to the school?' asked Hannah, unwrapping her supper and releasing the tang of hot fat and salt. A line of seagulls perched on bollards turned their necks in unison as if a bell had rung.

'I think maybe we should go together. Recent events have driven the whole horrible business from my mind. I know the term is almost over, but we still need to do something about it,' said Rora. 'Especially for Robyn, who is going to be there next year. I gather that the chief monster is the head teacher's own child. I think she is going to be defensive about the whole thing.'

'I'll ring up tomorrow and make an appointment with her. Nail those little shits,' said Hannah, putting a fistful of chips into her mouth.

'So Lionel didn't float your boat, then?' asked Hannah when she could talk again.

'Not really,' said Rora. 'His beard put me off, that and the neat way he cut up his food.'

'You're the limit. You'll never find anyone if you are going to be this picky,' said Hannah. 'He said he found you intimidating, and no wonder if you were scrutinising his table manners.'

'He just means he didn't fancy me. Men often use the word intimidating when they mean sexually unappealing,' said Rora.

'I think it's more to do with the kind of vibes you were giving off,' said Hannah.

'Well, if you mean I was giving off an "I don't like men with pointy little beards and fingers that dig into your palm" vibe, then you are right,' said Rora crossly.

'I don't think you are right about the intimidating thing anyway,' Hannah protested. 'Men are quite often turned on by powerful, inaccessible women.'

'They are more often turned on by soft, compliant ones,' said Rora sourly.

They passed the wine bottle back and forth in companionable silence. A man with trousers just an inch or so too short for comfort passed by them and said, 'Hello ladies,' in a nasal voice, as if he was trying to impersonate someone, which made them snigger into their chips.

'This is the second picnic I've had today,' said Rora.

'Really? Who did you have the other one with?' asked Hannah.

'Krystof,' said Rora.

Hannah stopped mid-munch and fixed Rora with a look.

'What manner of picnic was this?' she asked. 'Lots of people, a shared dish of coleslaw and a three bean salad, or wine and fine meats and lolling on a grassy bank à deux?'

'Who on earth says "à deux"?' said Rora.

'I do. You were lolling, weren't you, with that poor chap whose ears go red when you walk into a room?' she said accusingly.

'Don't be ridiculous, his ears don't go red!' said Rora, laughing.

'So, are you having a relationship with him?' asked Hannah.

'I'm not sure. Maybe. He's very nice ... I saw Carl,' she said and then realised that Hannah would wonder why she had mentioned him so apparently out of context.

'You saw him here, in Hastings?' Hannah asked in astonishment.

'Yes. He came to the house. He had heard that Dad died.'

Hannah put her chips aside, which was an indication of how serious the conversation was. She looked carefully at her friend, but Rora kept her face averted.

'Rora, look at me. Tell me that you don't still have feelings for him,' she said.

'No . . . I don't know,' said Rora.

'So which is it? No? Or I don't know?'

'We are linked together.'

'Oh. My. God.'

'He's not what you think he is.'

'I knew he was bad news the moment I saw him, and I was right. I was right wasn't I, Rora?'

'You don't know everything about him,' Rora said, wishing she hadn't told Hannah about seeing Carl.

'So tell me,' Hannah said.

'I was raped.'

It was the first time she had ever told anyone and saying the words out loud brought back the feelings of shame. She thought about how she had stood in the shower and scraped at herself with the sponge meant for cleaning the bath until her skin was red and raw. How she had kept scrubbing until she could no longer feel anything at all.

'When?' Hannah asked looking shocked.

'When I was eighteen,' Rora said.

'Oh God, Rora! Why didn't you tell me about this? Did you tell anyone?'

'No,' Rora said. 'I've never told anyone before.'

'But what's this got to do with Carl?'

'He was there.'

'What do you mean? He was there as in he was part of the rape?'

'No. He saw it happening.'

She thought of how it had been when he had finally come to find her on the beach. She had seen him walk towards them, cupping his hand over his eyes, as if he couldn't quite believe what he was seeing. Ian had still been on top of her. He was making that strange noise that was halfway between tears and laughter. She couldn't move. She couldn't make a sound. She looked at Carl over Ian's shoulder. She tried to make him go away with her eyes. She knew it would kill him to see her like this. Carl had always touched her as if she was precious, as if he couldn't quite believe his good fortune. But despite what she was trying to tell him, he hadn't gone away. She would never forget the way he had stopped short, as if he had been shot, nor the sound he had made – a kind of moaning in-drawn breath and then a scream of rage so loud she had thought the whole town would have heard him. But no one had come. Then he had started running.

'Why didn't you tell the police?' Hannah asked, still aghast that this had happened to her friend and she had not known about it.

'It was complicated,' Rora said, looking away again. She wasn't ready to tell Hannah any more. She wasn't sure she ever would be.

'When did it happen?' Hannah asked.

'Some time during the last year of sixth form,' Rora said vaguely, looking away again and picking up a stone and aiming it at a plastic bottle buried in the pebbles.

'I so wish you'd told me,' Hannah said looking at Rora sadly. 'I was only a stupid teenager, but I might have been able to help.

You must have been all over the place. No wonder you were always so strange about men.'

Rora knew that Hannah was referring to her pregnancy. She had told her friend that Ursula was the product of a one-night stand with someone she had met in a club in London shortly after she had left home.

Hannah shuffled over to her and put her arm around her shoulders.

'I'm glad you've told me now, anyway,' Hannah said.

'My chips have gone cold,' Rora said. 'Let's go and have a cocktail.'

She hadn't been able to tell Hannah everything, but she still felt a little lighter for unburdening what she had. She thought that perhaps one day she might be able to tell the whole story, but she wasn't ready yet.

Kiss 13

'They spun in and out of the light like lovely ghosts.'

29 June 2010

Ms Lincoln ushered Hannah and Rora into her office quickly, as if she was worried they might be spotted. She was tall and wide-shouldered and wore her hair in a severe bob. Rora wondered if the geometric cut and the dark trouser suit had been chosen in an attempt to counteract the effect of her voice, which was disconcertingly high and squeaky, as if a small child was trapped inside the head teacher's body. This impression was reinforced by the line of ceramic rabbits dressed in Victorian garb and a pen topped with silver and pink feathers poking out of a desk tidy.

'I'm very distressed to hear what has been happening,' she said. 'We work very hard here at Mayfield to create an environment in which children are rewarded for kindness.'

'Well, something's gone badly wrong, then,' said Hannah.

'How do you usually deal with bullying?' asked Rora.

'Well, girls can be a little cliquey at this age,' said Ms Lincoln. 'I'll have to hear all sides of the story before I can ascertain exactly what's been happening.'

'Exactly what's been happening is that my daughter has bruises all over her arms,' said Rora.

'I gather her grandfather has just died . . .' Ms Lincoln left her sentence unfinished, and Rora felt herself getting angry.

'Yes, her grandfather has just died, but that has no connection whatsoever with what has been happening here. Are you suggesting that my daughter has been harming herself?'

'No, of course I'm not suggesting that,' said Ms Lincoln.

'Four girls, and we know their names, have been systematically tormenting Robyn and Ursula,' said Hannah in a deceptively calm voice.

'There are certain children who seem to attract negative attention,' said Ms Lincoln. 'Without wanting to cause offence, Robyn can be a little, well . . . challenging and Ursula has problems too . . .'

'What are you saying?' asked Rora. 'How challenging and what problems?'

'Ms Lincoln,' said Hannah, still in the same unruffled tone of voice, 'we understand that one of the girls involved is your daughter Mia. Might this have a bearing on your apparent unwillingness to act on what we have told you?'

'I intend to fully investigate the matter,' she said. An ugly flush had started to climb up her neck and her hands skittered restlessly across her desk. 'It's just that I have learned, to my peril, that it's a mistake to have knee-jerk reactions to these things without being properly armed with the facts.'

'I'll have a knee-jerk reaction myself,' said Hannah, 'any moment now.'

'There's no need at all to take that tone of voice with me,' said Ms Lincoln on a rising squeak. 'It will do nothing to help matters. We all need to behave like adults in a situation like this.'

'I thought you said the school believed in teaching children to be kind to each other,' Rora said.

'Until we are satisfied that measures have been taken,' said Hannah, 'we'll be keeping our children away from school. It's nearly the end of the school year anyway.'

'I'm afraid you will be breaking the law if you choose to do so without a valid medical reason,' said Ms Lincoln.

'We expect a phone call within the next couple of days, telling us what you have done to punish the children involved and to make sure this doesn't happen again and if we don't I will be contacting the LEA to report the situation,' said Rora, getting up. Hannah had a glint in her eye that didn't bode well and Rora wanted to get out of the room herself before she said something she would regret.

Despite their frustration and anxiety, Hannah and Rora were struck with hysteria as soon as they got out of the school gates, making each other giggle by taking it in turns to mimic the head teacher's unfortunate voice. Hannah laughed so much she walked into a lamp post.

'Seriously though, I don't think I want Robyn to go back to that school,' said Hannah, rubbing her injured shoulder. 'I'm going to look into alternatives over the summer.'

'I know they are only nine years old, but I could hang those wretched girls up by their ears,' said Rora vengefully, which led on to a discussion about the creepy ceramic rabbits on Ms Lincoln's desk.

'Do you think Robyn is "challenging"?' asked Hannah in a worried tone of voice.

'What the fuck does that mean anyway?' asked Rora.

'Well, she doesn't say a lot and she can be a bit OCD about her hair and her clothes and her toys . . . and pretty much everything,' said Hannah, sighing.

'She just keeps her cards close to her chest. She's fine. She's got it all going on, you can tell, she just can't be bothered with small talk.'

'I love her so much,' said Hannah. 'I love both of them, but she has always had a special part of my heart. I'm not sure why. Paloma is so much less of a worry.'

'Sometimes you love children in a particular way because you know they are going to have to struggle a bit in life. You know that the other, less complicated ones are going to have plenty of people to love them,' said Rora.

'That's true,' said Hannah, giving a passing boy on a bike the evil eye for almost cycling into her.

'I don't know what's happening to me,' she said. 'Overnight I seem to have become the sort of miserable old lady who hisses at teenagers. How did that happen?'

'Sometimes I think that Ursula has inherited my mother's illness,' Rora said.

'You've never said that before,' said Hannah, who felt as if she was just getting to know the woman she thought she had known for years. This was the second thing Rora had confided in the last twenty-four hours. 'What makes you think that?'

'I don't know. Her intensity. The way she keeps so much hidden. She went sleepwalking the other night. I found her in the room where my mother died,' said Rora.

'I don't think she's much like Sandi, although I don't really remember her that well,' said Hannah.

'Flipping kids,' she said, after they had walked a little further. 'They prey continually on your mind.'

'They really do,' said Rora, thinking of the way her father had gone out and bought all of her books. She felt suddenly so knocked back with grief that she had to stop and breathe until the worst of the pain passed.

Rora spent the first half of the afternoon sorting through some of Frank's notes so that she could establish where further research was needed. Seeing her father's handwriting with its familiar curves and slopes, his odd little notes in the margins, made her feel close to him. Despite her absorption in the work – when she was writing time always seemed to stand still – the emptiness of the house began to impinge on her. Ursula had gone with Hannah and the girls to the cinema. The silence stopped being peaceful and began to have a noise all of its own. However many times she told herself to focus on her task, the thought of Carl intruded and became part of the silent clamour of the deserted house. She thought of the way he had seemed bewildered to find himself at her door, as if he had acted on a sudden whim and felt at a loss when actually confronted by her. She wondered what imperative had brought him there. Was it simply curiosity? Did he ever regret the decision he had made?

After she had piled up her father's notes into some sort of order and switched off her computer, she set off for the aquarium. She deliberately didn't look at her reflection in the mirror in the hall. He could take her as he found her, she thought, and then wished too late that she had at least run a comb through her hair.

On the seafront, a man lay spreadeagled on the grass verge clutching an empty can of beer, his face baked the colour of an old brick. Ten feet further on, another man slept curled up on his side, his arms wrapped tightly around a small canvas bag. Rora wondered what had brought them to this point. The instinct to dissemble so far eroded in them that they lay without protection in the glare of the sun and of passing strangers. It would no doubt be the most ordinary of journeys – a job lost, a failed marriage, a wrong that festered for too long, a lack of love. Despite the quality of the light and the new boutiques, Hastings was full of people who had simply ended up there – the town seemed not so much the end of a journey but a stopping-off point that had become permanent just because there was nowhere else to go. The new arrivals reached the sea and then lay down as if waiting for the tide to take them.

On the pond three swan boats were moving in erratic circles around a lump of concrete fashioned to look like an iceberg. Rora could hear a child shouting on one of the boats, whether in protest or in celebration it was hard to make out.

When she reached the aquarium a young man at reception with a name badge that proclaimed him to be Gary, a prematurely receding hairline and a resentful expression that suggested that he had been forced to work while others were having fun, told her that Carl was out.

'It's our colleague Serena's birthday and Carl's volunteered to "help" with getting the party set up.'

He made jabbing motions with his fingers to indicate the quotation marks around the word help, as if he was scratching the air in fury. He gave her an assessing glance. 'You're not one of his women, are you?' he asked.

'No,' she replied.

'It's just that you are so his type.'

'Could you tell me where he is?' asked Rora in as chilly a tone as she could muster.

'He'll be upstairs in the Green Man on Castle Street,' Gary said as he angrily resumed stacking leaflets on the counter.

The pub was already quite full by the time Rora got there and she made her way through the crowd at the bar and went up the stairs. The party hadn't started yet but the tables had been pushed against the wall and they had rigged up a disco ball, which illuminated the middle of the room in glittering tiles, leaving the edges in shadow. Carl and a girl with bleached blonde hair and golden skin were centre stage. She was laughing and nudging his legs into position, placing one of his hands in her own and the other on the small of her back, teaching him to do some kind of dance, a waltz maybe. A slow, swelling song she didn't recognise was playing on the CD player. Carl was looking fixedly down at his feet.

'Look up. How can you lead if you keep looking at the floor?' said Serena, the sort of woman who made a white shirt and jeans look elegant. Rora reflected that if she had worn the same outfit she would simply have looked a bit crumpled.

'I lose my place unless I can see what my feet are doing,' said Carl.

'No! Back a step, now forward. That's it.'

'Am a doing it right yet?' he asked, as they swayed and turned. She ran her hand in a proprietorial way along his shoulder.

'Not really, you have about as much grace as a carthorse.'

'I'm only doing this at all because it's your birthday, Serena,' he said, and swung her round flamboyantly, his leg spinning in a half circle. She made a sound of mock admiration and he laughed in response. They were beautiful. The light caught the side of their faces and sheened their arms and their shoulders.

It glossed their hair, and gave their less than skilful movements around the floor a kind of solemnity, a kind of grace.

All she would have had to do would have been to say something out loud or to make a movement and the spell would have been broken. She may even have been able to stop what she could see was about to happen, but she couldn't move. Neither of them noticed her there. They picked up speed, Carl becoming more sure-footed, beginning to learn the rise and fall of the movement, fitting his hips to the sinuous rub of hers. He slipped his hand under the back of her loose shirt and pressed her to him more closely. They spun in and out of the light like lovely ghosts. Or perhaps it was Rora who was the ghost, because it seemed suddenly as if she was no longer watching from the shadows but was being held instead of the other woman in the curve of his arms. She could feel his hand on her own back and the heat of his body against hers. His eyes were on her face, on her mouth. It was Rora's hair that his hand went up to stroke, her cheek his fingers grazed.

They stopped dancing. Rora heard the intake of Carl's breath as his teeth grazed his bottom lip. She saw the question in his dark eyes as he waited just a beat for Serena to raise her mouth to his. It seemed to last forever, that kiss. When Serena cupped the curve of his head, Rora could feel the spring of his hair under her own nails and the silkiness of it where it lay close to his scalp. Serena tugged his shirt out of his jeans and her hands went along his sides and up his back, and Rora knew the firm slide of him and the warmth of his skin. Serena put her face to his neck and Rora could smell his sweet smokiness. Still entwined, without taking his mouth from hers, he moved so that they were leaning against the wall. Rora felt the shudder of her body as Carl sank into her, the touch of his fingers between her legs and then the insistent, hard press of him.

It was only when Serena made a noise, a small, almost discontented sigh, that Rora was brought back to herself. It was like waking from a dream. She went out, closing the door quietly behind her. She pushed again through the Friday-night drinkers who also didn't seem to notice she was there, barely moving aside for her as she threaded her way – finding a gap under an arm, a space left by a turned back.

She went out onto the seafront, where a warm wind had whisked the sea to a foaming turquoise. She walked for a while along the beach, stumbling from time to time as the stones moved under her. She felt indistinct, her feet and her head unsteady. Far out to sea a fishing boat, brought high by a wave, crashed down, turning the water around it a sudden, clean white. It paused for a moment and then it began its familiar, hurtling turn towards the beach, heedless of the churning shallows that lay in wait for its slender hull.

She had never really sought intimacy, preferring always to be sufficient in herself, and she had long given up the possibility of the kind of love that she had once thought possible, but this afternoon she felt the sorrow of being alone. The very thing she had always avoided as being a disruption to the smooth running of her life felt, for the first time, like a comfort she craved. It seemed to her that nobody in the world knew or cared where she was at that exact moment. It was as if she didn't exist at all. She heard the shrill scrape of the boat across the stones and the hiss of the wave as it inhaled its portion of shingle, and as she turned back she could still feel the silky nudge of Carl's lips claiming hers.

*

Back at home and still suffused with the mysterious longing she had felt at the sight of Carl and the birthday girl, she soothed herself with a glass of wine and wondered why Carl had come looking for her. It was obvious she meant nothing to him. And why after all this time should she mean anything? He was a free agent. It would be Serena this week, and no doubt someone else the next. He was incapable of proper, lasting feeling. He was too damaged and too destructive to make anything work. What on earth had possessed her to seek him out? She felt a little shiver of shame when she thought of the way she had imagined herself into his arms. She told herself it was fortunate she had witnessed the scene because it had served its purpose – it had hardened and then broken off the last little nub of her weakness.

Just before she left to collect Ursula the phone rang. It was Krystof. The man seemed to have an uncanny knack of knowing when best to time his overtures. It was almost as if he had sensed her loneliness. His voice was comforting, like the sensation of softened wax in your hands or the feeling of entering warm water from a chilled room. She cautioned herself against too fervent a response. The man deserved more than being simply an antidote to Carl.

'I was sitting in my garden thinking of you,' he said.

She could tell he was smiling because his voice stretched and warmed.

'All good things, I hope,' she said, adopting the slightly bantering tone she always seemed to use with him. It was as if his seriousness made her perversely facile. His solemnity reminded her of being in social situations when the gravest moments prompt a fearful temptation to burst out with something wildly inappropriate.

'Now you are fishing,' he said, 'which is fitting, because I'm ringing to ask you to come out with me on my friend's boat on Thursday. I thought you might like to bring Ursula.'

She hesitated for a moment. She had always been so protective of her daughter that her first impulse was to suggest that she should leave her behind. She was surprised to hear herself agreeing to the plan. He was just a friend, nothing more, she told herself, and Ursula would like him, Rora was sure of it.

'You really are determined to get me into the sea,' said Rora. 'What if I fall off?'

'You won't. My friend has been fishing off this coast for many years. He supplies my restaurant and many others. There is nothing to be afraid of. There will be life jackets and me.'

'Ursula swims really well, so it would only be me you would need to keep an eye on.'

'I can manage that without too much pain,' he said.

On the way back from picking Ursula up from the cinema, with the sun still shining and with nothing much in the house to cook, they decided to buy sandwiches and fruit and go up to the East Cliff and eat their supper there. Ursula had been quietly pleased by the news she wasn't returning to the school, and now the summer stretched out in front of her as a glorious, unblemished thing.

'They don't know where I'm living, do they, Mum?' she asked as they entered the funicular that led up to the Country Park.

'Do you mean the horrible girls at your school?' asked Rora.

'Yes.' Ursula settled herself down on the wooden bench inside the carriage as it began its vertiginous glide up the side of the cliff. She enjoyed the thrill of the ride, pressing her face to the glass so that she could see the glitter of the stones beneath her and the grass hanging out of the cracks in the cliff face and the lift station growing smaller behind them.

'The school is going to deal with those girls,' said Rora, 'and in any case you are not going back there.'

'Are we going back to London soon, now that . . . Grandad has died?'

Ursula's face became sad at her own words. She hadn't known her grandfather for long but they had formed a strong attachment in the time they had been together and Rora knew she was upset by the loss of him.

'I always expect him to be in his bedroom,' she had said a few days after his death. 'I don't know why I keep forgetting,' and she looked puzzled – as if she couldn't understand her own reaction, but Rora knew that Ursula was looking for traces of him. She was seeking evidence. It was inconceivable that there should be nothing left.

'We're going to stay a while, until I've finished the book, at least until the end of the summer, then we can decide what we want to do,' said Rora.

Unlike her daughter, she didn't particularly enjoy the lurching sensation of the lift, nor the way the ground seemed to fall away under them, and was relieved when the carriage made its shuddering stop at the top. They walked a little way along the path into a wooded area with a bench to sit on. The town seemed a long way away, although the sound of activity still reached them and Rora could hear the grind of barrels across cobbles and the tinny music from the fairground rides. She had thought that the growth of summer had reached its highest point, but it seemed that the hedges and trees were even fuller than they had been when she was last here and everywhere she looked was a thick and clotted green.

'I used to come here when I was a girl,' she said to Ursula. 'I used to come with a friend and walk all over this park. I knew every nook and cranny of it.'

'Which was your favourite bit?' asked Ursula, reluctantly eating the banana she had been given. It was always a battle to get her to eat any fruit.

'There's a little building, just over there,' said Rora, turning round on the bench and pointing further along the cliff path. 'We used to sit in there when it was raining. I think it's still there.'

'Let's go and find it,' said Ursula jumping up and surreptitiously putting her half-eaten banana back in the bag.

'I saw that!' said Rora.

'Bananas are so slimy,' said Ursula and her small shoulders shuddered with distaste. The cabin seemed closer to the edge of the cliff than she remembered it and Rora wondered if perhaps the earth around it had been stealthily falling away. She had read that whole villages in some parts of the country were moving inexorably towards the sea – their foundations and garden fences helpless against the changing shape of the coastline. But the place exuded the same feeling of refuge it always had when Rora and Carl had made it their territory.

'I always felt that nothing could touch me when I was in here,' said Rora.

'What were you scared of? Were girls at school mean to you too?' asked Ursula.

'I was scared of a lot of things, but being here always made me feel better,' Rora said.

'Can we come again?' asked Ursula, when Rora made a move to go.

'Of course,' said Rora, 'but only if you hold my hand going back in the lift. My stomach feels even funnier on the way down.'

'Wus,' said Ursula, but she said it kindly and took Rora's hand long before they began their descent.

Kiss 14

'She felt his intake of breath against her lips as if he was readying himself to plunge into deep water.'

1 July 2010

Ursula was excited about the prospect of going on the boat and packed her furry bag with a number of extra items she thought would be necessary for the trip.

'We're only going out for a couple of hours,' said Rora when she saw what her daughter was taking, 'not making a journey to discover a new continent.'

'You never know what might come in useful,' said Ursula firmly, her bag straining at the seams.

'I hardly think we are going to need a torch and plastic survival sheeting for a jaunt in a fishing boat, and surely one spare pair of socks will be enough,' said Rora.

Ursula had insisted on cutting open two bin bags and taping them down the middle to make a sheet large enough to cover them all, and had packed chocolate bars, spare underwear and a roll of loo paper. Rora sighed but gave in knowing that Ursula always felt calmer when fully prepared.

They walked down to the harbour, which was already thronged with visitors drawn to the town for a music festival. A group of ladies in red neck scarves and striped tops were standing in a circle singing sea shanties, watched by three derisive boys with their arms crossed. The street was lined with stalls selling everything from olives to incense sticks. A group of Lindy hop dancers were

flicking their hair and jumping over the bent backs of their part-
ners. The air was a rich soup of fish, hot fat, burning jasmine and
the diesel fumes of the cars waiting in line to get into the rapidly
filling car park. Although the sun was shining, the balmy wind of
the last couple of days had picked up speed. The sea was crested
with dashing white foam and the waves when they hit the beach
smacked the shingle with a fine spray.

Krystof was waiting for them by the net huts and Rora intro-
duced him to Ursula, who shook his hand solemnly.

'I gather you're the swimmer who's going to save us all if we
fall overboard,' he said.

'I have all my badges,' said Ursula, 'but not my lifesaving one
yet. Mum's the problem,' she said confidingly. 'She thinks the
sea's out to get her.'

Krystof laughed, and led the way to a tubby boat – made
in the traditional style with overlapping wooden boards and a
flat bottom – which was waiting in the shallows, having already
been winched off the hardwood blocks on which it rested. Rora
recalled Frank's note about the way the fishermen used to hold
the copper nails in their mouths when they repaired their boats,
spitting them out into their cupped hands as they needed them,
and the way the fishermen's wives would string their washing up
between the beached boats to dry.

'Welcome to the *Fairwind*,' said Krystof. 'I'm afraid we're
going to have to wade into the water, so you'd better roll up your
trousers.'

They were helped on board by the boat's owner, Peter, who
hauled them up with burly arms. He had neat, crisp curls like
spaniel's fur and eyebrows that rose at the ends, which made
him look faintly diabolical.

'Do you think he's a pirate?' Ursula asked Rora in a whisper.

Two men on the beach pushed the boat out as easily as if they were throwing a net into the water and the engine started with an oily shudder. Krystof handed Rora and Ursula life jackets and they put them on. Rora spent ages checking and double-checking that Ursula's was done up securely until her daughter squirmed away from her and went with Peter, to whom she had taken an instant shine, despite his mischievous eyebrows, to have a go at steering the boat. As they left the town behind them the wind picked up and the boat assumed a different motion – a sway punctuated with a kind of tentative swell as if the boat itself wasn't sure if it could take the turbulence. Rora felt unsteady when she was standing and chose instead to sit safely at the helm surrounded by boxes and ropes. The sea they left behind was ploughed in great big watery furrows and the spray rose as fine as an aerosol and coated their faces and hair.

Rora had been invited to a party at Hannah's house at the weekend. She hadn't been looking forward to it particularly; she found it trying talking to strangers, but she suddenly thought it would be more bearable if she went with Krystof. The man had a gift – he seemed to lighten everything round him.

'Would you like to come to a party with me?' she asked.

'Will there be dancing?' he asked.

'Maybe,' she said.

'Will you dance with me?'

'I might,' she said.

'Then I would be delighted to attend. Now come and help me catch some mackerel,' said Krystof.

He was in his element. The sun shone on his face making it gleam and he walked along the boat as easily as if he was on solid ground. He helped her to the side and she was surprised by how quickly she became accustomed to the rolling motion of the deck. She still found it difficult to focus on a particular spot – looking from her feet and then out to the horizon made her feel light-headed. Krystof held the line between his finger and thumb, the reel firmly wedged under his arm.

'All we've got to do now is wait,' he said.

'How will you know if you've caught something?' she asked.

'It's not caught till it's in the boat,' said Krystof. 'You can feel the line going tight when something takes the bait.'

The fish were elusive. Nothing seemed to happen for ages and when, finally, in a sudden flurry of excitement, Krystof reeled the line in, all he had to show for it was a cod, too small to keep, that had to be thrown back into the water.

'I hope you don't mind me asking, but what happened to Ursula's father?' he asked, after they had abandoned fishing and Krystof had dispensed cold beer and a Coke for Ursula, who was already disposed to like him for supplying the much longed-for but usually forbidden beverage.

'He was just someone I had a short fling with. He wasn't interested in parenthood.' Rora trotted out the accustomed line.

'Are you in the habit of short flings?' asked Krystof, looking out to sea as he spoke as if he found the subject difficult.

'I am rather,' said Rora.

'Why is that do you think?' he asked, turning to look at her. His eyes in the full glare of the sun had resumed their golden hue. He looked as if he belonged on the boat, Rora thought, with the wind blowing his short hair up in tufts, his feet planted sol-idly on the deck, although she couldn't really imagine a place where he wouldn't look relaxed and exactly himself. He always seemed unperturbed, ready in an easy sort of a way for whatever might be in store.

'I've only ever had one near thing,' she said lightly. 'Other than that I haven't really met anyone who really got to me.'

'What would it take for someone to get to you?' asked Krystof softly.

'I'm not sure. Someone who really knew me and loved me despite it all,' she said jokingly, although she thought her answer was as close to the truth as she could manage. So many of her relationships had been based on not knowing and not being known, or at least being mistaken about the other person, often wilfully, so that each of them became the person they knew the other wanted them to be. It hadn't been like that with Carl. They had known the best and worst of each other. Ursula drank her second Coke with relish and then went to resume her duties at the wheel.

'Peter says I'm a natural,' she announced. She looked happier than she had for days and Rora smiled to see her face flushed with sugar and self-importance. At her best, with no shadows hanging over her, Ursula was able to recognise and enjoy pleasures as they arrived. Rora was glad of it. Other people didn't seem to find it as hard as Rora did to enter the moment and take it for what it was. She wondered why she was like this – always one step behind or one step ahead, never where she was supposed to be. She looked out at the sea and saw the beauty of it – the way it held itself apart, although it was all around her, in her mouth and on her skin – and tried to fix the look and feel of it.

The boat stopped and turned, beginning its journey back, and the movement made Rora stagger and lose her footing. Krystof caught hold of her and held her for a moment. Their faces were close together. She looked at the curve of his smiling mouth and suddenly there was something between them. A feeling as unexpected as the turn of the boat had been – a kind of waiting absence, as if something was on the edge of happening, like a drop of water hanging from a tap, or the tilt of a coin before it falls off the ledge into the bottom of an arcade game. The moment seemed to last forever. It hummed between them like static. She knew he wouldn't move to her. She lifted her mouth to his. She felt his intake of breath against her lips as if he was readying himself to plunge into deep water. There was a tender fierceness in his mouth and the wet, salty slide of his lips on hers made her want to push herself against him, but she held herself back – Ursula was nearby. She heard herself groan as they moved apart. He looked at her mouth and then looked away, as if it was too much for him. She felt disorientated, dizzy.

'I wasn't expecting that,' she said, her voice unsteady.

'I was hoping for it,' he said, and put his fingers into the high neck of her sweater and pulled the fabric aside and placed his mouth against the jumping pulse in her neck.

The sky had turned a strange inky blue when they arrived back and the clouds looked lit from behind with an unearthly golden glow.

'The weather's about to change,' said Peter as he helped them back down off the boat. 'The wind is northerly and it looks like rain.'

The crowds of earlier on in the day had thinned and the atmosphere had become more raucous as the pubs filled up and customers spilled out onto the litter-strewn streets.

'That was a perfect day,' said Ursula, her face still rosy, her curls in a great tangle around her head. 'I'm getting a boat when I'm older.'

233

They left Krystof at the harbour – he and Peter were going for a drink – and walked home.

'I liked Peter and Krystof,' said Ursula. 'Which one do you like better?'

'I don't really know Peter,' said Rora. 'I very much like Krystof.'

'I have a feeling he likes you too,' said Ursula.

'Did you use anything you'd brought in your bag?' asked Rora, seeing the speculative look on her daughter's face and keen to change the subject.

'I ate two bars of the chocolate and wiped some oil that had spilled on the floor with the toilet paper,' said Ursula.

When they got home Ursula fell asleep as soon as she got into bed, as if a light had been switched off.

The next day the rain still hadn't arrived. It seemed it never would. The promising wind had dropped and the air was as close and syrupy as it had been all month. On the streets and in the shops, people moved wearily, the elderly among them taking it in turns to fill up the benches, where they sat bemoaning the state of their gardens and their legs. Even the children seemed lacklustre, walking ten steps behind their parents, scuffing their tired feet along the ground.

Carl rang that afternoon and Rora was cold and uncommunicative, and so in the end he brought the awkward conversation to a halt. After he rang off Rora told herself that she had done the right thing. They couldn't be anything to each other now. He had someone else. Seeing him would only be hanging on to the past.

On the night of Hannah's party the weather was still holding fast against the rain. The air was full of grit and the sea had an oily sheen. Rora had a cool shower and then looked at her rather uninspiring collection of trousers and skirts. She didn't have time to go and get herself anything more suitable. She remembered seeing some of her mother's clothes crammed into the back of the wardrobe in her father's room and wondered if there might just be something she could wear. She still thought of the room as Frank's, even though there was nothing of him there now that she had moved his books and clothes and turned and aired the mattress so that even the shape he had left there had flattened out against the slats of the bed.

She found a few droopy dresses and some gaudy cardigans with mismatched buttons, but right at the very back was a dress she hadn't ever seen her mother wearing. It was made of green silk and was full-skirted with a narrow belt and a scooped neckline. It looked as if it had never been worn. Rora wondered what had prompted the purchase of a dress that was so unlike her normal garb, and why, having bought it, her mother had never worn it. She felt suddenly sad that there was no one left to ask. Perhaps it had been Isobel's – it looked like the sort of thing she might have worn in her youth. It was possible she had given it to Sandi in an attempt to wean her from her hippyish flounces. It fitted Rora as if it had been made for her, revealing the creamy line of her shoulders and her neat waist. When she looked in the mirror she found herself wondering what Krystof would think of it and was aware of a fluttering feeling of anticipation. She thought of the way he had held her, gathered up in his arms. She put on her mother's single earring and the garnet gleamed against the green.

'You look the most beautiful you have ever looked,' said Ursula seriously when Rora came downstairs to show herself off. 'You should wear that dress every day.'

'It might get a bit smelly,' said Rora, and chased a giggling Ursula into her room to get changed.

Krystof came to pick them up at eight. He paused on the step when Rora opened the door, as if he had been pinned back by a gust of air. He looked distant, as if he was remembering something rather than seeing what was in front of him.

'You look magnificent,' he said at last.

'Not like me at all, is it?' asked Rora.

'On the contrary, I think you look more yourself than ever before,' said Krystof.

He took her hands in his. She thought he might kiss her, but Ursula came bounding down the stairs in her neon shorts and sparkly top and they set off.

Hannah's blowsy garden was ablaze with lights. They were draped over the trees and shrubs and over the back door and the roof of the shed. Ursula went off to find Robyn and her sister and the other couple of friends that had been invited along. They started dancing in the front room in that unselfconsciously aware way of all girls that age – part child abandoned to the moment, and part teenager-in-the-making, ready to mock before someone else got in first.

There were a few people there that Rora knew through Hannah and some that she remembered from school. It was surprising how many of them had stayed in the town. It seemed Hastings hung onto its inhabitants like it hung onto the mists that gathered in the glen above the town and the grass that grew to the very edge of the cliff. She wandered from group to group introducing Krystof to the people she knew, and then the two of them took themselves off to explore the rambling garden. The long thin plot was a reflection of her friend's personality – each section led on to another, revealing itself fully at the very bottom where she had created a convivial space with a table and chairs and high hedges and a chiminea that burned with some sweet-smelling wood. They lingered there and between them there was the same static fizz that she had experienced on the boat. A fearful yet pleasurable anticipation of what they knew was to come. Rora felt the silk of her dress against her legs and the warmth of the night on her arms and throat. She felt beautiful and complete in herself in a way that she hadn't for a long time.

'I think I'm falling in love with you,' he said, and she felt an uncurling sensation inside her as if something was becoming unspooled. She didn't quite know how to answer him. She wasn't sure she could trust her fledgling feeling.

'Are you?' she said helplessly, trying to get the measure of him and of herself.

'Here you are! Look who I found lurking in the hedgerow!' said Hannah, who had a strange note in her voice – she sounded uncharacteristically nervous. Following on behind Hannah were the woman from the party at the pub and Carl. Rora was aware of the curious glances that were being cast in his direction by those people who had known him when he was a boy.

'I worked with Serena for two years at my last job,' said Hannah, looking studiously away from Rora, 'and it turns out she's seeing your old friend Carl.'

'Hello, Rora,' Carl said, and there it was again, the irrepressible twist of her heart as he spoke. The way he sabotaged her without even trying made her furious with herself and with him.

'Nice to meet you, Serena,' she said. 'This is my friend Krystof.' She spoke as perfunctorily as possible, wanting them both to go, wanting the evening the way it had been at the beginning. She could see Carl looking at Krystof with an assessing air, which flustered her.

'Well, just thought I'd get you all together,' said Hannah, looking at the group uneasily. 'I've got to go and mingle.'

Typical, thought Rora savagely. She throws a grenade and then pisses off.

'Have you two known each other for a long time?' asked Krystof, and Rora could tell he was a little puzzled by her awkwardness and her silence.

'We've known each other since we were at school together,' said Carl and he looked at her in the old, intent way as if there was nothing else in the world worth seeing. His face was unreadable but she could feel the tension in him.

'How nice! School friends!' said Serena kindly, but Rora disliked her voice with its sexy mid-sentence inhalation and the way her dress fell off her shoulder. Rora was floundering, trying to think of the best way of getting away, when she heard Ursula calling for her.

'I must just go . . .' she started, taking hold of Krystof's arm and almost dragging him along with her, but someone must have told Ursula where she was because a moment later her daughter emerged through the arched passageway.

'Mum,' said Ursula, her hair in a post-dance tangle, 'Robyn says she wants to go to bed now. Do I *have* to go with her? I'm so much older.'

'Well, that was the agreement,' said Rora, moving to her daughter so that she blocked her from the view of the others.

'I *really* don't want to go to bed yet. I'm not tired. The night is still young.'

Serena moved to Rora's side, laughing at Ursula's turn of phrase.

'I like that,' she said, her dress slipping down further to reveal inches of silky flesh. 'The night is still young,' she repeated in her silly voice. Rora felt her teeth clench.

'Why don't we go back to the house and discuss it?' she said.

'Robyn has no stamina,' said Ursula, trying out the new word.

'Something tells me that you have lots of stamina,' said Serena, bending towards Ursula in the way that people without children often do, as if they think it will help them to feel less intimidated. Ursula looked at her without smiling.

'I have, actually,' she said as if she suspected that the woman was laughing at her.

'I didn't know you had a daughter,' said Carl, and she could feel him moving forward to look at Ursula.

'Nice to meet you Ursula,' he said. She took his extended hand, a small frown between her eyebrows.

'Who are you?' she asked Carl.

'I'm an old friend of your Mum's,' he said.

'She's never mentioned you,' said Ursula.

'Well, I haven't seen her for a long time.'

'Let's go back to the house,' said Rora.

Ursula had a change of heart and decided she would like to go to bed after all, and so Rora went upstairs with her. All the promise of the evening had evaporated. Her dress was crumpled, the lights seemed suddenly garish. She felt hot and out of sorts, as if she might be sickening for something.

'Can we go home?' she asked Krystof when she came back downstairs. 'Would you mind very much if we cut the evening short?'

'Of course not,' Krystof said. She thought he seemed subdued. They walked home in silence. The day had been breathless, but now the wind suddenly picked up and a few minutes later, with almost no warning, it started to rain. They were both quickly soaked through, although Krystof seemed oblivious. He walked solidly on with his head down.

'Carl's the near miss, isn't he?' Krystof said suddenly, stopping in his tracks.

'What makes you say that?' asked Rora.

'I don't know . . . The way he looked at you. Your reaction to him.'

The trees along the road bent, one after the other, as if a giant hand had stroked the tops of them as he walked by. The rattle of the leaves, the creaking of the branches, the sound of a siren suddenly nearby all seemed horribly loud. Rora could feel the rain hitting her back. It had been too hot to wear a cardigan or even a shawl and she was exposed to the cruel fall of it, coming in great unforgiving sheets as if something held back had at last been released. The smell of wet dust and slowly melting earth was sweet and brackish.

'He was my nearest miss,' she admitted at last. 'But it was a long time ago . . . everything has changed . . .'

'It didn't look as if much has changed at all, not from where I was standing,' said Krystof, and he wiped angrily at his face with the sleeve of his shirt.

'It's complicated. It always was,' said Rora. 'We have this kind of can't be with each other, can't be apart sort of a relationship. It isn't a grown-up thing. It was because we were children together.'

Krsytof turned from her and started walking again. He was moving so fast that Rora struggled to keep up with him.

'Slow down!' she said.

'I thought there was something happening between us,' he said.

'There is. I think . . . I'm not sure,' said Rora, and he stopped again.

'Are you going to see him?' he asked, and looking at the stern lines of his face she wondered that she had ever thought him comical. She saw that despite his lightness and his almost child-ish openness, he knew his worth. With the rain falling on him he looked intact, immovable.

'I don't think I really want to,' she said, and then paused.

There was something about Krystof that made her want to tell the truth – she knew that the games she had become so adept at playing over the years would not impress him in the slightest.

'If there's anything between us still, it is a battered old thing. It's almost a habit in me to react to him. I can't really seem to help it.'

'I think you know how I feel about you,' said Krystof, 'but I don't think we should see each other until you have worked out what you want. My heart can't take it.' He spoke simply, but Rora heard the metal in his voice. An instinct for self-protection had triggered a new wariness. She found herself feeling sad that his good opinion of her had faltered.

'Did you come back to Hastings hoping that he would still be here?' he asked.

'No. I really didn't know he would be here,' she said, and she caught hold of one of his hands. 'It's like an echo of something. It's not real. We shared something once and it tied us together.'

'Maybe you should listen to the echo,' said Krystof and pulled his hand away and walked on at his previous hectic pace, so that before she knew it they were at her front door and he had said goodbye and gone.

The house in Pilgrim Street was loud with rain and wind. The chimney in the living room whistled and moaned and the windows rattled. All alone and as chilled as if she had been immersed in freezing water, Rora felt adrift. What am I even doing here? she thought. Where's my place? Not here in this house saturated with memories, but not, it seemed, anywhere else either. She peeled off the green dress and hung it up. Wrapped in a blanket from the cupboard, she went to run a bath. She lay in the water for a long time, topping it up as it cooled, so that after a while she felt formless, as if she was part of the watery night. There was no dam or stopping place – she would run with the rain through pipes and in gushing rivulets, down sloping roads to the sea.

Kiss 15

'The threat lay in what he could make her feel and hope for.'

5 July 2010

After a couple of days of procrastination, when she changed her mind almost from hour to hour, Rora finally decided that Krystof was right – she had to listen to the echo. She owed it to Carl at least to spend some time with him and work out if the way she reacted to him – that instinctive leap her body made – was simply due to the remnants of an old infatuation. They had been two lonely, abandoned children who had found solace and courage in each other's company. He had protected her. She had never even thanked him for that, although she couldn't imagine what she could possibly say now, so long afterwards, that would properly express what it had meant for her and for Ursula. She remembered the letters; she had them somewhere still; her private, unread account of sorrow and guilt.

Even though her head was full of Carl, she thought of the way the world fell into place around Krystof in the exact shape it was meant to be, and she knew that he could provide the stopping point that part of her yearned for. Beneath his dark grace and new confidence she knew Carl was still belligerent, still tightly braced against possible harm. They hadn't been good for each other, although for a while it had felt as if they were.

Maybe she should remain single and free from the burden of feeling too much. She and Ursula had managed perfectly well on their own, and the occasional stranger drifting through to provide a passing, counterfeit thrill had been enough for her. But then she thought about what her father had said about making her story as good as it could be. Perhaps it was time to test his theory about her capacity for love.

There hadn't been anyone since Nick, and that had been less about love and more about accommodation. In those days it was Nick's brand of ease and entitlement that she looked for in a man because it made her relax. Despite his inherent coldness, she had found it hard to tell him she couldn't be with him anymore. While he was at work she had packed away the few things she had accumulated in his flat and left the bag in the hall. He always noticed when things were out of place and she thought seeing it there would be a way of preparing him for what was to come. She didn't love him but she didn't want to hurt him, and she hated the idea of letting him walk into the room unaware and unarmed. She found witnessing other people's vulnerability difficult, almost painful. She had taken off her ring while she was waiting for him and was holding it so tightly in her hand that she could feel the imprint of it against her palm. He thought she was joking at first.

'Don't wind me up, Rora. Just tell me what's bothering you,' he said, and she heard again the doctor's edge to his voice. *Now, Mrs Lowther, what seems to be the problem?* She thought that at any moment he would put one of his cool, cuffed hands against her forehead.

'I thought it was what I wanted,' she said.

'We're getting married in three months,' he said.

'I'm sorry,' she said, and wished that she could at least cry.

It took him a little while, but then his features softened into the shock of it and she saw that he believed her. He only allowed himself a brief falter, like a dancer disguising a moment of wrong-footedness with a new spin, an extra turn, and then once more he was in control.

'I couldn't let us carry on,' said Rora, trying to explain.

'No, indeed. Although it might have been better if you had thought to put a stop to it before we sent out two hundred and fifty wedding invitations.'

'I'm sorry,' she said again.

'I suggest you work out exactly what it is you do want, Rora,' he said, and she was relieved to hear the bitterness in his voice.

Rora arranged for Ursula to spend the night at Hannah's and then rang Carl and suggested that they meet in a pub on the High Street. He was waiting for her at a corner table, sitting with his arm along the top of the bench, his legs crossed. She wasn't fooled for a minute by his air of relaxation. She went to the bar to get a bottle of wine and she could feel him looking at her. It made her self-conscious and she was aware of standing stiffly and of smiling too much at the barman. She had only been in his company for a few minutes and he was making her act like a teenager again.

'Thanks for agreeing to meet up,' she said, sitting down at the table and pouring them both a glass of wine. To her annoyance, she could feel a slight tremor in her hand and hoped he hadn't noticed.

'There's no need to be nervous of me,' he said.

'I'm not!' she said indignantly, but she knew she was. Being with him unsettled her, made her feel unsure of herself in a way that no one else ever had.

'I've seen you take a piss in a lemonade bottle at the back of the school coach, remember,' she said, trying to regain her equilibrium.

He laughed and she was dazzled by the way the hard lines of his face softened.

'I could piss pretty much anywhere,' he said. 'Still can, as a matter of fact.'

'So, how long have you been working at the aquarium?' she asked and then almost instantly regretted her question.

'How did you know I was working there?' he said.

'Hannah told me,' she said. 'Actually, that's not true. I saw you there once when I was with Ursula and then . . . I came to see you and was told by your colleague Gary that you were . . . elsewhere.'

'Ah Gary, the man who can make stacking leaflets an act of war,' said Carl.

'I came to find you at the pub when you were setting up for a party,' said Rora, wondering why she was disclosing this. It made her sound like a stalker.

'I didn't see you there,' he said.

'No. You were otherwise occupied,' said Rora, cross with herself for sounding so prissy. He looked at her and then he laughed again.

'You caught me dancing with Serena,' he said, looking irritatingly delighted by her reaction.

'Something like that,' Rora said.

'To answer your question, I've been working there for eight months or so. I was lucky to get a job . . .' He paused and went on, 'but I did an online course in marine biology and the friend of a friend recommended me. I love the job.'

'That's brilliant,' Rora said, thinking about the schoolboy who had thrown books and spent hours in detention.

'That's enough about me. Tell me about that bloke you were with at Hannah's party.'

'Krystof's a friend. I met him when I first arrived back in Hastings,' Rora said, blushing slightly under his scrutiny.

'Hmm . . . he looked a little too suspiciously at me to be just a friend.'

'Don't be silly. He didn't look at you any way at all.'

'Who's Ursula's father?' Carl asked.

'A man I spent one night with,' Rora said, topping up her glass of wine so that she didn't have to look at him as she spoke.

'Have there been many of those?' he asked, and she thought he sounded sad.

'I was seeing someone until relatively recently, a doctor. We were engaged, actually, but I broke it off,' she said, not wanting him to think she slept around, although she felt she had.

'A doctor . . . let me guess, reassuring manner, dab hand in the kitchen, frequent romantic breaks away, lager drinker, immaculately ironed polo shirts . . . what happened?

'I didn't love him,' she said.

'What possessed you to agree to marry him, then?' asked Carl. He had dropped his teasing tone and was looking at her closely.

'I don't know. It was the easy option. He was decent, good to me. I had no reason to turn him down.'

'Except that you didn't love him, the poor sod,' said Carl.

'I think that was the main attraction,' said Rora.

Carl had been fiddling around with his beer mat but when Rora spoke he became very still.

'Is that what you look for in a partner?' he said. 'Someone who leaves you cold?'

'My father stopped living after my mother died, and ... I don't need to tell you what can happen when you care too much,' said Rora.

The relaxed, almost mocking lines of his face changed at her words and he looked suddenly sombre.

'We were so young,' he said.

'We still knew right from wrong,' she said. Carl made a strange gesture with his hands as if he was warding off the memories her words were conjuring up. He looked vulnerable, just as he had all those years ago. This was why being together was impossible – they would be continually hauled back to the past as if they were tethered to it with rope.

'Why didn't you read my letters?' she asked suddenly, as if the question had burst out of her.

'I couldn't bear to. It would have been too much for me,' Carl said. 'I preferred to imagine you living a perfect life, somewhere a long way away from here.'

'How could I?' she asked and she met his eyes, feeling her own fill with tears. He reached over and touched her face. And there it was again, that same push-me-pull-you feeling of attraction that was also a kind of repulsion. He would forever be part of what she felt the most ashamed of in her life and the shadow hung over them, tainting them, despite the wine and the banter, despite the way he made her feel.

'Let's go for a walk,' he said. 'We'll take what's left of the bottle and find somewhere nice to sit.'

They walked along the front. The evening sun was hazy, the sea as still as a pond. People strolled hand in hand, lulled by the soft air and the romance of the seaside, into silence. They walked as far as Pelham Crescent and stopped at a bench by the crazy golf course. They talked about her father and about his aunt Mo, who had died five years ago, and her writing and his new hobby of BASE-jumping.

'What's that?' Rora asked, remembering how he used to look as a boy when enthusiasm for something took hold of him.

'It's basically parachuting from tall things,' he said. 'To call yourself a BASE jumper you have to have launched yourself off a building, an antenna tower, a bridge and a cliff. Building, Antenna, Span and Earth, hence the name.'

'Have you done all four kinds of jump?' asked Rora.

'Not yet. I'm a novice. I've only done three jumps, all in Norway.'

'What's the appeal?' she asked.

'It's hard to explain. Planning a jump is always very compli-cated. You need to focus on the detail – the equipment, where you are going to land. I like that bit. And then, during the actual jump, just before the parachute opens, I feel great. Like I'm untouchable.'

'I don't see how you can feel great when you are hurtling towards the ground moments away from being smashed to bits,' said Rora.

'It might sound strange, but it's almost peaceful,' he said.

He was still trying to find ways of diverting the pain. People never really change, Rora thought. They became better at hiding what they were, but that was all. Carl got out his phone and showed her a picture taken just after he had landed a jump from a cliff. He was running, body tilted against the weight of the tangled parachute trailing on the ground behind him. His face was transformed by some great feeling, a kind of fierceness that looked more like pain than pleasure. He was sharply in focus; the background was a blur. She felt that this was what would happen if they were together. He would be the sharp brightness that would make everything else but him indistinct. She felt afraid. She recognised him as the danger she had spent so long protecting herself from. The threat lay in what he could make her feel and hope for.

They lapsed into silence, passing the bottle between them until it was finished. An elderly couple passed by and smiled at them – almost identical beams, as if their years together had merged their happiness.

'Have you ever been in love, Rora?' Carl asked.

'I'm not sure,' she said.

'I loved you,' he said and looked at her, his face guarded.

She leaned towards him and put her mouth on his. She was aware briefly of his eyes widening, his face registering surprise. Almost as soon as their lips met, she became dizzy with lust. It was as if some longing she hadn't been aware of was switched on in her. She pushed her mouth hard against his, wanting to dispel his cautious, watchful air. It wasn't him creating the urgent pace between them. If anything she could feel him holding himself back from her, as if he knew he was on the edge of something he wasn't ready for, or as if he was too tense, too tentative to allow his body proper expression. It seemed to her that she couldn't get close enough to satisfy her overwhelming hunger for the shape and the feel of him. Everything she wanted seemed to be centered on his mouth, his tongue. The wine on his breath tasted like the honey from the gorse that blazes so brightly in certain evening lights; from the sea it looks as if the cliffs are on fire. She thought of walking with him there when they were children, and something turned in her and then settled. It might even have been love.

Kiss 16

'It was like the essence of a kiss.'

9 July 2010

Rora threw herself into working on her father's book. It allowed her to escape from her thoughts, which, left to their own devices, ran through her head on a maddening loop. When she and Carl had parted a couple of days before, he had said he was leaving it to her to decide whether or not they should see each other again.

'What about Serena?' Rora had asked.

'Serena's not the jealous type,' Carl said, but Rora remembered the other woman's brittle voice and tight face and wondered if he was right.

Rora had spent most of the intervening days exploring the places her father had written about. It calmed her to keep moving and she felt she was walking alongside him when she identified the section of wall in which a baby's body wrapped in brown paper had been buried 200 years before. Or when she stood on the site of the workhouse in which people had been forced to break boulders to earn their breakfast, or tried to find the remnants of the stone that used to be called Lover's Seat, which once jutted out of the East Cliff. These expeditions felt like her father's gift to her – as if he was offering her a new version of the town she had learned to despise.

She was deep in her work when she heard the letterbox rattle and went to collect whatever had been delivered. The envelope was addressed to Ursula in childish handwriting, with a smiley face in the corner where a stamp should be. It looked like a party invitation, hand-delivered. She gave it to Ursula as she was eating her lunch and watched as she opened it. Ursula read it without saying anything, then flung it down on the table with a wail.

'What's wrong? Who's it from?' Rora asked and picked it up to read herself. The note was unsigned, but it was clear where it originated.

You are a sneaky bitch and we know where you are.
From Your Enemies.

'How did they find out where I live?' asked Ursula, her face white and anguished. She had been so much happier since the decision had been made for her not to return to Mayfield, but now she looked as tense and stricken as she had when Rora first discovered what had been going on.

'Don't worry, Ursula, I'll sort it out,' Rora said as calmly as she could manage, but she felt a terrible sorrow on Ursula's behalf. As soon as you let your children out into the world they were vulnerable in all sorts of ways you never imagined.

Ms Lincoln was her usual evasive self on the phone until Rora raised her voice, and then she hastily promised to look into it. She said she had already talked to all the girls involved and they had been excluded for a week.

'In addition, we are running a workshop on bullying,' she said, 'and we've put a new bench in the playground called "Bully Buddy" where people can go if they are being bullied.'

'That'll help a great deal,' said Rora sarcastically. 'Soon the Mayfield playground will be lined with useless benches. You ought to have one for children suffering with terrible head teachers.'

'I don't think that's a very helpful attitude,' Ms Lincoln replied.

'What I would like to know is how the girls, including your daughter, know where we live and how they are able, at their age, to walk around town posting vile letters.'

'I'll look into it,' said Ms Lincoln in her squeaky, childlike voice.

'I want a phone call back before the end of the day,' said Rora and put the phone down.

She spent the afternoon cuddled up on the sofa with Ursula. After popcorn and the inevitable *Calamity Jane*, they looked through some old photo albums that had pictures of Isobel on her wedding day with a bunch of daises clutched in her hands, and pictures of Sandi and Frank – at a party with a group of other young people with smooth, shining faces, Sandi smiling exuberantly on the back of a camel, and then the two of them, arm in arm, under what looked like an apple blossom tree. Frank was wearing a wide-brimmed hat and Sandi was in the green dress Rora had worn to Hannah's party.

Ms Lincoln rang at the end of the afternoon. 'It seems that my daughter got her older brother to deliver the letter,' she said. 'How she got hold of the address I'm not sure, although she often sits in the office and waits for me if I'm not quite ready to leave . . .' Her voice trailed off miserably. Rora almost felt sorry for her.

'It was a joint effort with a couple of the other girls, but it does seem, I'm afraid, that she was the driving force . . .'

'Will they come here again?' asked Ursula when Rora reported back on what the head teacher had said.

'I'm sure they won't,' said Rora, but Ursula didn't look convinced.

'But they know where I am,' she said, her face pinched and her mouth trembling, and Rora had to promise to lie beside her on the bed until she was asleep, which took so long that Rora fell asleep herself and woke disorientated in the middle of the night with a crick in her back.

Hannah came round the following evening with a bottle of rum and a large bag of midget gems – a Hannah gastronomic special that was surely not going to end well.

'I thought hard liquor and sweets were the perfect antidote to the bullying blues,' she said, kicking off her shoes and collapsing at the kitchen table. Robyn had received an almost identical letter to Ursula, although hers was embellished with a yellowish stain and an arrow pointing to it, with the word 'WEE' in capitals.

'It's hard to imagine that nine-year-old children could be so inventively horrible,' she said, taking a gulp of the rum that Rora had poured out for her.

'I think Mia Lincoln has been driven to madness by her mother's voice,' said Rora.

'I kissed him,' Rora said when they were on their third shot of rum.

'Who? Your lovely Polish chap?' Hannah asked. She was curled up on the sofa neatly, her feet tucked under her. Rora felt a wave of affection for her friend. She might be a little blunt and heedless, but she had always been there when Rora needed her. Well, almost always – they had fallen out briefly when Hannah had found out about Rora's pregnancy.

'Why are you throwing yourself away like this?' she had asked, bewildered by Rora's new impenetrable face and remote voice. She hadn't realised that Rora had been barely coping and the only way she could get through the days was to let in only what was absolutely necessary. Rora remembered that she had felt jealous of Hannah's young, unblemished skin and her stories of misguided shags and her comprehensive knowledge of all the places in London you could go to get a fry-up at three in the morning. She had felt old in comparison.

'I'm not throwing myself away,' she had said. 'I'm rescuing myself.'

'How is having a baby at nineteen, on your own, rescuing yourself?' Hannah asked.

'You don't understand,' Rora said.

'No, I bloody don't,' Hannah said.

They bonded again over Ursula's tufty black hair and her seashell nails and the disconcerting sight of Rora's swollen, blue veined breasts. When Hannah met Rich and married him absurdly young and fell pregnant with Robyn around the time of her graduation, Rora refrained from reminding her how horrified she had been over Rora's early pregnancy. She sometimes wondered if spending so much time with Ursula had accelerated Hannah's desire to have children.

'Carl . . . well . . . both of them actually,' Rora said.

'Rora Raine!' exclaimed Hannah. 'You utter trollop.'

'Who the heck uses the world "trollop"?' Rora asked, smiling at her friend's scandalised expression.

'I do,' Hannah said, leaning forward eagerly to hear the details. 'I can't believe you are even countenancing the thought of Carl.'

'I'm not sure countenancing is quite the right word,' said Rora.

'You've got to prefer Krystof, surely,' Hannah said. 'Those lovely eyes. The sweet way he bows his head when he is asking something. Not to mention his way with almond biscuits.'

'I don't know,' Rora said. 'I think I might see what happens with me and Carl . . .'

'Oh my giddy aunt,' Hannah said. 'You're walking straight back into trouble. I can't keep up with you. I shall have to live my life vicariously through your exploits. The most exciting thing that has happened to me recently is that Rich and I have decided to have sex on Wednesday night now instead of Saturday morning, to be more spontaneous.'

'Would you be really kind and babysit for me tomorrow night?' Rora asked. 'Seeing as it's not Wednesday.'

'I really hope you know what you're doing, Rora,' Hannah said.

'That's just it, I don't,' said Rora, trying to ignore Hannah's worried look.

The rain had finally come, although it wasn't the deluge that had been forecast, only a damp, penetrating drizzle, and as Rora walked to the restaurant to meet Carl she could feel her shoulders getting wet through her thin jacket. The town had emptied as if it was on a curfew, leaving the streets to the odd dog walker and the clumps of teenagers who were not deterred by the weather when staying in was the only other option. He smiled when he saw her, but she could tell even before she sat down that he was tense.

'This is the only halfway decent place that had a free table,' he said.

'It's fine,' she said, and hung her damp jacket over the back of the chair.

'I wanted to take you somewhere better,' he said.

'Honestly, it's perfectly all right. I can eat anything,' she said, although the sight of him had caused her stomach to lurch in such a way that she thought it unlikely that she would have any sort of appetite. His hair was slightly wet and she could see a small razor cut on his cheek.

'It's as if the staff are zombies,' he said. 'It took ten minutes to get anyone to come and take a drink order from me.'

She recognised this restless, discontented Carl. He had always fretted when things were not as he had imagined they would be. She remembered he had become furious one night when they had gone together to see the fireworks in nearby Lewes. He had paid with great ceremony and some pride for both of them to go on the bus, but when they arrived it had rained hard all evening and the much vaunted fireworks were largely shrouded in fog. Although she was happy enough to get wet, and even enjoyed the smoke and mystery of the evening, he was unable to shuck off his disappointment and remained moody and uncommunicative.

'I wanted it to be perfect for you,' he said sadly in the bus on the way back.

Rora dressed more carefully this evening than she usually did. She had chosen a claret dress with a wide, scooped neck and long silver earrings that reached down as far as her collarbone. She had taken off the little key she usually wore around her neck. She didn't want him to know that she had worn it all this time. When she sat down she saw his eyes move over her face and then in a glancing way at the skin of her throat and the hollow between her breasts. His expression as he did so was strange, distracted. The contemptuous young waiter who dawdled with their drinks and got their orders wrong made Carl angry again until he saw that both his irritation and the waiter's absurd rudeness were making Rora laugh and so he relaxed a little. They ate the soggy pizzas with the random toppings they had been given without demurring and shared a carafe of red wine.

'Tell me what it is you like about this Krystof, then,' said Carl, trying and failing to sound offhand.

'He's kind,' she said, not wanting to talk about him to Carl because it made her feel disloyal.

'Kind. That's a terrible sort of a word. You say it about people when there's nothing much else to say about them.'

'That's not true. Kindness is the most important quality in a person,' said Rora. 'You're kind too.'

'Nothing could be further from the truth,' Carl said and his face grew sombre.

'What are Serena's good qualities?' she asked, keen to get Carl away from the subject of Krystof. 'Apart, that is, from her gorgeous face and splendid shoulders?'

'So you noticed those, did you?' said Carl laughing at her, and she was glad to see he had reverted to teasing mode.

'Well, she's very pretty,' she said, remembering with a stab of jealousy that surprised her with its intensity the way they had danced together across the pub floor.

'She's a good marine biologist too, and looks damn fine in a wetsuit.'

'I'm surprised you have made the time to come out with me, then,' said Rora coldly.

'That's another thing I remember about you,' said Carl smiling broadly. 'Your extreme haughtiness.'

'I'm not haughty!' she protested.

'You're like an ice queen when you choose to be. You give the best withering looks I've ever been on the end of,' he said, resting his elbow on the table and looking at her. Rora found it hard to stop looking at his mouth with its soft, curved, top lip, which contrasted with the stern lines of his face. It was as if, despite himself, his mouth was betraying a gentleness that he was trying his best to keep in check. At that moment, the last thing Rora felt like was an ice queen. She was astonished by the strength of the longing that swept through her. She wanted him to lean across the table and press that devastating mouth against hers more than she could ever remember wanting anything. He must have seen something in her face because he reached out and took her hand and then looking at her, he slowly traced one finger up and down her bare arm.

'Shall we go?' he asked and she nodded her assent, not sure she could altogether trust her voice. Carl insisted on paying the bill, and so Rora left an extravagantly large tip for their grim waiter and they went out laughing at his astonished face. Carl suggested a walk, despite the drizzly mist, and they made for an old haunt as if by instinct.

Battered by storms and beset by financial difficulties, the pier had been deemed unsafe and had been shut for several years, but Carl, with his usual disregard of the rules, persuaded her to wriggle through a gap in the fence at the entrance.

'Do you really think we should be doing this?' Rora asked, knowing that he would ignore her objections. 'What if our extra weight causes the whole thing to crumble?'

'It'll be fine,' Carl said, and so they made their way along, taking care to step over the gaps where the boards had given way. Beneath them the sea churned and sucked as if it was trying to claim for itself what was left of the shaky edifice. Despite the bedraggled ballroom and the peeling railings, the pier still had glamour, like a woman whose looks have faded but whose bone structure still hints at her past beauty. The wind from the sea was icy, but Rora barely felt it. When they got to the end of the walkway, on the other side of the pavilion, Carl stopped and took her hand. They stood for a moment, looking at the mysterious dark swell of the waves. The wind skimmed the surface, throwing up a fine spray that wet their faces.

'Are you cold?' he asked, putting his arm around her.

'No,' she said and turned her face to him and her hair had gathered a thousand glittering drops.

'Come on, I'll walk you back to Pilgrim Street – you're shivering,' he said.

'Can't we go back to your place?' Rora asked, surprised at her own boldness.

'I don't think that is such a good idea,' he said.

'Why not?'

'This is us you're talking about, Rora. You're not just some woman I have sex with and then decide the next morning that I don't like her laugh or her politics or the way she brushes her teeth, and then spend several weeks trying to disentangle myself from.'

'Do you even try and talk to women before you go to bed with them?' she asked.

'Of course I do,' said Carl. 'I'm not a complete sleaze.'

'I mean proper talking. Not just rubbish about how beautiful their eyes are. Or how much you admire a woman who can hold her drink.'

'Don't be ridiculous,' said Carl, although he didn't sound terribly convincing.

'My feet are so cold I can't feel them,' said Rora.

'We'll go back for a drink and then I'll get a taxi for you,' he said, as if he knew he was making a bad decision.

They walked down the almost deserted streets to Carl's flat, which was a grand name for what was just a room with a partitioned-off kitchen and a bathroom attached. It had a tiny balcony with a view over a roundabout and a Kwik Fit garage. Rora sat on the sofa while Carl unearthed a half bottle of whisky from the back of the kitchen cupboard. The place was almost completely empty. There were a few books on the shelf and some clothes hanging on a rail in the corner of the room. Carl's wash things were in a sponge bag in the bathroom and his rucksack and boots were by the door. It was a place made for a quick exit, not a place for living in.

'You have quite a minimalist style,' said Rora.

'I don't really need that much,' he said, handing her a glass of whisky.

'I've got to get my shoes off,' Rora said and shucked them off along with the wet tights that had turned her feet a bright, painful red. She considered her feet ugly and was a little shy of exposing them to Carl's scrutiny, but she knew she had to get them warm. Carl looked at them and then fell back in mock horror.

'They are truly awful aren't they?' Rora said. 'I keep them covered so as not to upset small children.'

'What you need is a footbath,' he said, and ignoring her protests he set about filling the plastic basin at the sink, carefully putting a tea towel on the floor before placing the warm water down.

'Are you sure you want my trotters in your washing-up bowl?' she asked.

'Just do as you are told,' he said, and sprinkled baking soda and salt into the hot water and stirred it round.

'How come you have baking soda in your cupboard? Can't imagine you rustling up a Victoria sponge,' said Rora, feeling the warmth of the water penetrating her frozen feet.

'The last person left it behind,' he said. 'I sometimes use it after long hikes. It works like magic.'

When the water had cooled Carl got a towel from the bathroom and then sat down next to Rora on the sofa and spread it over his knee.

'Take your feet out, one at a time,' he said, 'and put them here.'

Rora did as she was told and he rubbed them, carefully drying between each of her toes. The touch of his hand on her feet was light and yet it set a tremor along her legs.

She caught hold of his hand and held it and he looked at her for a long time, as if he was trying to read what was in her face.

'I can't resist you,' he said.

He gathered Rora's still wet hair up with one hand and held it so tightly that she could feel water dripping down inside her collar. He rubbed his thumb on the back of her neck, tracing a line from the bone to the silky first hairs. Rora undid the back of her dress and let it fall from her shoulders and his mouth went to her skin as if it was seeking somewhere to rest. His breath and lips mapped her out, finding the hollows and the ridges of her throat and then the soft curves of her upper arms.

'So beautiful,' he said, his voice deep and unsteady.

'Carl, I need to tell you something,' Rora said.

'Tell me later,' he said, his face soft and dazed.

She took him by the hand and led him to the bed. He stumbled slightly as if he wasn't quite in control of his body. They lay down next to each other and then Carl sat up and leaned over her so that his face was at right angles to hers. No part of his body touched her other than his lips, which he laid softly against her mouth. With the absence of other distractions, with no rub of skin on skin or grind of limb against limb, all sensation was focused on the slide, the swell, the push of their lips. It felt like something new and something innocent. It was like the essence of a kiss. A kiss distilled.

They kissed as if they didn't need to breathe, and then his mouth came down harder and she felt the thrust of his tongue between her lips, then the sting of her bottom lip against his teeth. At last, as if he could no longer help it, his hands were on her, cupping her chin, his fingers in her mouth, in her hair. Her skin sang against the roughness of his cheek and her body arched towards him as he stroked the top of her breasts. She felt a spread and a beat between her legs. She pushed him back then, wanting to slow down her own reaction, which felt too hot and fast. She got on top of him and he looked at her and made a kind of hissing sound as if the pressure was too great, the sensation too acute. She found the seam of his jeans and rubbed herself against him so that he bucked beneath her and his arms went around her back to hold her closer. She rolled off him and put her hand into his waistband and then undid the fly, pulled down his boxer shorts and stroked the hard smoothness of him until he stilled her hands. Looking all the while at his face that was at once familiar and yet strange, she lowered herself onto him slowly. It was as if her body remembered his. As if the memory of how he felt against her had been imprinted. They matched each other movement for movement, rocking to their own immaculate beat, and she held him in her until she knew that one more motion would take them both. It came to them in one unstoppable quickening that spiralled so high it seemed for a moment as if they had been lifted up and then thrown back down. For a long time afterwards they laid still, as if stunned.

When Rora woke Carl wasn't in the bed and at first she thought he had left, but then she noticed that the door onto the balcony was ajar. She got up, wrapping the sheet around herself and went to join him. He was leaning on the rail looking out across the allotments that ran along the back of the flats. Each small piece of territory had been marked out with sheds and railway sleepers and concrete breeze blocks. Even from this distance you could see the differing personalities of the plot holders: some had neatly boxed beds with immaculate lines of vegetables, others had given over much of their soil space to tall purple poppies and couch grass. There was the odd supermarket trolley doubling up as a wheelbarrow and compost bins made out of wooden pallets topped with cardboard. These allotments didn't look much like the herb-lined patches in which TV chefs made marrow tasty with nothing more than an outdoor stove and the evening sun. Rora put her arm around Carl.

'Do you want a cup of tea?' she asked smiling at him, letting her sheet slip a little from around her shoulders in the hope that she might be able to tempt him back into bed.

'In a minute,' he said absently and looked away from her. She stood for a while with her head against his shoulder.

'It's strange isn't it, the way people mark up a bit of earth and make it their own,' he said. 'That plot over there has a kettle and a table and some sort of a lamp,' he said.

'I think a lot of people use allotments to escape,' she said. 'It's nothing to do with growing vegetables.'

'We all have to have our versions of that,' he said.

'Only if we have something we need to escape from,' said Rora.

The silence grew between them. Downstairs someone started playing the piano and then broke off abruptly.

'Why don't we just see what happens?' said Rora.

'Coming from Miss "Let's Make a List" that's almost funny,' he said without smiling. He looked at her in the flimsy covering and she could see the flare of desire in his face, which he quickly suppressed by turning away again.

'It might be best if we just walk away. Give each other the chance to start again,' he said. 'Being with each other would be like trying to stick together something that has shattered into a thousand pieces. We can never be perfectly one hundred per cent again.'

'We've only ever been ninety-eight per cent,' said Rora, trying to smile at him, although her heart had twisted at his words.

'I've spent these last few years thinking about you. Hoping that one day we could be together, but it is harder than I thought it was going to be,' Carl said.

Although Rora put her fingers inside his shirt and let her sheet drop so that he looked at her and groaned, and then picked her up in his arms and took her back inside, and although she felt her body melting as it always had when he touched her, his words lingered in her mind. Was it love she wanted from him, or just some sort of absolution? Was she hoping that being together would wipe them clean?

Kiss 17

'Their phantom kiss warmed the glass and she imagined that she could feel the press of his lips against hers.'

17 July 2010

On Sunday morning Carl rang and suggested that he take Ursula and Rora to the caves.

'I think we should take this thing a little slower. Let's see if we can do normal,' he said, and she knew he meant that he thought it would be safer if they did something that didn't involve drinking wine and ending up in his flat.

'We need to get to know each other again.'

'I'm not sure about the caves,' said Rora.

'Come on, Ursula will love it there.'

Ursula heard Rora say the word caves, and started jumping up and down. She had been asking to go there for weeks.

'Can we go? Pleeease.'

Carl heard Ursula and said, 'There you are. She's keen. We'll have fun.'

At around the time he was due to arrive it started raining again and Rora wondered if perhaps the weather would put him off – part of her would have been glad for the reprieve – but he arrived promptly at eleven, dressed in a waterproof jacket, the hood pulled over his head.

'Once we get inside we'll be fine,' he said in response to her suggestion that they might postpone. 'Anyway, it's due to ease off later.'

Ursula presented herself at the top of the stairs dressed in her red mac and matching sou'wester. Rora smiled to see that she had covered her bag with a shower hat.

'Clever!' said Carl admiringly, indicating Ursula's plastic-topped bag. 'You'd be great on an expedition.'

It was a very different town that they walked out into. After weeks of opened windows and doors left ajar, of fans blowing curtains aside and umbrellas shading pavement tables, the town had shut down and turned in on itself. A few harried families cursing their holiday timing walked with their heads down, their summer dresses covered with plastic ponchos. The roads had oily rainbows where idling cars had left their ghostly traces. A wedding party outside a church gathered round a gamely smiling bride in a strapless dress as she picked her way across the grass in sodden satin shoes.

They walked up the slippery steps to the West Hill, Ursula leading the way.

'Ursula's lovely,' Carl said to Rora. 'She's a miniature version of you.'

'Do you really think she's like me?' said Rora, her heart beating hard in her chest. 'I don't see it myself. I think it's just the hair.'

'She's a dead ringer,' said Carl.

'She was being bullied at school,' Rora said. 'She's stopped going there. Term finishes soon anyway.'

'Who was bullying her?' asked Carl.

'The head teacher's daughter, no less. She put stuff in her hair and pinched her and all sorts of other things.'

'Horrible creature,' Carl said. 'Do you want me to go to the school and give the head a good talking to?'

'No, it's fine. I'm dealing with it,' Rora said, almost smiling at the fierce look that had come over Carl's face. She could imagine him marching into the school and creating a scene – sweeping Ms Lincoln's rabbits off her desk, or punching a hole in the wall. When they reached the top of the stairs she felt hot and she stopped to take off her scarf. Carl stopped with her. His eyes went to her throat and neck to the key that was hanging from its silver chain. His eyes widened in surprise. He put his hand up to touch it.

'Is this what I think it is?' he asked, his mouth set in the old tender lines. She found she was close to tears.

'There's something I must tell you,' she said.

'Come on, you're being *really* slow,' shouted Ursula, who had retraced her steps to see what was holding them up.

From the top the town looked smeary and insubstantial. The sea, the sky and the roofs were one indeterminate grey, as if the rain had washed away the character of the place. They walked up the hill across spongy grass to the entrance of the caves, where two or three groups of people – drawn more by the promise of shelter than the instructional value of the museum – were waiting to go in. The air inside was humid and musty, as if despite the light displays and the mannequins and the push buttons activating information the earth still claimed the caves as its own and was only temporarily tolerating the artifice. Ursula seemed a little fearful at first, hiding behind Rora for protection.

'It's very dark,' she said nervously, as they walked down the first tunnel, past a somewhat unconvincing tableau of smugglers rolling barrels of rum across a beach. Carl acted as guide and his string of terrible jokes put Ursula at ease, so much so that she was soon darting ahead, pushing buttons and exclaiming in horrified fascination at the more sensational aspects of the exhibition. There was a skeleton, which sat up in a half-hearted fashion, and some flogging that involved a fair amount of technicolour gore and various bloody skirmishes with customs agents.

Carl took the opportunity when Ursula was otherwise occupied to put his arm around Rora. Her skin contracted as if a length of silk had been passed across it. She thought that perhaps now was the time to tell him, in the half dark so that he wouldn't be able to see her face clearly. Just then a group of people reached them, and they were forced to move on along the tunnel into the next cavern where lights illuminated the wall and the marks – the little scratchings made by smugglers or the soldiers who had taken refuge there during the war, or 21st-century vandals – were thrown into sharp relief. The jumbled story was evidence of the eternal impulse to make a mark, stake your ground, to leave something of yourself behind.

They came upon Ursula wearing a pair of comically large headphones, and the moment to tell him passed. They went to the gift shop and Ursula chose a plastic figure in smuggler's stripes and a postcard of the gallows where the hapless men were sent when their luck ran out. When they reached the exit, they saw the rain had stopped and the sun had come out again. They walked eagerly into it. After more than two hours underground, it felt like a gift. The waterlogged grass steamed, the town below had revealed itself again in all its tainted glory.

Ursula lifted her head up to the sky and sneezed four or five times, sharp little explosive sneezes the way she always did when she went from darkness into light. Carl did exactly the same at almost the same time. He stopped short. She saw his eyes widen as he looked at Ursula. His face went white.

'How old are you, Ursula?' he asked, and she could hear astonishment and something very like fear in his voice. Not fear surely, since this was the man who claimed never to have been scared, who jumped from edges of cliffs in an effort to feel what he couldn't.

'I'm nine,' said Ursula. 'Nine years and two months and four days.'

Carl looked at Rora. He didn't say anything; there was no need to. The question blazed from him. She nodded her head and the reaction was immediate, the air seemed to go out of his body and he stumbled.

Ursula chattered all the way home, seemingly oblivious to the tension in the air and so taken up by the wonder of the caves that she didn't notice that Rora and Carl were walking in complete silence next to her. Rora saw Carl looking at Ursula as if he was checking out something he thought couldn't possibly be true. When they got back to Pilgrim Street, Carl asked if he could come in. Rora could tell that he was angry. It had been building in him all the way back, and now it was in the hunch of his shoulders and the clench of his fists.

'Why don't you go and watch a video?' Rora said to Ursula, dreading the moment when she and Carl were alone and she would have to look at him. He waited in silence until the sound of the television went on in the next room. She marvelled at his self-control. He had clearly learned something over the years about mastering his feelings.

'Why didn't you tell me?' he asked. His voice was low but she could hear the animosity fizzing through it.

'You didn't even open my letters,' Rora said, and then felt ashamed of being so disingenuous. She hadn't mentioned her pregnancy when she had written to him. At first the omission had been because she wasn't sure whether the baby was Ian's or Carl's; there seemed no point in giving him another reason to feel despair on her behalf if the child wasn't Carl's, although after the first shock of the discovery she had felt nothing but happiness. She had made the decision to keep her child regardless of parentage. She had seen it as something positive to cling to, a way of helping her to heal, and then, after Ursula was born with Carl's almond-shaped eyes and long fingers curled into furious fists, her overwhelming feeling had been a desire to protect her. How would she explain to her daughter what had happened? How could she tell the story without disclosing her own part in it? She wanted nothing to cloud Ursula's clear-eyed gaze, although she knew now that she had been foolish. You can't arrange life for your child so that they are safe from harm – the bee would sting regardless, people would be cruel and the day would inevitably come when they would feel the pain of loving and not being loved back. Children have to go out into the world skinless and develop their own protective covering in order to survive.

'You could have got the news to me if you had really wanted to,' Carl said.

'Yes, I could have,' said Rora, turning away from him, knowing the hurt she had inflicted.

'You knew what happened to me when I was a child and yet you allowed me to abandon my own daughter.'

'You didn't abandon her,' Rora said. 'You did the best you could for her and for me.'

'Don't rewrite the story, Rora,' Carl said harshly. She had never heard him speak like that before, not to her.

'I'm sorry,' she said. 'I didn't know what to do for the best.' She was horrified to see that Carl had begun to cry.

'What have you told her about me?' he asked, rubbing his sleeve across his eyes as if he was ashamed of his tears.

'Nothing,' she said. 'She just thinks it was a short relationship and her father wasn't ready to be a parent.'

'Hasn't she asked about who he was?'

'She has from time to time,' said Rora, remembering with pain her daughter's fear that she was only half a person. Carl seemed to gather himself up into some sort of resolution.

'I can't deal with this now,' he said. 'I've got to go.'

She watched him walk down the street away from the house. Just as he reached the corner, he stopped and she thought he was going to turn back, but then he changed his mind and walked on.

Rora didn't hear anything from Carl for five days. She spent the time working on the book and taking long walks along the beach and wondering if perhaps she should ring him. She thought it was possible that he wouldn't ever come back. Part of her thought it was better if he didn't. She had set her life in motion the way it was. How could the three of them pick up the pieces now? Did she want him to be in Ursula's life? Did she even want him in her own? She thought of the way she reacted when he was near her, the almost instinctive way her skin clamoured for him, and she felt a kind of despair. It seemed to her that the way he made her feel had little to do with how she was now or how she wanted to be, but was a habit that was cut so deep in her it felt like part of her flesh. She had thought for so many years that he knew her better than anyone else and that this was what love was, this deep recognition, an acceptance of all frailties, and yet now she wasn't so certain. What would they build on? They would share Ursula. She owed him the chance to learn to be a father and to see his daughter grow up, but what could they be to each other? She thought it might, after all, be possible to love someone and not be able to be with them.

Carl turned up on Friday. He had the burnished look of someone who has been out in the elements. He had clearly come straight to her house because he still had his rucksack on his back. He still retained that old habit of carrying what he required. He was as ready as ever for a quick getaway.

'Can I come in?' he asked, and she opened the door wider. He brought with him the smell of damp clothes and a smoky odour, as if he had been sitting by open fires.

'I've been away,' he said, 'thinking about things.'

She took him into the kitchen and busied herself making tea so that she didn't have to look at him for too long. She didn't want to let herself be dazzled by him. She wanted to keep herself apart to give herself the chance to be clear and sure. He moved around the room, looking through the window out onto the waterlogged garden, then at some books Ursula had left on the table, and then finally at her.

'I went to Glencoe and did some jumps. Quite a short fall. Only two hundred and sixty feet.' He spoke defiantly, as if he wanted his words to provoke some sort of reaction in her.

'Oh yes,' she said in a neutral voice.

'The bloke jumping after me knocked himself out on the side of the cliff. He was lucky to make it.'

Rora refused to give expression to the horror she knew he was expecting from her.

'You haven't changed at all, have you, Carl?' she said.

'Doing the jumps helped me to think a bit more clearly about this situation,' he said.

Rora felt suddenly furious with him. His reaction to finding out he was a father was just what she would have expected. She had been right not to tell him about Ursula. She was just sorry that he had found out.

'You're a complete idiot,' she said. 'I thought after everything you would have learned not to be so irresponsible and reckless.'

'Have you told Ursula about me yet?' he asked.

'I haven't yet. Now that I know what you've just been doing I don't think it's a good idea,' she said. 'Ursula has been through enough, the last thing she needs is a damn fool of a father who goes and kills himself just when she has discovered him.'

Carl gave Rora one of his belligerent stares. The kind of look he used to give anyone who displeased or crossed him when he was a boy. Rora felt her anger slide away. She realised he had done what he had not to break records or even to boast, although he was pretending to be arrogant with her now, but because he wanted to wear down his rough edges and find something that passed for peace.

Rora was aware of being clumsy. Her hands didn't seem quite to be doing what they ought. She dropped the teapot lid into the sink and then splashed herself with boiling water from the kettle. She let out an involuntary cry.

'Put it straight in water,' he said, taking her burned hand to the sink and holding it under the running tap. As her hand went numb, she found that in contrast the rest of her body was feeling too much. She was aware of every detail of him – the way his fingers curved around the edge of the porcelain sink, the tendons in his arm and the small dark hairs on the side of his neck. She wanted to touch him. It was the same impulse that is transmitted to fingers by the curve of cool stone or the soft spring of spun wool.

'I think that's OK now,' she said, taking her hand away from his.

'I want to get to know her,' he said. 'I want her to know that I'm her father.'

'I don't know how she will react.'

'I'll do it any way that you think is best,' said Carl. 'I can't promise I'll make a good father, but I want to try.'

Rora could see the desperate hope in his face and, despite her misgivings, she relented. They decided that the three of them should spend some time together before they told Ursula. It was going to be confusing enough for the child anyway without presenting her with someone she hardly knew. Rora said she would bring Ursula into the aquarium the next day so that she could get to know Carl a little. They sat for hours discussing the possible ways of telling her.

'You can tell her I wasn't ready until I actually saw her,' said Carl. 'And that when I did see her, I really wanted to be her dad. It's almost the truth.'

The ever-present Gary was at the reception desk when Rora and Ursula presented themselves at the aquarium.

'Back are you?' he said rudely. 'I thought you would be.'

'Why do you say that?' asked Rora.

'I said you were his type, and hey presto, here you are again,' he said.

'Where can I find Carl?' asked Rora, ignoring his rudeness.

'He's with Swifty,' said Gary indifferently.

'Who's Swifty?' Ursula asked, fixing Gary with a glare. Rora could tell she wasn't too impressed with him.

'He's a seal,' said Gary.

'Why's he called Swifty?' asked Ursula.

'Because he's very, very slow,' said Gary, who looked a little disconcerted at the gimlet look Ursula was giving him. 'He needs to be sung to at least twice a day or he starts to pine.'

They found Carl by the seal enclosure. He was singing 'Abide With Me' in a deep baritone. Rora didn't think she had ever heard him sing before and was surprised at his ability to hold a tune. He was standing in front of a window where a mottled looking creature was slowly crossing and criss-crossing in front of him.

'How long do you have to keep that up?' asked Rora and Carl turned at the sound of her voice. He smiled at her and Ursula. It was one of his rare, wide smiles that made his normally shadowed, rather stern face suddenly merry.

'How's Swifty?' asked Ursula.

'Swifty is fine,' said Carl, 'and seeing you has made him feel even better'.

'Carry on singing,' said Rora, grinning.

'I think he's had enough for today,' said Carl.

The seal hung around for a few moments as if hopeful of another verse or two, then did a couple of desultory back flips and swam off as if he knew his moment in the sun was over. Just as they were turning to go he made one last hopeful pass across the window, one ragged flipper tucked tightly into his side, which made Ursula laugh.

'I love him!' she said and Carl smiled over her head at Rora.

'Would you like to come and play with the rays?' Carl asked Ursula and she nodded eagerly.

He led them through to the stingray enclosure where a deep tank housed the larger fish and a shallow pool contained the smaller of the species. The water teemed with the strange, almost mythical creatures with their undulating fins and their neat, smiling mouths, which only became visible when they flipped round and showed their white undersides. They moved smoothly, navigating the polystyrene rocks and lobster pots that littered the bottom of the tank in Disney fashion.

'You can touch them if you like,' Carl said, putting his hands in the pool.

'Don't they sting?' Ursula asked.

'These small ones have had their barbs cut,' he said.

He touched the sides of the fish tenderly, his hand movements looking as if he was propelling them puppet-like on their way through the water. Rora put one hand reluctantly into the tank and touched the side of a passing fish and withdrew it hastily. The skin felt slippery, almost glutinous, and the rays had a darting, heedless way of moving, although Carl assured them that the fish were skilful navigators and trawled the seas aided by a sophisticated sense of smell. He took Ursula's arm, rolled up the cuff of her shirt and placed her hand in the water.

'Just feel them. They are soft and hard at the same time,' he said.

Afterwards they sat and watched him cleaning the sides of the big tank. Ursula had been very impressed when he changed into his wetsuit.

'I think I could do with one of those,' she said.

'I'll get you one,' he said.

He misted the windows with a spray and then wiped them clear with a cloth. The sleek movement of the fish was so hypnotic that Ursula's eyes started to droop. She hadn't been sleeping well since she had received the letter. She lay down on the bench and closed her eyes. Carl unhooked the scuba diving mask attached to his belt and put it over his head. He walked up the stairs at the side of the tank and then opened the gate to the enclosure. He sat on the edge and carefully put on flippers and let himself down into the water, making as little splash as possible so as not to disturb the fish.

Rora watched through the glass as he moved among them as if he was taking comfort from their company. He looked remote, untouchable, almost in another world than the one in which she was standing. He took hold of a large fish, looked closely through his mask at something on its underside and then released it. It spun off with a flick of its rigid tail. Carl kicked his flippered feet down to the very bottom of the tank and smoothed the layer of small stones and then swam around until he located a gathering of lantern-jawed fish hovering timidly outside a cave, as if a sudden movement would send them back into hiding. He reached into the bag at his waist and took out some pink matter, which he fed to them, individually placing the food carefully on the edge of their eager, open mouths. When he had finished he kicked for the surface, but then stopped as if he had remembered something and swam to the side of the tank, tapped on the glass and beckoned Rora over.

Carl's eyes were magnified by the effect of the mask and the water. The skin of his face was stretched slightly giving him an expression of mild surprise. Bubbles rose around him like stars. A pair of bright yellow fish swam by very close and he crossed his eyes at them. Rora responded by opening and closing her mouth in her best cartoon fish fashion and he smiled and the movement of his mouth sending up another series of silvery trails as if his laughter had a visible residue. He steadied himself against the window and traced a line on the glass around her face. Even through the rocking water and shifting, greenish light she could see his eyes become suddenly intent. He took out his mouthpiece and put his hands against the side of the tank and held himself there, waiting for her.

She was worried about him running out of air. She put her hands on his – her palms against his palms. Their faces came close together, nose to nose. She could see the little scar under his eye, white and silvery, and the soft indent of his top lip. Her mouth found the shape of his. Their phantom kiss warmed the glass and she imagined that she could feel the press of his lips against hers. Their fingers moved together and there was an echo of what it was like to be touched by him, his hand cupping her chin and smoothing back her hair, and although they were miming it now, their movements mirrored. Rora stroked the place where his forehead was, the line of his jaw. She traced the shape of his mouth with her finger and it seemed he couldn't help opening his lips. She held him there for a moment more, and then at last she released him, and he rose to the surface with two swift kicks of his feet, displacing water so that the passing rays rocked slightly and then followed the unfamiliar current like dogs scenting the wind. The sea anemones attached in clumps to the sides of the rock shuddered and pulsed as he passed by. He put his head out of the water and even from below she could hear the great gasp he made, as if he had stayed there against her for as long as he possibly could.

Kiss 18

'His mouth was urgent, even angry, but as her lips moved beneath his, she felt him soften, as if, despite himself and the depth of his feelings, he couldn't be hard to her.'

22 July 2010

'Why are we suddenly spending so much time with Carl?' asked Ursula.

'Don't you like him?' Rora asked

'He's extremely nice and he said he was going to get me a wetsuit,' said Ursula.

'You'll need it just to go for a walk if it carries on like this,' said Rora, looking out of the kitchen window at the flattened, grey garden.

The rain had been relentless for the last five days and Rora and Ursula were getting cabin fever. Rora had run through her inventory of rainy day activities, but now the pair of them were painted and crafted out and were longing for the weather to change. They were baking a cake for Carl, who was coming round that morning, although there was hardly anything left in the mixing bowl after Ursula had insisted on regular taste tests. Rora and Carl had decided on the phone the night before that the time had come to tell Ursula the truth, but now Rora didn't feel so sure. She believed that Carl wanted to play a part in Ursula's life, he seemed enraptured by her, but she was worried about how Ursula would take the news. She hadn't recovered from the shock of getting the letter from her tormentors and still started, wide-eyed, every time the letterbox rattled, even though Rora had tried to reassure her that she would never see the girls again.

'I'm going to make up for all the time we have lost,' Carl said when she asked him for the tenth time if he was sure they were doing the right thing, but she knew it wasn't possible to catch time up like that. There would always be things he had missed. She couldn't give him Ursula's wriggling entrance into the world, nor the wonder of her first words and first steps. She had caught him looking at her from time to time in the old, intent fashion, but he had kept his distance, as if he thought a sudden movement might frighten her away. She wasn't sure if it was his chance with his daughter that he was protecting, or his chance with her. Maybe both.

'Is he going to be your boyfriend?' asked Ursula with her disconcerting ability to pick up on her mother's thoughts.

'He used to be my boyfriend, a long time ago,' said Rora, taking the bowl from her daughter and whisking the remnants with more ferocity than was required.

'Will it be like the story of Rapunzel who lost the prince but walked and walked until she found him again and kissed his eyes so he wasn't blind anymore?'

'It's very hard to go back, Ursula,' Rora said. 'Sometimes it's better to carry on moving forward.'

'If Rapunzel had thought like that the prince would still be wandering in the desert,' said Ursula.

'Fairy tales are not the same as real life,' said Rora.

'Doh. Obviously,' Ursula said indignantly. 'In fairy stories people are always hanging around in woods when everyone knows it's better to stay on well-lit roads.'

Rora smiled at her practical child.

'Don't you think it might be a good idea to wash the chocolate from your face? I'll put the cake in the oven,' she said, and Ursula ran upstairs just as Carl's knock came at the door.

'This was on the doorstep,' he said as he came dripping into the hallway, holding out a parcel addressed to Ursula. 'It had been put under the porch, so it is still almost dry.'

'Oh god,' said Rora taking a look at the handwriting on the front and hastily throwing a tea towel over the top of it and putting it down on the work surface just as Ursula came back into the room. Carl looked startled by her reaction, but was diverted by Ursula's entrance.

'Hello, Ursula, I have something for you,' he said, taking a wetsuit out from under his anorak.

'Oh brilliant, thank you!' Ursula beamed at Carl. 'Can I swim in the tank with you now?' she asked.

'We might be able to arrange it,' he said, delighted that she wanted to do something with him. He looked meaningfully at Rora, but she avoided his gaze and busied herself by washing up the contents of the sink. At Ursula's request Carl set up a game of Coppit on the table, and when Rora declined to play the two of them started without her. It amused Rora to see that they were competitive in the same way – both prone to miscounting the squares on the board to their own advantage.

'Oh, we've forgotten the cake. I'd better take it out,' said Ursula suddenly, leaping to her feet and picking up the tea towel before Rora could stop her. She stood staring blankly at the parcel underneath it for a couple of seconds.

'When did that come?' asked Ursula.

'Just now,' said Rora. 'Let's throw it away, without looking at it.'

She wished she had had the presence of mind to put it in the bin as soon as Carl had handed it to her.

'I want to see what's inside,' said Ursula, stubbornly. She was white-faced and her mouth had closed up into a thin line.

'I don't think you should,' said Rora gently. 'It's just allowing them to upset you. They're not worth it.'

'I want to see what's inside,' said Ursula again.

Reluctantly Rora gave her the parcel, and watched as Ursula tore at the brown paper. The parcel contained a sun hat, squashed flat, its brim cut in jagged slices and scribbled all over with the word 'snitch'.

'That's my hat,' said Ursula looking dumbly at it. 'They stole it weeks ago.'

'I really think we have to go to the police,' said Rora. 'The bloody head teacher of the school doesn't seem able to control her own daughter.'

'Oh please, don't go to the police,' said Ursula, her eyes wide and imploring. 'It will make them even worse.'

'We have to do something,' said Carl.

'Do you think they will ever stop?' asked Ursula piteously, tears coming to her eyes, though Rora could see that she was trying not to cry. 'Mia is perfect. She has hair that shines in the sun and a bike with sliver and pink tassels and no one can stop her.'

'I'll stop her,' said Carl.

'I don't think anyone can,' said Ursula, and she went over to the oven and took out the cake, which was now less sponge and more wafer, and placed it carefully on the table. Her care broke Rora's heart. She might have taught her daughter how to carry hot things safely, but there was no lesson she could offer on how to stop Ursula feeling the way she was. It was no good telling her that it would pass, because although of course it would, the feeling of injustice and the fear of being singled out would stay with her forever.

Rora and Carl abandoned their plan to tell Ursula that afternoon – she had had enough upset for the day. Instead Carl ate the burned cake and was so tender and kind to Ursula that Rora began to believe he had the makings of a good father.

'The thing about bullies,' he said, 'is that they are scared. They might seem full of bluster and ready to take anyone on, but inside they are cowering.'

'They don't seem very scared to me,' said Ursula.

'They hide it well, but take my word for it, they are quaking.'

'What have they got to quake about?' asked Ursula in a disbelieving voice.

'The things we all quake about,' said Carl. 'Not having friends, feeling small, thinking everyone else is better.'

'Do you ever feel small?' she asked him, as if she thought he was teasing her.

'Often,' he said, and he looked at Rora with such sadness that it made her catch her breath.

'What do you do to make yourself feel better?' Ursula asked.

'I do something distracting,' said Carl smiling at Ursula, and Rora was reminded of the boy who had jumped ditches and hung from door frames every time she had asked him about his parents.

'I wish I was Calamity Jane,' said Ursula. 'Then I could shoot them and ride away on a horse.'

'How about we go to the school gates and you point this Mia person out to me? It's just about going home time now, isn't it?' said Carl.

Rora looked up at him in alarm.

'Carl, I don't think that's such a good idea,' she said.

Ursula looked questioningly at her mother.

'Come on, I'd like to see her,' said Carl. 'I won't say a word to her, I promise, scout's honour.'

'You were never a scout,' said Rora, and was surprised to see Ursula sitting down and putting her shoes on. 'They wouldn't have let you in.'

'That's it,' said Carl approvingly to Ursula. 'It won't take long. Do you want to come too?' he asked Rora.

'I think I'd better,' she said.

When they reached the school gates the first few children were coming out. They stood for a while on the other side of the street. Rora took hold of Ursula's shaking hand.

'Don't be scared, Ursula,' Carl said. 'I'm just going to fix her with one of my evil looks. She won't know what's hit her.'

After a few more moments a group of girls came out of the school door and walked over to the bike shed.

'That's her,' said Ursula in a tremulous voice. She pointed to a girl at the centre of the group. 'The one with the bow in her hair.'

Mia pulled out her bike from the rack, smoothed down her already neat hair and put on a pink bicycle helmet. She swung her leg over the bike and set off with an efficient stamp of her white-socked leg. The rest of the group shouted goodbye after her, as if they were seeing off a visiting dignitary. Rora saw Carl staring very hard at the girl, and if looks could kill, she would by rights have been lying collapsed on the pavement.

'You see, she is untouchable,' said Ursula despairingly. 'She smells of mint and flowers.'

'Does she now,' said Carl thoughtfully.

Later, after Carl had walked them home and then gone, Rora had lain a full hour next to Ursula until she had at last fallen into a fitful sleep. Then she had a quick supper and settled down for a couple of hours of work on the book. The house was completely silent – even the seagulls had been washed away by the rain – but it wasn't the ominous quiet that she had felt when she first arrived. She had released the house from the encroaching garden and now there was some sort of lawn, even though the sun had yellowed great patches of it, and recognisable flower-beds edged with pebbles from the beach. She had also hired a van and driven all the broken furniture from the attic room and elsewhere to the dump, and now the house felt clearer, more known, as if she belonged there. The peal of the bell broke the silence, and she went to the door to find Krystof standing there.

'I know I said I would stay away, but I can't do it,' he said. He looked tired, and she thought that perhaps he was a little drunk. He had a slightly too purposeful way of talking and he was leaning on the doorframe. She was surprised by the spurt of happiness she felt when she saw him. She showed him into the living room, moving her computer off the sofa and pushing books aside to make a space for him to sit down.

'I've interrupted your work,' he said, standing in the middle of the room, as if he couldn't make up his mind whether to stay or not.

'It's fine. Really,' she said. 'I was about to finish anyway.'

'It's late. What can you think of me turning up like this?' he asked.

'I think it's very nice to see you,' she said, and he sat down heavily on the sofa, slightly misjudging the move so that he almost toppled sideways. She saw that he was more than just a little drunk.

'Can I get you a coffee?' she asked.

'It might be a good idea,' he said and smiled his disarmingly open smile. 'I've been drinking vodka.'

He got up and followed her down to the kitchen and watched while she put the kettle on and scooped coffee into mugs.

'Have you seen Carl?' he asked, scanning her face as if he was looking for evidence of change. She didn't know what he was expecting to find there.

'We've spent quite a bit of time together, actually,' she said and saw his face fall.

'It's a little more complicated than I told you before,' she said. 'Carl's Ursula's father, you see.'

'I see,' said Krystof, taking a deep breath as if he had been winded, 'that would explain a lot about why you were like you were with him at the party.' He looked so sad that Rora was tempted to hug him.

'I think I have my answer,' he said, getting to his feet and holding on to the edge of the kitchen table.

'What was the question?' Rora asked.

'The question was . . .' Krystof hesitated and then said, 'Never mind now. It doesn't matter.'

'It does matter,' said Rora.

'I love you,' said Krystof. 'I've tried not to because I can see that you are tied up with someone else, but I can't help it. I love the way you are soft and prickly. I love your horribly ugly feet. I love the way you eat food as if you are always hungry. I love your face the way it looks so stern and then smiles and my heart melts,' and he put his hand to the breast pocket of his shirt. 'You have crept into here, and I can't get you out.'

'Krystof, you barely know me,' Rora said.

'I do know you,' he said. 'That's the point.'

'Can you just give me a little more time?' Rora asked. 'So much has been happening to me. I'm in a muddle.'

'I think if you don't know now, then you won't ever know,' he said, 'and tomorrow morning when I wake up with a terrible head I will feel mortified that I came here and spoke to you like this.'

'There's no need to feel mortified. You are my friend.'

'Your friend!' Krystof exclaimed, banging down his coffee cup so that it slopped all over the table. 'That's it. I am doomed.'

Rora couldn't help smiling at his woebegone expression, and seeing this seemed to make Krystof furious.

'It's not funny Rora,' he said.

'Of course it's not. I'm sorry.'

He stood up and moved towards her and then cupped her face in his hand, lifting her head so that she was looking directly at him. His hold was tight on her; she could feel his fingers pushing into her skin. His eyes had lost their yellow flecks and were green and serious. He suddenly seemed a lot less drunk than he had a few minutes before. For the first time since they had met she felt unsure, even a little nervous.

'I'm not someone you can play with and then put down.'

'I don't think of you like that,' she said, although she felt that she deserved the rebuke. She knew she had used him as an antidote to the turbulence that Carl had stirred up in her. She found that she didn't want him to think of her as someone who would toy with another person's affections. She felt ashamed of how she had been behaving – blown this way and that, with no regard for what she was doing to him. She realised as she looked into his strong, sure face that she cared more for him than she had realised. He wasn't simply a diversion from Carl; he was someone who was worth loving.

'You are driving me mad,' he said, and he put his lips to hers, as if he knew he shouldn't be doing what he was doing, but couldn't really help himself. His mouth was urgent, even angry, but as her lips moved beneath his, she felt him soften, as if, despite himself and the depth of his feelings, he couldn't be hard to her. It wasn't in his nature to confuse love with ownership. He understood the value of tenderness. He made a noise deep in the back of his throat and she felt light with desire, which was partly provoked by the pleasure of being desired. Kissing him felt right. Their lips matched each other's, as if this was simply the beginning of a conversation that would last. His hand went into the neck of her shirt and she felt her body arch towards him. He pulled away from her as if it cost him a great deal to do so.

'Next time, you will have to come to me. I'll not bother you again,' he said.

'You're not bothering me,' she said, but he put up an unsteady hand as if to ward her off.

'Just forget it,' he said. 'Blame it on the rain and on the vodka.'

The next day Ursula was still subdued.

'What if they come and leave something else when we're out?' she said, and a visible tremor ran through her body.

'I've rung the police this morning,' said Rora. 'No, don't worry,' she said when Ursula made a sound of dissent. 'They're not going to go charging in there, all guns blazing, Calamity Jane-style. I spoke to a lovely policewoman who knows all about how to deal with this kind of thing, and she said she would go and have a quiet chat with Mia's parents.'

'But they'll know it was me that told,' said Ursula.

'But it wasn't you that told, it was me. Don't worry, she won't mention your name.'

Just then the doorbell went, and Rora discovered a grinning Carl on the doorstep.

'I thought we'd go to the fair in Brighton later on today,' he announced. 'But first we are going on a little detour.'

Brushing aside Rora's demands to know where they were going, they set off down the road with Carl leading. When it became obvious that they were once more heading to the school, Rora stopped.

'What are you going to do?' she asked Carl. 'I really don't think you should get involved.' It was there still; that glinting restlessness had never left him. It never would.

'We are not going to do anything at all,' said Carl. 'We're simply going to watch.'

It was the last day of term and the children were gathered outside. The older ones who were leaving to go to secondary school the following year were in damp, clutching embraces, their shirts covered with the names of people that they couldn't imagine living without, but would soon forget. Mia was in the centre of her adoring group, who followed her obediently, as they had done before, to witness the grand bike embarkation. Mia shoved a small child who was holding her lunch box to her chest out of her way as she passed and wheeled her bike to the gate. Her acolytes gathered to see her off. She straightened the bow in her hair, pulled up her socks, took her helmet from her basket and put it on her head like a queen putting on her crown. There was a pause and then Mia let out a terrible scream. Her hair and her face were covered in black, oozing liquid. It covered her eyes and dripped down onto her chest. Still screaming she spun round, trying to get her helmet off her head. It was the diminutive child she had pushed earlier who started laughing first. It was just a nervous titter, the sort of laugh you give when you can't really help yourself, but one by one others started laughing too until it seemed everyone had joined in, even the gang of sycophants were looking at her and shaking with mirth.

'Not so pretty now, is she?' said Carl with satisfaction. He looked at Ursula and she gave a tiny smile that started at the corners of her mouth and then spread so that she was grinning so widely it seemed to reach her ears. It was Carl's smile. The one he gave when everything was right with the world.

After a while they walked on to the station.

'You are a very kind person,' Ursula informed Carl.

'I do my best,' he said.

'He's a very terrible person you mean,' said Rora reprovingly, although she smiled too.

'Mummy says you were once her boyfriend,' Ursula said after they sat down in their seats on the train to Brighton.

'Yes, I once was,' said Carl, and he looked at Rora with his dark searching gaze until she dropped her eyes.

'Would you like to be her boyfriend again?' asked Ursula.

'Ursula! It's none of your business,' said Rora feeling embarrassed.

'Of course it's her business,' said Carl. 'The thing is, Ursula, I don't know if she would have me.'

'He already has a girlfriend,' Rora said.

'Actually, Serena and I have parted company,' he said.

'That poor, poor woman,' said Rora.

'She took it quite well, really. I think she was a little fed up with hanging around waiting for me all the time.'

'You would have him, wouldn't you Mum?' asked Ursula turning to Rora, and Carl laughed delightedly, the sound so loud that a couple of people in the train compartment turned to look.

'Why do you never take anything seriously?' Rora asked Carl, speaking crossly to mask her discomfort.

'What makes you think I'm not being serious?' he asked, and his eyes dropped to her mouth and he gave her one of his slow, seductive smiles.

'You just can't help yourself, can you?' she said, and was relieved when the ticket inspector came into the compartment and created a diversion.

When they got to the fair the rain had eased off to a fine drizzle that soon transformed Ursula's and Rora's hair into masses of uncontrollable curls.

'It's like being with a couple of circus clowns,' Carl teased, earning a swipe from Ursula, who was desperately trying to smooth her hair down. She clamoured to go on all the rides that Rora hated but Carl relished.

'She's clearly got a head for heights,' he said, pleased, and the pair of them whooped and gurned through the twists and turns while Rora waited below. After the daredevils in the group had had their fill of excitement, and they had eaten hot dogs longer than Ursula's arm, the three of them decided they would go into the hall of mirrors. Rora had imagined a tent with a few bendy metal plates along the sides, but this was a discomforting tunnel with dead ends at every turn, which quickly made Rora feel dizzy. She fell back while Ursula and Carl raced ahead, Ursula holding Carl's hand.

'Let's look at ourselves in this one!' Ursula kept saying. Rora was just happy that she was having a good time. She resolved to check in with WPC Bentley again tomorrow. There was no way she was going to let Ursula suffer any more horrible deliveries. She caught up with Ursula and Carl just as they were both standing in front of a mirror that elongated their features to comic proportions. She heard Ursula laugh and then fall abruptly silent. She came up behind them and saw that her daughter was transfixed by her reflection. She kept looking at herself and then at Carl's image next to her, as if she couldn't quite believe what she was seeing. She turned slowly towards Carl.

'Are you my father?' she said. 'We've got the same eyes and chin and you sneezed just like I did when we came out of the caves.'

Rora held her breath, waiting to see what Carl would say.

'Yes, I am,' he said.

Ursula stared at him for a moment or two and then turned on her heel and walked on down the hall of glass to the exit. Carl and Rora followed behind, Carl giving Rora a worried look.

'Not quite the reaction I was hoping for,' he said.

'Give her a chance, she's had a shock,' said Rora. 'You didn't really imagine she was going to throw herself into your arms murmuring "Daddy", did you?'

'Nothing so easy, if she's anything like her mother,' said Carl.

Ursula was waiting for them outside, her hands crossed in front of her, her face closed.

'I would like to go home now,' she said.

'Listen, Ursula, I know it's a lot to take in and will take some time to get used to, but Carl's really pleased you are his daughter,' said Rora.

'Have you known you were my father all along?' she asked Carl, ignoring Rora.

'I told him a couple of weeks ago,' said Rora.

'How long have you known Carl was my father?' asked Ursula, looking at Rora with her scarily shut down face.

'Ever since you were born,' said Rora.

'Why didn't you tell him before? Where's he been all this time?'

Rora tried to put her arms around her daughter, but Ursula turned on her savagely.

'You told me he didn't want to be my dad,' she said. 'So why does he want to be my dad now?'

'It's difficult to explain,' Carl said softly. 'Grown-ups do the strangest things for all sorts of strange reasons.'

'When were you going to tell me?' she asked, and Rora could see that this was what was really upsetting her – the idea that they knew something that she didn't.

'We were going to tell you really soon,' said Carl. 'We were just waiting for the moment to be right.'

'I don't want you to be my father,' she said, 'and I don't want you to be my mother either.'

All the way back to Hastings Ursula kept up a stubborn silence, turning her face away and ignoring Rora and Carl. Carl kept giving Rora worried glances and she mouthed reassurances at him. Through one of the windows Rora got fleeting glimpses of other lives – someone sitting in a conservatory with a view onto the railway line, a boy in an orange shirt playing football alone on a fenced-off patch of bright AstroTurf, a young man carefully seeing an elderly woman into a car – thousands of houses and rooms in which people were working out stories similar to her own.

Ursula asked to go to bed almost as soon as they got back. She still wouldn't look at Carl, and eventually they decided it would be better if he left and gave Ursula a chance to absorb what they had told her.

'I think she feels betrayed by us,' said Rora, seeing Carl out. 'She thinks we have been keeping secrets from her.'

'We are both expert at that,' Carl said. 'I just wish we'd told her before she discovered it for herself.'

'She always needs time to think things through.'

'I wonder who she gets that from?' asked Carl, smiling at Rora.

He gazed at her for a moment as they stood on the steps, moving restlessly from foot to foot as he always did, as if he was getting ready to run, and Rora felt a swell of affection for him. The two of them would always be bound together, not just by Ursula but also by all that they had shared. Although she couldn't quite face it now, not when she had only just found him again, she knew that despite the way she was tied to him in knots too tight and intricate to untangle, it wasn't going to be enough. They had missed their chance.

'Thank you,' she said, and her whole heart was in the words. Her eyes filled with tears and she felt an inconsolable grief. She was crying for what they had been and what they had lost. He smiled his crooked, heart-breaking smile and pulled at a strand of her hair.

'You know I love you, don't you?' she said. 'You know I'll always love you.'

He nodded and his face moved strangely. She saw that he was on the verge of tears himself and she reached up and touched him. He held her hand against his face for a moment, then turned and walked away. She knew he had understood what she hadn't said. He had always known what she was thinking.

Rora woke the next morning at eight o'clock, wondering why Ursula hadn't come into her bedroom as she usually did. She thought she was probably tired from the shock of the day before and went in to rouse her. Her bed was empty. Surely she hadn't been sleepwalking again?

'Ursula, where are you?' she called, going down to the kitchen. Ursula wasn't there either, but there was a note on the table, written in Ursula's rounded, careful hand.

Dear Mum,
    Don't worry. I've gone away somewhere safe to think.
                                                    Ursula

Rora opened the drawer in the dresser that contained all the miscellaneous objects there was no other place for and saw the torch was missing. She felt her stomach lurch. Where could Ursula have gone? Rora made another frantic search of the house, calling out her daughter's name as she ran from floor to floor, but she had clearly left the house. She went outside and looked up and down the street. Ursula had run away from home once before when they were living in London, and Rora had found her sitting on the edge of the pavement five doors down with a plastic bag full of pilfered biscuits. Rora ran back indoors and phoned Carl.

'Ursula's run away,' she panted.

'I'm coming straightaway,' he said. 'Don't panic. She's very sensible. Call the police though, just in case.'

Rora made the phone call and was told someone would be with them very soon, then paced up and down the hallway waiting for Carl to arrive.

Somewhere safe to think – where did Ursula mean? Where would Ursula think of as safe? Rora stopped pacing as an idea struck her – the cabin on the East Cliff – it had to be there. Rora had told her that it had been a refuge when she was a child and so maybe Ursula had thought to go there too, when she was feeling at her most bewildered and upset. Carl arrived just as Rora was putting on her anorak.

'I think she's gone to the cabin,' she said. 'I took her to see it the other day.'

They ran down Rock-a-Nore. The rain was so hard and heavy Rora could barely see in front of her. The sea was a great foaming mass and the waves crashed against the harbour wall and sent up spray that seemed to reach as far as the ominous sky. As she ran she heard a grinding, thunderous fall and an answering shout from the small group of people who had gathered on the edge of the beach by the railings. A huge plinth of rock had peeled itself away from the cliff and toppled into the sea creating a dirty-coloured mist over the water. The stones continued to move down the cliff in little rivulets like sand from a giant hourglass.

'What's happening?' she asked, stopping and holding on to Carl's arm.

'It's not finished yet!' she heard someone in the crowd shout, and a second wave of falling stone picked up speed, taking with it another great slice of the cliff. This was greeted by the watchers with an awestruck yell, part terror and part excitement. The air was filled with the smell of something hidden being released, as if an enormous beast had opened its mouth and expelled a massive breath. She thought with horror of the picture in one of Ursula's storybooks of a girl sitting on what she thought was a grassy mound, oblivious to the open yellow eye and the scaly tail of the creature beneath her.

'She's up there, Carl!' Rora cried, watching the cliff shifting. The stones ran down as far as the sea and stopped there as if waiting to be taken.

'Come on,' said Carl, grabbing hold of her hand.

They ran up the steps alongside the funicular, slipping on the wet stone. Rora had a tearing stitch in her side, but she kept up with Carl all the way to the top. They ran together towards the cabin, but stopped in their tracks when they saw it was no longer there. The cliff around it had given way and taken it along with the ten feet or so of earth around it. All that was left was a jagged edge of rock and torn-up gorse bushes.

'Where is she?' Rora cried, panic wringing its way through her so that she could barely think. Carl was expressionless. He fell to his knees and looked over the crumbling edge.

'What are you doing? Be careful,' Rora cried behind him. The landslide had not yet run itself out. They could hear the sound of stones falling in bursts, punctuated by episodes of stillness, as if the cliff itself was wondering if it was time to settle down once more. The town below was shrouded in a wet mist and it felt as if they were alone, standing on the very edge of the world. The days of rain had saturated the ground and now the cliff had reached its tipping point.

The once familiar cliff walk now looked like another country. The beast was holding its breath. The trickle of moving matter had stopped.

'Ursula!' Carl suddenly shouted, and Rora came instantly to his side.

'She's there,' Carl said, 'about thirty feet down, she's landed on a rock.'

At first Rora couldn't see Ursula – she was looking in the wrong place – but then she caught sight of her daughter's red coat and her legs sticking out over the ledge. She didn't seem to be moving. Her phone went. It was the police ringing from outside her house and she explained where they were and what had happened.

'Come quickly,' she said. 'Please come quickly.'

'The cliff could shift again at any moment,' said Carl. 'I'm going down to get her now.'

Rora watched in terror as he carefully inched his way over the edge, finding places to put his feet among the debris. His slow progress downwards triggered another small slide and Rora's heart stopped.

'Perhaps you should wait for help,' she shouted, but she knew that there was no stopping him. He looked up once or twice and his face was white and scared – he looked more vulnerable than she had ever seen him. She took comfort from the fact that Carl had always been at home on the edges of things – he had no fear of heights and had chosen to throw himself into the air countless times when BASE jumping. He had described to her with great relish the small hesitation he always felt just before he launched off, the last little earth-bound kick and then the transformative power and beauty of the fall. This was his terrain.

After ten minutes of agonising descent, he reached the rock where Ursula was lying. He tentatively put half his weight on the stone to test it, then moved across so that he was sharing the ledge with her. There were the occasional little flurries of rockfall, like small coughs coming from the centre of the earth, and each time the sight and sound of them made Rora's stomach clench and her breath come fast and uneven.

'Please let her be all right,' she said. 'Please, please, please.'

She saw him bend over Ursula, put his hand to her neck.

'She's breathing,' he shouted up and Rora's heart lifted.

It seemed that Ursula had only been stunned because after a couple more moments Carl was able to sit her up. In the distance Rora could hear the sound of approaching sirens.

'Help's coming,' she shouted down, 'wait there.' But it seemed Carl wasn't listening. He had Ursula on his back, her arms clenched around his neck as he began the slow climb back up. Rora watched in agony as his feet slipped from time to time, unable to get purchase on the loose stones and the sliding mud. There was a shout behind her and she turned to see three or four firemen approaching with ropes. Rora could see the effort in Carl's strained face and Ursula's wide and terrified eyes. As they reached the top, she leaned down to haul her daughter to safety. She could feel Ursula trembling in her arms.

'Come away from the edge,' said the fireman who reached them first, and he pulled Rora and Ursula to safety. She had just turned round to check where Carl was when there was another terrible scraping noise, much louder than before, and she saw him fall back, taking another foot of the cliff edge with him.

Kiss 19

'She touched the cool slope of his cheek, his forehead, the dark line of his brows in his pale, luminous face and put her lips against his lost mouth.'

24 July 2010

She had wanted to stay and wait until she saw he was safe. She struggled hard in the fireman's arms, but he pulled her from the crumbling edge and hustled her away.

'There's nothing you can do here. We'll take care of it now,' he said firmly, business-like, even though the rain was dripping off his face and he looked shivery. It was extraordinary that amid the noise and shock of it all she had noticed this – the drop resting on the tip of his nose, his mouth chapped and sore looking. It was as if she couldn't see beyond the detail of things because looking any wider would make her lose herself.

'Your daughter is going to need you at the hospital.'

She sat in the ambulance, holding Ursula's hand, managing to talk to her daughter in a soothing voice, even though the voice didn't feel like her own, but rather that of a person who knew they were supposed to talk like this in this situation, being carried through the spitting streets, the siren sounding as if it was coming from somewhere else.

She waited while they checked Ursula, not wanting to take her hand away, and then walked down shining linoleum to the X-ray department with Ursula on a gurney beside her. She expected to see him at any moment, moving fast down the corridor after them, running to find out how Ursula was. He would be all right. He would be all right. This was Carl, the Teflon Kid. The boy who balanced along edges.

Ursula had a broken leg and a few minor cuts and abrasions.

'No lasting damage,' someone said kindly, though Rora thought surely there would be. She could hear the slide of the cliff in her head – its great, throaty rumble.

She asked at reception where he was. She went from person to person with the same question but she couldn't find anyone who could tell her what had happened, so she waited. The hospital buzzed around her, pain running down tubes, along electrical currents. He would come. He would come. He would smile his crooked smile.

'You are always such a worrier,' he would say, and jam coins into the coffee machine and flirt with the nurses whilst moving restlessly from foot to foot.

Rora knew as soon as she saw them coming down the hospital corridor towards her. Their shoes were tapping in unison with a clicking sound, as if they were marching into battle. She got to her feet. She would have run away if she could, but there was nowhere to go. The walls moved and bent. She thought she might be falling.

'Aurora Raine?' the policeman said. He had bad skin and a stiff little moustache. She nodded without saying anything. She couldn't have spoken.

'I'm very sorry to have to tell you that Carl sustained terrible injuries in the landslide. I'm afraid he didn't make it . . . He's dead,' he said more loudly, as if he thought he had to make himself absolutely clear. There was no room for embarrassing ambiguity. She felt herself sway, saw a pattern of black dots floating in front of her.

'Are you sure?' she asked. 'Are you sure?'

A policewoman sat her carefully back down and crouched beside her with her hand on her shoulder.

'I'm terribly sorry, but we are,' she said, and Rora slid off the chair onto the floor. She covered her head with her arms. It was impossible. He had been in her heart and head all her life. He had climbed up a cliff with Ursula on his back. He was more alive than anyone she had ever known.

They let Rora see him after a while. It seemed that although his body had been crushed by falling stones, his face hadn't been touched, and when she went into the room where he lay covered in a sheet, she could almost imagine that he was sleeping, until she moved closer and could see the waxy absence. She realised that she had been hoping it had all been some sort of mistake, because the sight of him came as a terrible shock, as if this was a new discovery, not one that had been explained to her several times by strangers. She had absorbed the words she had been told, but not the meaning. She had expected him to be there, at least enough of him to get comfort from, but he had been and gone and taken part of her with him. It would be that way forever.

She hated the polite room with its polished floor and its closed window – a room for damming up grief so it didn't spill out into the corridors. She was torn between wanting to get away and staying and hanging on to all that remained for as long as she could. His shape was all that was left, and she knew that the moment she walked out of the room Carl would move into her past, and the slow blurring of the lines of his face, the un-remembering of the exact shade of his eyes, the placing of his ears against his head, would begin. She touched the cool slope of his cheek, his forehead, the dark line of his brows in his pale, luminous face and put her lips against his lost mouth. The kiss felt like a ritual – the sipping of a shared cup or the folding of a flag, but it offered her no solace. *I would feel your kiss even if I was dead,* he had said when they were children. She waited just a little for the impossible to happen. Even now, she clung on to his certainty, the memory of the way he had cartwheeled down the hill, and then she felt the wave of grief rise up and extinguish her.

Kiss 20

'I send you all my love, always, and this last kiss.'

6 October 2010

Ursula only stayed in the hospital as long as it took to plaster her leg and tend to a few cuts and scrapes, but she spent two weeks in bed at Pilgrim Street, beset with some sort of fever that came and went in waves and caused her to scream at night with terrible nightmares. Rora hardly slept the entire time, lying between episodes wrapped up in a duvet on Ursula's bedroom floor. She was glad that she had something to do and someone to care for. It stopped her having to think too much about what they had both lost. One morning, when Ursula seemed to have got over the worst of her illness, Rora lay down next to her on the bed and held her in her arms and told her about Carl. Ursula received the news with quiet sadness.

'I'd only just got him,' she said. 'He was only my dad for a few days.'

'He was always your dad,' said Rora, holding Ursula close, her tears wetting both their hair.

'I'm so sorry, my darling.'

A few days later, when Ursula was strong enough to go downstairs, Rora found her sitting on the sofa holding her wetsuit in her arms and sobbing.

'If I hadn't run away, he wouldn't have died,' she said, and although Rora's heart broke, she took comfort from the fact that her daughter had been able to say the words.

'Listen to me, Ursula,' she said. 'I thought something I did made my mum die, and it made me feel so bad for so long. It doesn't work like that. Carl loved you and wanted you to be safe. None of it is your fault.'

The days ran into each other so that Rora barely knew how much time had passed since Carl's death. She had taken to walking around town late at night when Ursula was with Hannah. It was the only thing that gave her any relief. When she was in the house she felt an almost constant agitation in her body, even when she was lying on her bed or in a bath intended to soothe. Her restlessness exhausted her and yet she couldn't sleep. It was the same sort of dogged walking that she used to do with Ursula in the first weeks after her birth, carefully maintaining the pram at the exact speed designed to transform her daughter's furious, red-faced screaming into hiccupping sniffles, and then, finally, to surrender and deep, stunned sleep. Now it was she that needed to be walked into oblivion. She almost always went out when the revelry was over; the restaurants shut, the pubs emptied, the rides stilled, the heads of the pedal boat swans covered in their dark hoods. She walked wherever her feet took her, but more often than not she made for the West Cliff. From there she could be completely alone, with only the lights of the town and the dark mass of sea beyond.

This evening some impulse sent her down to the front rather than up to the cliffs. She smelled the smoke long before she knew where it was coming from. It was not the mellow smoke of burning wood. It had a sharp, acrid edge that caught in her throat. It thickened and heated the air. It smelled of chemicals and paint and hot metal. A crowd had gathered all along the beach, watching with quiet awe as the pier blazed into the sky. This was not a peaceful death. The pavilion sent up a hissing lament as the fire tore into it. Several boats were alongside, pumping water into the flames from thick hoses, but this did nothing. Any chance to halt the progress of the fire was thwarted by the breeze that fanned the flames. Parts of the edifice, the bones already laid bare by the fire, fell in bright burning chunks into a sea the colour of a tropical sunset. Rora leaned against the balustrade that ran alongside the beach, smoke and tears turning her view of the fire into a softer, more watery thing. It was on the pier all those years ago that she had first seen him. It seemed to her now that their time together had passed so quickly that the memory of it was as indistinct as her vision. As she watched the little shards of burning wood that blazed for a while on the surface of the ocean, and then disappeared, she tried to hold on to the feeling of how it had been.

The next morning she returned to the scene of the fire. She had dreamed that she and Carl were walking along the pier, and in this dream its boards seemed to stretch forever into the sea. They kept moving along, pushed by a gusty wind that was so strong that it filled their laughing mouths and pulled at their hair. Although it seemed as if they had been walking for hours, they never reached the ballroom, which was always just a little further away in the distance, glistening in a way that it had never done in real life.

Ursula was with Hannah, and so Rora dressed quickly, filled with a kind of urgency she couldn't quite explain. She felt she needed to make sure. She thought if she had imagined the fire of the night before she might perhaps have imagined Carl's death too. But when she arrived at the front she saw that the pier was still smouldering; the collapsed ballroom looked like a caved-in face and the boards they had walked along such a short time ago were scorched.

Weeks ago she had received a curt letter from the council informing her that there had been complaints about the state the beach hut was in and asking her to take immediate action. At the time she had put the letter aside, but now she wanted to go there. It seemed to her that if Carl was anywhere at all, he must be there. She thought about one of the last times they had visited. It had been bitterly cold but beautiful; the sea a lilac grey, the beach deserted. They had sat under three blankets, the door of the beach hut open to the view, their hands cupped around mugs of tomato soup. She remembered the way they had laughed at his efforts to get her jeans off under the blanket, the cold on her bare skin and then the heat of his mouth on her.

Kiss me quick was the fifth hut along and bore very few traces of its bright yellow paint, and the words on the sign above the door had almost been washed away. She fished around in her bag for the key she had found in the kitchen drawer, tied to a label by a length of ribbon. Wind, salt and rain had swollen the wood and she couldn't get the door open. She had to throw the full weight of her body behind the endeavour and finally, after the fifth time of taking a running jump and using her shoulder as a battering ram, the door opened with a sudden pop, like a released cork.

Rora had the strangest sense that she was letting Carl's breath out and that the last of him was escaping forever into the atmosphere. Stiff towels lay over the backs of the chairs. There was a bottle of water half drunk, a teapot with furry green teabags fastened to its side. A thermos flask lined with a dark residue and two mugs with mouth marks on the rims stood on the small table. The mobile she and Carl had made together from small bits of worn wood and shells shifted gently, as if tentatively trying out movement after a long paralysis. She saw the armchair with its cabbage rose pattern that she and Carl had found outside a house with a 'take me' sign on it, the deck-chairs stacked up against one wall, and the cupboard above the tiny sink with its collection of beach finds – little plastic objects from China or Africa or Bexhill-on-Sea that had been washed up on the shoreline.

In the corner, almost hidden by a rolled-up towel, she saw Carl's old tin box – the one that contained the remnants left by his mother and then their later hoarded treasures. She felt for the key she still wore around her neck and took it off and opened the box. She touched each memory in turn: the faded bunch of knapweed, the menu they had thought so excitingly grand, the wand of a spent sparkler with which she had written his name in the damp night sky. Right at the bottom was a folded piece of paper. Rora sat down on the armchair and read the letter Carl had left for her.

21 September 2000

Dear Rora,

I don't know when you will find this letter. It seems strange that I am writing to you without knowing what the world will look like when you read it. Maybe you will discover it a week from now. Maybe it will stay undiscovered for a long time and only come to light when you are toothless and old and I am dead, and this won't mean anything. Or perhaps two hundred years from now, a stranger will find it and make up a story to fit the words.

Tomorrow I will be sentenced. They have warned me that I will be in prison for at least eight years, maybe ten. I told you not to get in touch with me but I have broken my own rule. I wanted to write this last letter and have one last visit to our hut. It is the place that I will take with me. The place I will think about when things get tough.

I hope you know that I don't blame you for anything that happened, although I know that you will blame yourself. It is the way you are made. I told them I was on my own. That Ian and I had a fight and that it went too far and I killed him. No one knows that you were there on the beach that night or what it was that provoked me to attack him. This is the way I want it to be. If I can think of you being happy somewhere it will make the next few years more bearable for me.

I know what I have done will always be part of who I am, but I hope it is not all of me. I think that who we are is a lot to do with who we love, and I think that loving you has made me better than I might have been, despite everything.

I send you all my love, always, and this last kiss.

Carl

X

Seeing his words written down provoked in Rora the final unsealing. She thought of the night on the beach and the way Carl had hit Ian over and over again, as if he was trying to beat something out of himself. At first she had been glad of his defence of her and had encouraged him, wanting Ian's perfect skin broken as hers had been. She had even joined in – hitting Ian's face with her fist. They were in a kind of trance, but then she saw the blood and it brought her back to herself. She tried to stop him dragging Ian into the sea, but Carl was implacable. He looked ferocious, as if he was fighting for something that had been stolen from him. His anger was endless. She should have stayed. She should have stopped him, but she hadn't, and that was why she shared the blame. They were both culpable.

She remembered the terror of the days after, Isobel telling her in a shocked voice that Ian had died and that Carl had been arrested for his murder, asking Rora how much she knew, and where she had been when it happened. And the weeks and months that followed, during which she had so feared discovery that she had shut down against any mention of Ian's name, refusing to go to the funeral, even though so many of her classmates had gone to pay their respects.

For a while Rora sat in the beach hut, frozen in the horror of that night, but then slowly those memories shifted and were replaced by others – she thought instead of Carl's hand on hers as they trailed petals into the sea, and of the way he always looked at her as if she was home.

Kiss 21

*'She blew him a return kiss over the head of his oblivious
companion, and he smiled as if he knew what she had been
thinking about in the space between his kiss and hers.'*

12 September 2012

Frank bequeathed 14 Pilgrim Street to Rora in his will, and during the process of clearing it for sale she discovered she had actually been making it ready for her and Ursula all along. It was still the house it had always been, with its creaking stairs and resident seagull, its tendency to shift when the wind blew and its banisters worn to a golden sheen by generations of hands, but by the time she had made good the cracked walls and replaced the window frames she felt as if it was where she and Ursula belonged.

The town that had always filled her with dread seemed to have acquired a new beauty, or perhaps it was only that she had rediscovered the old one. She loved its makeshift air, its tatty merriment and the great, smeared skies that arched over it. There were still days when what she had lost became too sharply present to her again, but the town seemed now to be on her side, holding her up until the swell of pain passed, and then putting her gently down.

In between her house renovations and finding Ursula a school she could be happy in, Rora finally finished her father's book, and was delighted when it was accepted for publication. The day she rearranged the local bookshop window putting it in the most prominent position possible, despite the muttered objections of the shop owner, was a proud one. Frank would be glad, she thought, to see it there – his name on the cover, all his careful notes, his discoveries and stories captured at last between hard covers.

It was a while longer before she could bring herself to do the other thing she had promised him. He had left written instructions on how to reach the village on the edge of the North Yorkshire Moors, and on one bright, blustery day she and Ursula made the trip there. She tried to make a holiday route of it – stopping on the way at Sherwood Forest for a quick walk, and then again to eat steak and chips in a pub with a fire. It wasn't so much that she was delaying their arrival, nor that she was happy to travel without knowing exactly where she was going, more that she had discovered the value of making the journey as good as it could be.

The tree where her mother had first told her father that she loved him was easy to find. It stood alone in the middle of a stretch of green by a river, where the water ran fast over brown boulders that looked like the shoulders of bears. She thought of her mother in her green dress and of her father full of joy at knowing his love was shared. They poured Frank's ashes into the running water, and then Carl's too – she didn't think her parents would mind sharing their river with him.

'Now we can always visit,' said Ursula, whose heart had taken a lot longer to mend than her broken leg.

'Yes, they are all here,' Rora said, looking around her at the bright, moving grass, the shining water, the tree above them sheltering the people she had loved, and fixed it all in her mind. There was no chance she would forget but she wanted to be able to conjure up, as you would a prayer, the peace and comfort of the place. As they walked back to the car, Rora felt the wrench of what they were leaving behind, but alongside the sadness, like the sound of distant whistling, she could also feel the tug of what might happen next.

There was bunting hanging outside and a noisy crowd had spilled out of the restaurant onto the pavement. Where there had once only been two tables, there was now a line of them under a blue canopy. Rora went in and looked around for him. She saw him straightaway – he was walking around the room with a tray of food, stopping every now and again to talk to groups of people, urging them to try something new. Now that she was there she felt suddenly shy. She didn't know what he would think about her coming. Perhaps she had left it too long and now someone else was by his side, sharing this day of triumph. She touched her hair, smoothed the front of her dress flat. He looked up and saw her, and his face stilled.

'I wondered if perhaps you needed some help,' she said, walking towards him and taking the tray from his hands.

They edged forward together. He was cautious of her, as if he thought she might shatter. They went for long walks and she showed him the Hastings she had recently rediscovered. It was easier to share the almost forgotten passageways, the hidden buildings, the beautiful view from a little-known vantage point than it was to tell him what she was feeling.

She admired his restraint – he never asked her the question she knew she would have asked if she had been in his position, but it lay like a wedge between them. Would she have chosen Krystof if Carl had lived? Wasn't that what she had been trying to tell Carl during that last conversation at the door of the house? She had known then in her heart that it couldn't have worked. There were too many shadows on them. Or would she have decided despite this that she and Carl and Ursula had a chance of being the family she had denied her daughter? Rora churned the questions over and over and wondered if the fact that she wasn't completely sure of the answers meant that she wasn't ready yet to love someone else. She thought sometimes that it would maybe fizzle out, this almost relationship she had with Krystof, under the burden of not properly knowing.

Meanwhile they danced around each other cautiously. They hardly touched and in fact, almost went out of their way to avoid any contact at all. Rora scrambling quickly over obstacles in case he thought she needed help; Krystof going abruptly when they parted in case a lingering goodbye would be misconstrued and taken as an invitation for intimacy. They talked about their families, their hopes, the work they had done and still wanted to do, but it seemed that they couldn't get beyond the surface of things to what really mattered. She knew she would have to tell him what had happened all those years ago on the night of the party. She wanted him to be the first person she told the whole story to, even though she thought he might not like her anymore when he heard what she had done. She had to take the risk. It was the only way they would get beyond skittering over the tops of things.

She chose to tell him as they were walking around the summer fair that had arrived in the town, as if the noise and bustle of it and the hot smell of wires lying across grass and *Greensleeves* pumping out of the Victorian accordion would deaden the impact. He listened to her stumbling account in silence. The words were hard to reach. Nothing quite did justice to the pain and shame of it. When she finally ground into silence, hardly daring to look at him, he said, 'I understand now why you often look so sad. It was a terrible thing you had to endure.'

'Do you think less of me now?' she asked.

'I think the same,' he said. 'Less and more doesn't come into it.'

She felt suddenly as light as the brittle candy floss spinning in its churn and as high and free as if she was sitting on the top of the big wheel. She felt young.

'Do you still miss him?' he asked her one evening when they were sitting at the bar in his new and improved restaurant, watching other couples edge towards each other or sit in silence at the end of what they had once had.

'I will always miss him,' she said, knowing that her answer would cause him pain but wanting above everything else to be truthful with him now.

'He was the other half of me.'

Krystof looked at her and she could see the battle going on in him. He was holding on, but only just. She knew what this was costing him.

'Does that mean there is only half of you left?' he asked, as if he wasn't really expecting an answer, and she didn't give him one. But later, as she was walking home in the soft night air, she thought about what he had asked her.

She went down one morning a couple of weeks later to meet him after his swim, waiting for him on the beach until he had stopped his metronomic crawl and put his head up for long enough to notice she was there. She took off her dress and went to join him in the water.

'I've come for a lesson,' she said.

'I thought you had given up trying to learn to swim,' he said, smiling at her.

'I really think, as a resident of Hastings, I should be able to at least keep afloat for a few minutes,' she replied and launched herself into the water. For a few seconds it seemed that she would do as she had always done before, splash ineffectually for a while and then sink to the bottom, but her new resolve must have paid off because she managed at least five minutes of almost leisurely breaststroke, remembering to breathe through her nose and keep her arm movements slow and steady.

'You've done it!' he said when she got back to her feet in triumph. They looked at each other and Rora felt something shift. It was the slightest, almost imperceptible of changes, like the judder on the hand of a clock before it moves properly into position, but they both felt it.

'I've got something else to show you,' she said, and waded quickly out of the water and wrapped herself in her towel. He followed her, drying himself vigorously.

'Where are we going?' he asked.

'You'll see,' she said and dressed quickly, her skin sticky with salt against her cotton dress.

They walked along the front to the beach hut, which now gleamed with a new coat of yellow paint. The roof, which had developed a hole through which years of salt spray and rain had penetrated, was now safely covered in felt. Rora put her key in the lock and opened the door, which had been shaved and oiled so that it no longer stuck.

'Is this yours?' Krystof asked. 'You never said you had a beach hut.'

'I've had it for years. Ever since I was a child, when I came here with Isobel. Later on Carl and I used to come here. My grandmother's idea of sex education was to warn me that I should always leave the door open. I've been giving it a facelift,' she said.

Inside, all traces of mildew had gone and there were new deck chairs and fresh curtains at the window. Rora had arranged Carl's treasures along a shelf and added new junk shop finds – a line of red Swedish horses, a blue glass vase full of sea holly.

'It's beautiful,' Krystof said.

'It's always been a special place,' said Rora. 'I wanted to bring you here.'

He looked uncertainly at her as he stood in the door, until she made a small movement towards him. There must have been something encouraging in her face because she heard his breath catch.

'I've been thinking about your question,' she said.

'Which question?' he asked, his face open and hopeful, the yellow flecks in his eyes dancing.

'The answer is that I am not a half. I'm an imperfect whole.'

'You are perfect to me,' he said.

'I want to be with you now, at this moment, more than I want anything,' she said.

'That's more than enough,' he said, smiling at her tenderly. 'Shall we shut the door?'

The party room was full and noisy, the first such event they had been to as a couple, and they would have preferred to remain together but became separated when Rora was whisked off by an excitable Hannah dying to hear all about the latest developments in Rora's life. As she was passing on her way to the kitchen to get another drink she caught sight of him, leaning against a wall, his arms crossed, his shirt unbuttoned under his best black jacket. She knew he was bored from the way he was nodding his head. She knew the more he agreed with someone, the less he was actually listening. He looked at her standing there in Sandi's green dress for longer than perhaps was polite, considering he was mid-conversation with someone else, then he blew her a kiss.

Rora thought it was perhaps the sweetest kiss she had ever been given. It went across the room and into her heart and in receiving it she relived everything that they had shared that evening, until this moment, at this party, among people who knew nothing of it. It was as if this scrap of blown love had caused time to stop, and then to reverse.

An hour ago they were at home and the scramble to find a clean shirt for him and something she could bear to wear was underway. The sitter was perched politely on the sofa in a tiny skirt, wondering when she could safely text her boyfriend to come round. Rora's body was still warm from Krystof's hands, still sleepy and languorous and smug. She had emptied the entire contents of her wardrobe onto the floor. She couldn't find anything she felt happy wearing. He was asking her whether he should leave the top buttons of his shirt undone. She was standing in front of the mirror with a different shoe on each foot, asking him which pair looked best.

'Don't ask me about shoes, Rora. I don't have the necessary qualifications,' he had said and his hand lightly stroked the back of her neck. 'You look beautiful in everything you wear.'

'What's the use of saying that?' she said. 'I need specifics.'

'If you don't hurry up and get dressed, I will be tempted to get you back into bed.'

'Done or undone?' he asked a moment later, looking handsome with his hair messed up and with the wiped-clean look he always got after they had made love.

'Leave the top button open,' she said, settling his collar flat.

An hour and a half before the party they were still in bed, cocooned in the warmth of their bodies, their legs wrapped around each other.

'We should really get ready,' she said, not moving.

'Let's just stay here forever,' he said, his hand on the curve of her stomach.

'They won't even notice if we don't show up,' Rora said.

'We could send a card tomorrow saying how much we enjoyed it,' he said.

'I think that's the sitter at the door,' Rora said.

Before that, rolling back further in the dim, intimate light of the bedroom. Lying stretched out across silky sheets. Side by side, joined from chest to curling feet – their breath coming fast. The slide of fingers, a palm flat across her breast, the soft hardness of them both, the way it felt unstoppable, the rush, the love.

Two hours before the party and Rora was lying on the sofa trying to generate enough energy to run a bath, thinking about whether she had time to go to the corner shop and pick up some flowers to take with them. Wondering if Ursula's sitter would arrive when she said she would, and whether, really, at fifteen she was old enough to react effectively in all possible disaster scenarios. Krystof came into the room and looked at her and there it was, the flicker of desire that she couldn't suppress, despite the lack of time and flowers, despite the fact she knew she had nothing suitable to wear.

'I love you,' she said.

Time rolled forward again and Rora was back in the room, the party still in full swing all around them. She blew Krystof a return kiss over the head of his oblivious companion, and he smiled as if he knew what she had been thinking about in the space between his kiss and hers.

EPILOGUE

Kiss 22

*'He was only just taller than her in her ridiculous shoes
and he didn't seem at first to know which side
his face should go.'*

12 April 2016

Rora drove along the front on her way to pick Ursula up from the party. Work was almost complete on the brand-new pier. Krystof had been right when he said it would be splendid again – it would stand out in the sea as boldly as ever and there would be lights and music and dancers. Maybe there would even be a fortune-teller to pore over hands and look for stories in a glass ball, and a game to work out couple compatibility, although Rora knew now that there was no such thing as a perfectly one hundred per cent couple. The lost percentages contained the hidden parts, the parts of each other we can never really know. Most of all, the new pier would give all those walking across its boards the feeling of being in a special kingdom, separate from the real world.

The days flicked past – click, click, click. It was the sound that the machine had made on the old pier – Hastings Through The Ages. She and Carl used to put their eyes to the hooded aperture and press the button to move each image along. The cliffs changed shape. The harbour widened then narrowed. The town grew so that it filled the valley. The river became a road. This shifting would never stop, like a flower spreading its petals and then dropping them, the town would reinvent itself again and again, making new shapes out of the old.

Rora stopped a short distance from the house and switched the engine off. She looked at her watch and saw that she was a little early. She knew better than to actually approach the premises. She had made that mistake once before and had been roundly told off for her foolhardiness.

'*None* of the other parents actually *come in,*' said Ursula, who was fifteen and never missed an opportunity to be embarrassed by her mother.

'I'll come out to you at the *exact* time,' she had said earlier in the evening, tossing her dark mane of hair and clipping off into the spring night in her absurdly high shoes. There were times when Rora thought her daughter was even more of a control freak than she used to be. She had neither encouraged nor discouraged her daughter's tendency to marshal the world and other people. Rora had learned that her job as a parent was less about shaping her child and more about discovering the person she already was. They had had a long journey, the pair of them, to come to terms with what had happened. But they had managed it, after a fashion ... what was it her father had said? '*We blunder through,*' and it was true.

Rora felt something fly into her eye through the open car window and pulled down the visor mirror with its little light to have a look. A tiny insect had lodged itself right under the bottom lash-line and Rora had to twist the corner of a tissue into a sharp point to get it out. In the dim interior of the car she could almost imagine she hadn't changed much. She still had her mass of curls, although now their gold was a little muted. Krystof said she looked exactly the same as the day he saw her wading in the shallows, but then the man always did see the best in things. The door of the house opened and Ursula emerged from the party as she had promised, on the dot of twelve, with a boy with dark hair and a jacket two sizes too large for him. Ursula ran a hasty eye down the street, but she must not have seen her mother because there was no way she would have kissed him otherwise.

The light from the open door framed them. He was only just taller than her in her ridiculous shoes and he didn't seem at first to know which side his face should go. Rora was touched by his clumsiness. She had understood that fifteen was considered a venerable age when it came to sex. If you believed everything you heard, then her daughter and this young man should have been well versed in such matters, but it was clear from their awkwardness that this was new to them. In the end it was Ursula who took hold of his face and pulled him to her and they kissed. Rora looked away. She thought of her first kiss with Carl and all the kisses she had given and received in the time since. The touch of lip to lip was fleeting and yet it existed out of time, forever preserved, forever intact.

The boy went back inside and after waiting a discreet minute or two Rora honked her horn. Ursula ran towards the car and got in, slamming the passenger door behind her, despite the fact Rora had told her again and again it didn't need to have such force applied.

'Was it a good party?' Rora asked.

'Not bad,' Ursula said nonchalantly, and then she turned to look at her mother.

'Have you been crying?' she asked suspiciously, scrutinising Rora's face.

'No, darling,' Rora said. 'It's only that a fly flew into my eye.'

Acknowledgements

It takes so many people to write a book. I would like to thank my agent Luigi Bonomi who, against the odds, continues to believe; my editor, Joel Richardson, at Zaffre, who saw a glimmer of something and knew how to make the rest better; my early editor, Sam Bulos, for her accomplished help; my friends Andrea and Katie, who have listened to me drone on endlessly and with whom I have shared many cheering evenings; my chum Theresa, who I never see enough of but who always says the right thing; my sisters Tania and Thomasina, who enhance my life in so many ways; my lovely boys Felix and Jack; and, of course, my husband, David, for more than words can say.

We hope you loved

this last kiss

Why not kiss and tell us
your thoughts on Twitter?

🐦 Tweet us at @BonnierZaffre and include #ThisLastKiss